She threw a
beautifully
executed flying
kick right into
the horned
bear's gut.

"Wha...
wha...
wha-
wha-
what...
the...?"

"HYAA

The second she made impact, Weapon Skill: Charge automatically activated. Cayna was insanely powerful and high-level despite being one of the weaker races. Her kick bent the horned bear's massive body in half and sent it flying.

✦ IN THE LAND OF ✦
LEADALE

1

Ceez

[ILLUSTRATION BY]

Tenmaso

YEN ON
NEW YORK

✦ IN THE LAND OF ✦

LEADALE 1 Ceez

Translation by Jessica Lange
Cover art by Tenmaso

This book is a work of fiction. Names, characters, places, and incidents are the product of the author's imagination or are used fictitiously. Any resemblance to actual events, locales, or persons, living or dead, is coincidental.

RIADEIRU NO DAICHI NITE Vol. 1
© Ceez 2019
First published in Japan in 2019 by KADOKAWA CORPORATION, Tokyo.
English translation rights arranged with KADOKAWA CORPORATION, Tokyo through
TUTTLE-MORI AGENCY, INC., Tokyo.

English translation © 2020 by Yen Press, LLC

Yen On
150 West 30th Street, 19th floor
New York, NY 10001

Visit us at yenpress.com
facebook.com/yenpress
twitter.com/yenpress
yenpress.tumblr.com
instagram.com/yenpress

First Yen On Edition: October 2020

Yen On is an imprint of Yen Press, LLC.
The Yen On name and logo are trademarks of Yen Press, LLC.

The publisher is not responsible for websites (or their content) that are not owned by the publisher.

Library of Congress Cataloging-in-Publication Data
Names: Ceez, author. | Tenmaso, illustrator. | Lange, Jessica (Translator), translator.
Title: In the land of Leadale / Ceez ; illustration by Tenmaso ; translation by Jessica Lange
Other titles: Riadeiru no daichi nite. English
Description: First Yen On edition. | New York, NY : Yen On, 2020.
Identifiers: LCCN 2020032160 | ISBN 9781975308681 (v. 1 ; trade paperback)
Subjects: CYAC: Fantasy. | Virtual reality—Fiction.
Classification: LCC PZ7.1.C4646 In 2020 | DDC [Fic]—dc23
LC record available at https://lccn.loc.gov/2020032160

ISBNs: 978-1-9753-0868-1 (paperback)
        978-1-9753-0869-8 (ebook)

10 9 8 7 6 5 4 3 2 1

LSC-C

Printed in the United States of America

IN THE LAND OF LEADALE

1

IN THE LAND OF LEADALE   Contents

ILLUSTRATION BY Tenmaso

"…Well, I'm stumped…"

Feeling feverish, Keina Kagami listlessly cooled herself by the window. It wasn't a matter of staying in the bath too long, but rather the result of wisdom gained through a long, confusing, and self-powered brainstorming session.

The fluffy clouds drifted across the blue sky before her. It was truly a marvelous day.

Beneath that azure sky, a forest spread across the foot of a long mountain range, and as she gazed farther down, she could see a dozen or so wooden houses standing in a row. Such a sight was unheard of in the twenty-second-century world she knew, and it seemed pretty rude to question whether the town was peaceful or on the decline.

Even someone like herself, who was part of that very landscape, couldn't help but scoff.

Attempting to understand the situation she now found herself in, the girl thought back to the other morning in that plain, sunlit room where this recent mess started.

Prologue

"Miiiiss, it's morning!"

Keina weakly opened her eyes at the bright light suddenly pouring in and the young, lisping voice. She stared up at the blurry outline of a grained wooden ceiling. Sliding her gaze to the right, she caught sight of a shuttered window. To her left and beyond the expanse of white sheets, the upper half of a young girl was greeting her with a big smile and cheerful "Gooood morning!"

"*Yaaaawn... Gwud mornin'?*"

"Hee-hee! Time to get up, miss!" the young girl replied, her smile dazzling.

Sleepiness began to naturally ebb away. Keina stretched her torso and bathed in the morning light as if trying to soak it all in, then looked down at herself and immediately froze. The young girl standing by the bed tilted her head at Keina's odd stiffness.

"Morning sunlight...and a wooden room?"

Until just the day before, or recently anyway, she'd always fallen asleep in that white-walled hospital room she was utterly sick of.

But more than that, Keina was dumbfounded by the fact that

someone who couldn't even stay awake on her own was getting up and stretching.

Whether seconds or minutes, the shock didn't last long. Keina's gaze became downtrodden, and she felt the eyes of the girl who had come to give her a wake-up call.

"Are you awright, miss?" The little girl seemed truly concerned.

Keina considered how she might dispel the sadness in the girl's dark eyes. Casting aside her own concerns, she opened an Item Box and clumsily took out a Candy, which would restore a small amount of MP. She placed it in her palm and presented it to the girl, just like the head nurse used to do for Keina when she was a child, since she was always crying. Keina smiled and gave the Candy to the young girl.

"Th-thanks, miss!"

"Not at all," she replied, her smile bright and her face slightly flushed. Getting up from the bed, Keina patted the girl's head lightly.

The young servant placed the Candy in the pocket of her loose smock. She stripped Keina's bed of its sheets and blankets, folded them neatly, and went to leave the room with a happy heart. However, she made sure to remind Keina, "Breakfast's ready, so hurry on down, 'kay?"

Logic urged her not to become too immersed in this heartwarming atmosphere, and Keina ruminated over what had just happened.

…Open the Item Box?

As soon as the thought came to her, a translucent display window appeared on the right side of her field of vision. Then, fifteen smaller boxes popped up at once. As she used the scrollbar in the top right corner to scroll down, a vast number of items appeared.

"No…way…"

She pinched her cheek.

…Ouch. Okay, no question this is real.

Having employed a classic reality-check technique, she had confirmed that the situation she now faced was no dream. There was no choice left but to accept it.

Since she'd thought this might have been a dream, she opened the Magic Skill tab next to the Item Window. Keina blanched when saw something called Dream Dropper: Nightmare displayed.

Wasn't this that online game she'd just been playing? *Leadale*?

The fact that she could move and feel pain proved to her that everything was all too real.

You can't fight on an empty stomach. Keina—or rather, Cayna—decided she would deal with her problem after breakfast.

She timidly descended the steep, creaking stairs and made her way to the tavern's dining hall. There, she found the girl from earlier and a plump middle-aged woman she assumed to be the proprietress.

Within the dining hall was a round table with a set of eight four-legged chairs. There was also a counter with four seats facing the kitchen. It was surely difficult to weave through the crowds when the place was filled to capacity. However, at the moment, there were only two farmer-looking men sitting in the tavern eating their breakfast of soup and bread.

"Come now, miss, have a seat," the proprietress urged. "Otherwise, your soup will get cold."

"Y-yes, ma'am."

Cayna deliberated for a moment over where to sit before taking a spot at the counter. Bread and soup in a wooden bowl were soon placed before her. The young girl from earlier gave her a wooden cup of water, completing the breakfast set.

There were already several things Cayna found strange about this online world. She went over them as she began digging in.

Come to think of it, how many years has it been since I last fed myself?

7

She broke off pieces of the slightly stale bread roll and dipped it in the stew-like soup as she ate. After living without a sense of taste for so long, she couldn't help but vocalize her feelings.

"…It's delicious…"

"Well, miss, ain't you just the sweetest?"

The proprietress's surly face immediately brightened. She put her elbow on the counter and began chatting amiably.

"If it's so good that it can put a smile like that on your face, what kind of disgusting food have you been eating until now?"

"Huh…?"

Cayna had apparently broken into a large grin and didn't even realize it until it was pointed out to her. Thinking back on her usual diet up to that point, the only things she'd ever ingested were water and pills, plus an IV drip. Ruminating about her life after the accident, she felt a keen emptiness over all the fine cuisine she had missed out on.

"Um, well…there just wasn't a whole lot that I wanted to eat…"

"Now, that's a sad tale. Without good food, you're only halfway living! Here, this is on me. Have as many seconds as you want."

"Ah, I will. Thank you very much."

The woman patted Cayna's shoulder. Cayna's cheek twitched as she looked at the stew/soup that was now almost filled to the brim.

I—I wonder if I can eat all this…

She thought it would be too much for her stomach to handle, but the enticing smell alone seemed to give her the strength to smash through her limits. Cayna realized she was a lot hungrier than she thought and unintentionally stuffed herself.

As she settled her full stomach with a cup of water, Cayna surveyed the first floor of the inn.

There was no question this village sat on the border between the White Kingdom of Felstes and the Green Kingdom of Gruskeilo.

Though remote, the region's position as a key trade route should have kept the borderlands thriving. The world setting likely included plenty of inns and carriages to account for the constant stream of merchants.

So why was this place so down on its luck?

The last time she logged out, she remembered seeing multiple NPCs and hearing a bustling background soundtrack that gave the inn a lively atmosphere.

Another stark difference from in the game was that the NPCs, who normally could only say their set dialogue, were responding to her with true emotion. At this point, you couldn't even call them NPCs anymore. It was then that Cayna realized this world was both a game and not.

The real question for her was *How long can I live in this world?*

Having reached this conclusion, Cayna decided to investigate matters as much as she could. First, she opened her Item Window and checked how much money she had on hand. After seeing a ten-figure number, she took out twenty gil, which was the game's currency.

Intent on finding out whether the twenty pieces of silver would even be accepted, Cayna presented them to the proprietress.

"Um, excuse me…"

"Hmm? What is it?"

"I'd like to stay here for a little while. Can I use these?"

The silver coins, each carved with some sort of flower design on the front and back, clinked as she put them on the counter.

The money had nothing more than numerical value in the game, but Cayna thought they actually looked pretty cute.

""What?!""

This reaction came from both the proprietress and the little girl, whose eyes grew large as she stared at the coins. The woman timidly picked one up and turned it over in her palm, examining it closely. She put it back with a sigh.

"You can use it if you like, miss, but don't go flaunting your deep pockets, okay?"

"…Pardon?"

"Deep pockets"? This? That's ridiculous.

Going to a shop and selling one pill that boosted your attack power for thirty minutes could earn you about forty gil, and even a shovel cost less than ten gil. However, Cayna's plan to take these numbers and mentally approximate the cost of a night's stay had completely backfired on her. When the proprietress said four coins were enough for ten nights, Cayna realized how badly she had to reassess her financial know-how. She was beyond relieved that the first person she encountered in this world had been an upstanding NPC like the proprietress.

There was no end to the questions running through her head, but her top priority at the moment was finding out why the village had fallen into decline.

"I feel like this village used to be livelier, no…?"

"It's been about four generations since we had business like that. Ever since the nation of Felskeilo was established, no one needs us anymore."

"…Buh?"

Cayna's brain short-circuited the moment she heard this completely foreign name. It sounded like a mashup of the White and Green Kingdoms' names, and she once again found herself wondering in bewilderment, *Huh? Am I not inside the game?*

The proprietress left the lost Cayna in the dust and continued on. "They say that two hundred years ago, seven nations constantly waged war with one another and stirred upheaval anywhere and everywhere. The gods were so angered by their unsightly fighting that they chose leaders from among humanity to lead the people. These people worked hard to unite the world into three countries, and now here we are."

One of the farmers who had stayed even after finishing breakfast began heckling the proprietress about her impromptu history lesson.

"Quit tellin' Li'l Miss Adventurer here stuff she already knows!"

"Shut yer trap! Get back to the fields, all of you!" she shouted.

The farmers got up and hurriedly left the inn.

Cayna was now the only customer. The information from that exchange sank her deeper into thought.

Aren't those seven nations part of the World of Leadale *VRM-MORG I was just playing yesterday?*

There were no set classes like soldier, priest, or mage; instead, you obtained four thousand different skills. The game had a high level of freedom that allowed you to play as an avatar whose race, equipment, and skills were completely customized to your specifications.

That freedom earned it the mockery of netizens who sarcastically referred to the game as a Wild West of sorts. A large-scale Battle Event held each month decided the gain or loss of territory among the seven nations, and every player went crazy over it. When a nation took a certain domain, they were granted special, limited-edition event items. Even though so many people logged in to discuss detailed strategy the day beforehand that it would crash the server, it was also pretty funny to see countries that couldn't manage to get online until the day of the Event end up in the dust.

To hear that those seven nations—White, Green, Red, Blue, Brown, Black, and Purple—had existed *two centuries ago* shattered Cayna's grip on reality. How was she supposed to live in a game she used to play now that two hundred years had passed? Anxiety loomed over her as her prospects turned increasingly grim.

First, it was imperative that she familiarize herself with this world. There was no question the list of things she needed to learn in order to find her footing was growing longer by the moment. A certain someone would totally laugh in her face if she froze up because of nerves.

When that despicable face that got its jollies from other people's misery came to her mind, she couldn't help but feel that a little anxiety was more or less the spice of life.

"...At any rate, if you're speaking of such bygone days, I take it you've been here before?"

"Huh? Um, well..."

Cayna knew it would be flat-out foolish to answer *I logged out just yesterday!* so she kept it ambiguous.

"You're an elf, right, miss?" the proprietress asked.

"Ah, yes, I am," Cayna replied.

Her current body was that of her game avatar. Before leaving her room that morning, she had used her Truth Mirror—an item distributed during certain events—to confirm this. As the name implied, a Truth Mirror showed your true form. It had no other functions.

When she nervously stared into it, she'd expected to see the emaciated girl who had been laid up in a hospital bed. Seeing her avatar reflected back at her, Cayna was momentarily overwhelmed. When she tugged at her bangs, the strands had shone with a subdued golden hue. Her hair was shoulder-length. She had deep-blue eyes and, of course, distinctly pointy ears that stuck out like a sore thumb. These ears were proof she was from a race of long-lived demi-humans.

Cayna had chosen the high elf race, which, unlike regular elves, specialized in fighting from the back line. She went with this simply because high elves had the highest possible INT and MP stats.

Even though each race had its own basic battle moves, once some users deemed a particular one to be the "lamest," no one would pick it. High elves like Cayna were tanking in popularity of late, and it was quite common to hear of fans forming high elf–only teams.

"Yes, I came here just once in its heyday...," Cayna started. She answered honestly, since she figured there was no reason to hide it.

The proprietress beamed.

"I see. So, miss, you know how the village was back in the day. To think a regular would return to our inn after all these years. It warms my heart."

Cayna just smiled awkwardly and let the woman assume she visited the inn often.

"Oh, right, I'm Marelle, and this here is Lytt. Relax and enjoy your stay."

"Thank you, I appreciate it. My name is Kei…Cayna." She adjusted her posture and introduced herself with a bow.

"Quit bein' be so formal!" Marelle replied, thumping her on the back. It made Cayna a little happy.

As soon as Cayna excused herself and returned to her room, she quickly set about checking herself and everything she had on her. When she pulled up the stats screen, the initial information read:

Name: Cayna
Level: 1,100
Race: High Elf
Title: Third Skill Master

In *World of Leadale*, you could exceed the maximum level of 1,000 by another one hundred levels by completing a special quest.

This level-breaking quest was a serious beast, and most people considered the event a necessary evil. Even Cayna's own guild had recruited members and nonmembers alike to take it on and failed countless times.

Finally, a huge four-party group of twenty-four managed to clear it. Some had even legitimately cried, which provided a pretty good picture of the quest creators' sadism. When they at last succeeded, each party member had shouted, "Screw you, Admins!"

After that, no rumors of anyone else beating the quest surfaced, so those members were essentially the strongest in the game.

The merits of a high elf were 10 percent Battle and Skill Bonuses when surrounded by nature and the use of Eagle Eyes.

The deficits were found in Craft Skills, since it was impossible to cultivate necessary plant ingredients by your own power. Cayna often gathered these by asking available guild members or buying them from vendors.

The title of Skill Master was an honor bestowed upon those who mastered 1,500 Magic Skills and 2,500 Craft Skills to equal 4,000 total skills (though the designers continued to add more). Cayna had been given the title of Third Skill Master, since she was the third out of the fourteen people to master every skill.

That title was the very reason Cayna preferred logging in and out of this remote region as she pleased without venturing into other territories.

Along with the honor and title came the automatically obtained Skill #4,001 called Scroll Creation.

Therein lay the problem. With this ability, Skill Masters like Cayna could record the skills they possessed onto parchment, making it easy for other players to obtain them without embarking on annoying quests.

However, whenever she met players face-to-face, they constantly demanded she "give me this" or "give me that." The Skill Masters got fed up with this and submitted a petition to the Admins to do something about it.

The Admins had tried to deal with it, but an incident occurred in the process where one person ended up having a nervous breakdown and quitting the game altogether.

In the end, their solution was to have the Skill Masters take on part of the Skill Transfer Quests normally handled by NPCs. Each Skill Master was then assigned a location of their choosing.

The goal of these Skill Transfer Quests was to reach the summit of each location. Word of the new rule that anyone who succeeded in these difficult quests could have any skill they wanted spread throughout the game like wildfire.

The locations of the Skill Masters differed greatly and tormented the players to no end.

A beautiful building filled with lethal traps at random intervals.

An undersea fortress known as the Palace of the Dragon King that was unreachable without magic that allowed one to breathe underwater—and of course, there were the sea monsters inhabiting the depths.

A castle in the sky that was completely hidden unless you used Flight and Eagle Eyes simultaneously.

The entrance to a temple whose location changed every day. Even after you finally managed to pinpoint it across the entire mountain range where it was located, the inside turned out to be an enormous dungeon.

Half these quests were too frustrating to be any fun.

They were clear manifestations of just how much resentment the Skill Masters harbored after having to deal with the other players' heartless *Gimme, gimme* attitudes.

With this in mind, Cayna conscientiously chose a silver tower in the middle of a vast forest as her base. If the objective was to reach the very top of the tower, it was certainly feasible. However, it took twenty-four real-time hours to do so.

It was important to note that the long stairs did not match the height of the tower's exterior. Players immediately started circling up the entire tower as if it were a drill bit, but since the speed matched their set pace, running wouldn't make the journey any shorter. If you stopped at any point before reaching the top, you would be instantly returned to the starting point outside the forest. This was considered a relatively tame trick compared with some of the gimmicks employed by Cayna's fellow Skill Masters.

The owners of each location had rings and passcodes that allowed them to directly access their most central regions, so coming and going was no issue. Cayna told herself she'd have to visit hers later and moved on to inspecting her items and equipment.

Currently, she was wearing a high-level Fairy King Robe that only female high elves could equip. Even within the entire game itself, Cayna was probably the only one who could wear it. She wore leggings that were visible down to her knees and sturdy boots. Both were treasured pieces imbued with several status boosts.

On her left arm was an arm guard that she could attach a bow to with a command key; by expending MP, she could turn the normal arrows into magic ones. On her right side, she wore a headband with a feather attached. It automatically rendered her invisible when faced with an external threat, though this cost MP.

Her weapon was a lightning dagger displayed at the very top of the Item Screen. It was an optimum weapon that paralyzed an enemy after only a few hit points.

"To be honest, I'm way too well equipped here…"

Basic battle strategy said she didn't need to be this armed when she could just blow everything away with magic, but Cayna couldn't be too careful now that she'd lost everyone from her guild in one fell swoop.

Even if her race wasn't as suited to a vanguard position as normal elves, she could still form a party with low-level players and act as a pretty good tank.

All that was left was to consult the toolbox at her tower and decide what she'd keep.

"…Oh!"

Suddenly, Cayna realized she had completely forgotten her support AI.

Her uncle had made it special for her when it became difficult for her to move on her own in real life. It was an assistance AI that aided her with daily tasks even though she was bedridden. Attached to the hospital bed, "he" was an extraordinary construct that could act of his own volition and do everything from raising and lowering the back of the bed to calling a nurse in an emergency. He could even assist her with in-game commands, keep detailed logs, scratch itches, and let Cayna know if she had visitors when she was either sleeping or being examined.

He had been with her longer than any gaming companion, and she considered him a partner of sorts. She called out nervously, unsure of what she'd do if he didn't respond.

"…Kee, you there?"

"Yes. I am here."

Cayna's heart eased as Kee—whose name came from a cat her mother once had—replied. He spoke in a concise, robotic tone devoid of any affectations.

"You have two urgent items."

"I figured. What's up?"

"Item one: You have disconnected from the hospital system. Item two: You have been disconnected from Leadale's *master system."*

"I see… Thanks."

She had already guessed that this place was both part of the game and not. The question was why Cayna was here to begin with. Even within the past day or so, she hadn't heard anything about *Leadale* ending service. It didn't matter if you were far from the royal capital or your friends; if there was important information or a big Event coming up, any logged-in player would hear about it from either the Admins or their guild and friends.

Cayna thought back to her most recent memory.

Her AI assistant had informed her that her uncle and a cousin had come to see her, so she must have logged out. She'd spoken with them for a short while, then logged back in. Fatigue had quickly taken hold of her, and she'd gone to bed without logging out. Her last memory was of setting her status to Away.

Whatever had happened between then and when she'd woken up must have brought her to this point.

"Hmm… Kee, did anything strange happen last night?"

"Yes, there was one item."

"There was?!"

Since her partner (?) himself couldn't tell if it was an emergency, he must have been uncertain whether to report it.

"After you retired to bed, the power cut out for approximately two seconds. That is when the previous two items occurred."

"Cut out?"

"I am eighty percent certain it was a blackout."

"Oh, right, a blackout. Okay… Wait, a blackout?!"

The gravity of her strange situation became clear, and Cayna could easily surmise what had happened. This forgone conclusion robbed her of all hope.

"Cayna?"

Keina Kagami's body was so weak that she couldn't survive without life support. Cayna herself knew this, and the doctors had warned her as well.

If interrupted by some outside source, whether it be a lightning strike or otherwise, it took about two seconds for emergency generators to resupply the hospital's equipment.

In that time, her spirit alone had escaped reality and fled to this world.

In other words, Keina Kagami's body was dead.

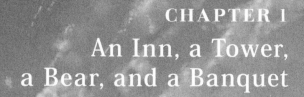

CHAPTER 1
An Inn, a Tower, a Bear, and a Banquet

"Huh?!"

As Cayna let this shocking truth sink in, she realized the sky had begun to take on an orange hue. Shocked that she'd wasted almost half a day, she forcibly convinced herself anyone in the same position would have been crushed. No names actually came to mind, but Cayna simply banished this to the furthest reaches of her thoughts and pretended it never happened. One might say she simply refused to accept reality.

The buildings had no glass windows, so the closed shutters quickly plunged the room into darkness. She opened them halfway and let in some of the orange light from the setting sun. Cayna took another look around the room and came across a lantern fixture on the wall.

"Ah, right. They use lanterns here, don't they...?"

Cayna had never taken a survival course or slept outdoors, so she had no idea how to light the lantern in her room. Naturally, this was where magic came in handy.

The Light spell was a skill obtained through relatively easy quests and essential for anyone who specialized in dungeon crawling.

Without it, all you had at your disposal were lanterns—incredibly fin-
icky, inconvenient items that used up fuel, provided meager light, and
had to be switched out in an emergency so you had a free hand. Only
total beginners used them.

Magic, on the other hand, had plenty of uses: Some people made
weapons and armor, while others crafted magic items for their equipment. Others still would just have fun with it and sell gag items with
hilarious descriptions. Being all business and taking your role as a
support class seriously was well and good, but there were always a few
simpletons who preferred to skip out on battle and light themselves
up all the colors of the rainbow.

"Bow down, fools!"

"Gaaah, I'm bliiind!"

"Your halo… It's so bright!"

"Shall we leave those idiots behind?"

"Sounds good."

""""Don't gooo!!""""

Remembering the conversation made her feel as if it had happened just yesterday and brought a smile to Cayna's face.

There were times when such nostalgia brought tears to her eyes,
but she shook her head and pulled herself together.

It wasn't as if she wanted to forget. She was simply setting those
memories aside and searching for similar joys that lay ahead.

First, she would test whether magic was feasible in this world.
As Cayna focused all her attention on the lantern, she evoked a spell
from her mental skill arsenal.

**Magic Skill: Additional White Light Level 1:
Light: Ready Set**

"Activate!"

"?!"

Cayna was relieved to find she could cast spells in the game as she always did. What *didn't* ease her mind was the small cry that came from the slightly ajar door of her now well-lit room.

Lytt, the little girl from the inn, was timidly peering through the crack in the door and gave a startled look as she glanced at the shining wall lantern.

Perplexed by her reaction, a curious Cayna walked over to her.

"What's wrong, Lytt?"

"Um... I-is it safe?"

Realizing the light had startled her, Cayna waved her hand dismissively to assure her visitor it wasn't dangerous.

"Oh, this? It's only light; it won't explode or hurt anyone. There's nothing to worry about."

Upon hearing this, Lytt slowly entered but clung to the wall with no intention of pressing forward.

Could it be that normal villagers rarely see magic? Cayna thought with a tilt of her head.

"Lytt, is this your first time seeing magic?"

The girl's small nod confirmed this. Cayna also realized why Lytt had come in the first place. The plate in her hand held a thread dipped in animal fat with a flame burning at one end like a candle. Lighting all the lanterns in the guest rooms must have been part of Lytt's duties.

"...Oh no, did I interfere with your chores, Lytt?"

"Nuh-uh, this one's even brighter now. You're incredible, miss!"

"O-oh, well...I'm glad you enjoyed it so much."

They looked at each other and smiled. Lytt had a visible twitch in her cheek, but pointing that out would be insensitive. It had been a while since she'd done any female bonding with anyone besides her cousin, and it filled Cayna's heart with warmth.

Even so, new doubts swelled within her as she wondered what in the world had happened to the players who once dotted this continent.

If there had been some sort of announcement from the Admins like *Hey, starting tomorrow, this world will be two hundred years in the future!* it wasn't hard to imagine that the majority opinion would be *Quit screwin' around!* After all, the Battle Event between the seven nations was undeniably a big part of *Leadale's* popularity.

"I think I'll stretch my legs a bit and head on over to the tower tomorrow... Hmm?"

As Cayna formulated a plan, she felt a sudden tug on the sleeve of her robe and saw Lytt draw close.

"Um, um, also, I came to tell you dinner's ready."

"Oh, sorry to hold you up."

"That's okay. After all, you're the only guest here, miss."

Cayna was struggling with thoughts like *This place really is in trouble* and *Should the innkeeper's daughter really be telling me this?* when she felt Lytt tugging at her hand. It turned out that Lytt had finished closing and latching the shutter windows while Cayna was busy fretting. She then began leading Cayna down the stairs.

Unlike that morning, Cayna could hear the muffled chatter coming from below. The villagers likely came here at night to relax and wind down. When she peeked into the dining hall from the stairs, she saw that a dozen or so men of varying ages had filled the seats. They were drinking, eating, and conversing merrily.

Apparently, a guest in the inn really was a rare occasion. Feeling the villagers' stares, Cayna crossed the tavern and sat in the same spot at the counter where she'd taken her breakfast that morning.

Without skipping a beat, Marelle placed her supper in front of her.

"Sorry 'bout the noise. Don't worry, though—these guys wouldn't hurt a fly," Marelle informed her with a jovial smile.

However, objections immediately began rising up around them.

"That's harsh, madam!"

"Yeah, we give ya a lot of business, y'know!"

"Better watch out, missy. He may not look it now, but back in his heyday, he was the village's bravest... Guh!"

This last comment earned the speaker a tray to the face from Marelle herself. Strength like that meant she'd probably be pretty good with a Frisbee. Knocked from his seat, the head of the villager who'd been struck stiffly jostled back.

Naturally, this sudden comedy act left Cayna in a slack-jawed state of shock. The dining hall (or since it was night, maybe *barroom* was more appropriate) roared with the villagers' laughter.

"Eat it while it's hot. My dad's cooking is the best."

"Oh, I will. Thank you very much... Huh?"

Cayna cocked her head at the younger, slimmer version of Marelle who now praised the still-steaming dish.

Her expression must have obviously read *I don't remember ever seeing her this morning,* because the girl gave a wry smile and began introducing herself.

"I'm Luine, the eldest daughter at this here inn. I'm already married, so I only come at night to help out. Are you one of our rare long-term guests?"

"Yes, my name is Cayna. It's a pleasure to meet you."

"Hey now, that's ain't no way for a guest to talk to staff! Where ya from, young miss?"

Cayna didn't think she'd said anything especially polite and found herself at a loss for words.

She'd been fairly upper-class back when she was human, but any suitably genteel manners had slipped away after her parents died. Furthermore, her personality had changed quite a bit since she'd started interacting with other people in the game. Cayna herself hadn't noticed this at all, but her cousin had cautioned her on numerous occasions.

The proprietress, Marelle, helped Cayna out of her current predicament by chiming in.

"C'mon, Luine! Don't bother the regulars. A lot of work went into that meal, and you're gonna let it go cold. If you've got time to prattle on, then at least carry a drink or two."

"Okay, okay, I'm coming. Honestly, Mom, a minute or two ain't gonna hurt anyone…"

Cayna watched Luine muttering as she returned to her waitressing duties, then looked up anxiously at Marelle behind the counter.

Although it seemed as though she had scolded her daughter harshly, the proprietress wasn't the least bit angry. She turned to Cayna good-naturedly.

"Hmm? If you want to talk with my daughter, make sure you eat that first."

"I will, thank you."

The menu included that morning's soup mixed with a small portion of meat and vegetables for a more savory flavor, as well as a small plate of salad. And just as at breakfast, Cayna was all smiles from beginning to end, constantly praising its deliciousness. Marelle gladly gave her one helping after another.

A few hours later, when it was obvious the villagers were thoroughly smashed…

Luine sat down next to Cayna, and they began chatting like old friends. Cayna did most of the talking. The rush of orders had died down, so Luine seemed to use this time to temporarily escape her waitressing duties. There was plenty of free time until closing.

"Wooow, you used to stay here two hundred years ago?"

"This was a border trading town back then. It was a bustling place full of carriages, people, and inns."

Cayna was actually a mess inside. After all, Luine had suddenly begged her to talk about life two hundred years ago. Even if she'd asked Cayna about just the past few days, Cayna would have been as fuzzy on the details as if she'd been told to describe a photo she'd seen only once. She felt bad that most of what she told Luine was a combination of lies and conjecture.

"Hey, I wonder if you ever met Great-Granny. They say she was a real looker back in her day."

"Um, I-I'm not sure if I did…"

Pretty impressive that people were still talking about this great-grandmother's beauty two hundred years later. In fact, Cayna was more intrigued by the fact that such an NPC even existed.

"So why'd you come to a backwoods place like this in the first place?"

"Ah, well, um, I'm looking for something…"

"Looking for something?" Marelle asked Cayna as she passed behind her with a handful of tankards.

Cayna hadn't meant to answer so bluntly. She didn't even know what she was looking for.

Lytt listened intently as she carried a tray and tilted her head cutely. Cayna couldn't help but pat her head, and the girl looked back at her sweetly.

Cayna had said she was looking for *something*, but it was more like *someplace*. A facility, to be exact.

According to her support AI, Kee, Cayna was cut off from the master system and could no longer access location services like the World Map. In other words, she was more than just lost; she was at the mercy of the world itself.

She wanted to know the location of her tower base and how far it was from this village. Nevertheless, Cayna thought it best to stay here for the time being until she was more familiar with the lay of the land.

It wasn't as if there was any problem with her ring. It would still take her directly to the tower regardless. However, she would have no choice but to pass through the surrounding forest if she wanted to get back to the village.

Initially, Cayna thought maybe she could use Flight to soar high above the trees, but based on Lytt's reaction to her earlier spell, she realized she was getting her priorities mixed. The villagers would likely mistake her for a monster and end up stressing unnecessarily. She needed the reassurance of knowing she wasn't interrupting people's peaceful lives.

"What're you lookin' for anyway? I'd be happy to help if I can," Marelle offered.

"Um, well, it's a silver tower in the middle of a forest."

""?!?!""

Cayna's honest answer left the old Marelle and her eldest daughter, Luine, speechless. Their faces expressed shock, but their eyes held distinct fear.

"N-now why would you wanna go to a terrifyin' place like that?"

"J-just give up now! Who knows what you'll find?!"

Their trembling voices indicated a definite fear of the place, and based on their warnings, it was clear they were worried for Cayna.

However, those concerns were being directed at the master of the silver tower herself. Cayna couldn't begin to guess what was driving their terror, and her mind swam with questions.

Huh? What? Did a dragon or something decide to move in after it sat neglected for two hundred years?

Dragons were a quintessential popular monster, but in a VRMMO like *Leadale*, dragons weren't Active-type monsters that openly roamed the fields.

Basic dragon-type monsters could be called upon using Summoning Magic. Most were found in places like player- and guild-run dungeons, where they were generally used as guard dragons in place of guard dogs.

In other words, if you wanted to fight a dragon outside of raiding someone else's tower, you had to get a player with the Summoning Magic: Dragon spell to do it for you.

Thus, Cayna couldn't rule out that someone had decided to occupy the empty tower and use it as their base.

However, Luine's next words overturned that concern.

...And not in a good way.

"Legend says the fearsome Silver Ring Witch lives there!!"

THUNK!!

It was Marelle and her daughters' turn to look baffled. Cayna had slammed her forehead on the counter as if she'd suddenly passed out. They stared at her for some time, but she only twitched slightly with seemingly no sign of getting up.

Worried their guest might be coming down with something, Lytt tugged at the sleeve of Cayna's robe. As the girl did so, not only did Cayna sit up, she rose from her chair entirely.

"A-are you okay? ...Feelin' a bit under the weather?" asked Marelle.

"YesI'mfineperfectlyhealthynoproblematatllwellthengoodnight!"

The three ladies blankly watched Cayna quickly rattle off an excuse and rush up the stairs at top speed.

"I wonder what's wrong...," Lytt said.

"Some trauma related to the Silver Ring Witch, maybe?" Luine suggested.

"Could've fooled me... Well, what can ya do? Let's call it a night."

Marelle's word was law. The girls started cleaning up and quickly forgot about Cayna's odd behavior.

Meanwhile, back in her room, Cayna lay on the bed with the blanket over her head and trembled in agony.

"I can't believe *that* lasted two hundred years into the future! This is sooo embarrassing..."

Moreover, she couldn't help but think it was a perfectly timed, wicked stunt someone had pulled solely to humiliate her.

The "Silver Ring Witch" was Cayna's infamous alias.

As a bonus prize for earning the title of Skill Master, players were given an Artifact of their choosing. Of course, there were some limits to how powerful it could be, but the unique equipment given was nothing short of extraordinary.

Cayna had requested an item that would increase her Magic Stats and give her a constant Magic Barrier. She left the design up to the Admins, and they came up with a giant silver ring that floated around the user. Just looking like a silver ring of Saturn was fine, but...

Whenever Cayna equipped it, the floating magic would activate on its own, and all the first-time ally players fighting in the Seven Nation Battle would see her as a Big Boss, as if they were in some kind of FPS game.

However, her current appearance and how people now saw her didn't really make a difference either way. As it was, her race traits were already elevated, and she had plenty of stat-boosting skills unique to her as a Skill Master. Moreover, thanks to level-breaking Synergy effects, Cayna's Attack Magic value was head and shoulders above that of other players.

These were only further powered up by the Silver Ring, and her super magic blasted everything away. Enemy players naturally trembled in fear, and thus, her notorious moniker formally came to be.

It was a dark stain on Cayna's history that she wished to seal away, but it seemed to be carved into legend even after she'd traveled worlds and space-time...

As the saying goes, *Anyone can start a rumor, but none can stop one.*

Though she trembled with shame, Cayna shook her head to chase away those negative thoughts and switched to something else. She hadn't yet been able to ask where the tower was located, so she vowed she would try tomorrow.

Still, the fact that her nickname hadn't faded into history was proof that players had existed in the past. As for those that might still remain besides Cayna, humans and werecats only had a life span of about two hundred years.

There were surely a number of dwarves and elves still around, though, who she could potentially find.

"There's no point dwelling on it. I can't confirm anything and don't see an end in sight, so I might as well just stop now."

Her mind was spinning around in circles, and since she didn't even have anyone to talk to about it, she decided to put the issue on hold until she could meet a mutually long-lived peer.

Cayna locked her door and, not having anything better to do, tried to go to sleep.

It was still too early for bedtime, and this world was full of endless fascination for someone like Keina, who grew up in a science-based civilization. Leadale itself had always been a continuous source of pleasure.

The light would pose problems once it was time for bed, however. The magically fueled lantern shone brightly and lit up every corner of the room. The Light spell she'd cast would last for roughly another six hours.

Players used the spell during dungeon crawls and the like, and when it ran out, that was usually a sign to finish things up. When party members came to a good stopping point, it was pretty standard for everyone to bring their light back outside and leave it there.

Since Cayna was trying to get some shut-eye and needed darkness, she cast the spell Black Light Level 2. Finding relief in the pitch-black room, she slipped under the covers.

"It'll go out before morning anyway."

Cayna figured she didn't need armor to sleep, but she didn't exactly have pajamas, either. She took off only her jagged arm guard and put it in the Item Box. Marelle had said that things like baths were a luxury, so she cleansed herself with the spell Purity and went to sleep.

It was the early hours of the morning, and as the village lay sleeping soundly, two shadows darted behind the buildings.

"I dunno, Zena. I been hearin' she's an adventurer. Sneakin' up on 'er seems sorta crazy."

"Dumbass, what's one little girlie like that gonna do? She's a sittin' duck for guys like us."

Zena and Lyle were the village misfits who the locals called punks and thieves whenever they were out of earshot.

The pair's target was the fat purse they'd seen Cayna flashing about that afternoon. She looked like nothing more than some little greenhorn adventurer girl, so anyone meeting her for the first time tended to underestimate her.

Little did they realize that her innocuous frame housed a transcendent being of a bygone era. To put it bluntly, their reckless endeavor was akin to a mouse challenging a monster. Even so, the two thugs lacked either the insight or competence to realize this.

They pilfered a ladder from a neighboring barn and laid it against the roof that would lead them to the window of Cayna's room. The two of them quietly climbed up. Lyle inserted a thin gold plate into the gap in the shutters and undid the window's inner latch.

As soon as he finished this delicate work, though, a pitch-black darkness radiated from the open window. Lyle let out a pitiful little yelp and fell backward. Naturally, there was nothing there to support him, and a painful-sounding *thump!* interrupted the silence as he tumbled to the ground.

The blow had knocked the wind out of him. He couldn't even answer his partner's questions.

"The hell are ya doin'? ...Hey, what's that?"

The darkness radiating from the room and beginning to seep outside made for an eerie spectacle in the moonlight.

Zena hesitated for a moment, but his greed was greater than his fear. He stepped into the gloom...all without noticing the magic immediately starting to rise within it.

Cayna's equipment was packed with a plethora of EX Items that gave her additional skills and special effects. Among them was a silver bracelet on her right arm that could automatically call upon an Active monster with Summoning Magic: Lightning Spirit Level 3. It was originally meant to be used when the player was Away and gained the nickname "Pervert Blocker."

She had this for a couple of reasons: Sometimes the Admins would, on a whim, hold events where monsters attacked all the towns. Other times, people would pull mischievous pranks like doodling on players who had their statuses set to Away. All the more proof that your safety wasn't guaranteed even within the towns.

At that moment, the spell identified the thieves as a threat and instantly summoned a Lightning Spirit whose threat level was somewhere in the 330 range (calculated by multiplying the caster's highest level and the Summoning spell level by 10 percent). You'd need four level-330 players to handle something like that.

The jagged 3D frames converged in front of Zena and materialized with an electric spark to form the silhouette of a lion. The wave of electric aftershocks zapped the intruder, who fell backward with a shout. The lion nimbly pursued.

Zena landed and twitched spastically in front of Lyle, who had finally managed to recover. The electric lion, which was almost double the size of a bear, soon caught up to them. The two flustered hoodlums spurred their aching bodies on and made a break for it.

The electric lion chased the two around the village and only returned to Cayna's side once they were beyond its perimeter. It deftly used its front paws to close the window that had been left wide-open before sitting in the center of the room.

The magic power that had been circulating while the Black Light was in effect had been used up and was now dissipated. Of course, Cayna had no idea any of this had happened during the night, and by the time the morning rays broke through the gap in her window, she woke energized and ready to take on the day.

Kee, who kept watch outside day and night, knew all about the incident. He had intentionally determined it was Not Important, and the truth remained hidden in darkness.

"Wow, it sure is nice out."

Cayna opened her window to let in the fresh air and verdant scent of the outdoors. The sight Mother Nature wrought soon after this new dawn moved her heart. It reminded her of the spectacle she'd once seen when she went mountain climbing with her parents as a child. Tears began to well in her eyes.

She stared at the marvelous scenery for a long while without feeling the least bit bored but noticed something flashing out of the corner of her eye. Cayna turned to the right and used Eagle Eye to magnify it.

"…Ah, there it is."

Although only the top half was visible from the village, a silver tower clearly stood at the foot of the mountain range to her right.

"I guess that's our mission today, huh?" Cayna said with a quiet laugh. A knock came at the door, and she left the window to answer it.

"You've barely got any equipment. Are you sure you're going to be okay?"

"There's no need to worry. Even with this, I'm pretty capable on my own."

In front of the inn, Cayna was engaged in a verbal tug-of-war as Marelle fretted over the girl leaving the village. It all started with her lack of anything beyond basic equipment. She didn't even have a tool bag.

She couldn't exactly say she had an Item Box in another dimension that housed vast stores of goods, and she was at a loss over how to free herself of this predicament.

Help came from a most unexpected source.

"Well then, miss, you could at least take this!"

"Huh? Lytt?"

Lytt held a leather canteen out to her. Unable to say no to those eyes swimming with deep concern, Cayna accepted it with a bright smile.

"Thank you, Lytt. I'd be happy to borrow it for a while. I'll make sure to bring you back a present, so look forward to it."

"Take care, miss."

"*Sigh*. Honestly… Listen, Cayna. My husband's going all-out for dinner tonight, so make sure you're back by then."

"I will, Marelle."

The mother and daughter saw Cayna off at the village entrance and watched her cheerfully wave at them down the main road. She finally vanished from sight, and they turned back the way they came.

Considering Cayna had told them just the day before that she was going to look for the silver tower, it wouldn't have made any sense for her to suddenly announce the next morning that she was going to pick medicinal herbs instead. Marelle had heard from Lytt that Cayna could use magic, so she figured their lodger wouldn't be in too much danger so long as she didn't run into too many monsters.

Given Cayna's base specs, the monsters in this area were by far the ones in *real* danger.

…Not that Marelle had any way of knowing that.

"I wonder if this is far enough?"

After walking down the main road for some time, Cayna checked to see if the village was out of sight and turned down a side path that led into the forest.

She stepped out into an open meadow as if somehow guided there.

Along the way, Cayna had heard strange whispers that she told herself countless times were all in her head. This was surely due to high elves' natural affinity for the trees and flora, which made some Craft Skills quite difficult.

After checking that no one was around, just to be safe, she raised her Guardian Ring and recited the secret code.

This code was a spell the Skill Masters had devised together, and it worked for every ring, hence why Cayna didn't want anyone from the village overhearing her. It was at this moment that she most clearly grasped the phrase "Loose lips sink ships."

"One who protects in times of trouble! I beseech you to rescue this depraved world from chaos!"

Upon finishing her chant, a silver sparkle began dancing around Cayna. Countless bands of light rose up from beneath her and created a glittering silver cylinder that wrapped around her like a cocoon. High above, the remaining beams came together in a complex pattern to form a mandala-like magic circle. It was reminiscent of an ice field brimming with silver powder that fluttered like snow and was as dazzling as an ice show.

Each Guardian Ring had its own unique effect—this was Cayna's.

The master of the Palace of the Dragon King, for example, would apparently become surrounded by an impressive waterfall.

"Does it have to be this pointlessly fancy each and every time...?"

A black space opened up in the center of the mandala overhead and steadily approached Cayna with every spin of the magic circle. Swallowed up along with the cylindrical veil, she passed through momentary darkness before finding herself in a completely ordinary stone-walled room.

She gave a huge sigh and let her shoulders droop, then turned her ring toward the wall right in front of her.

After profuse rumbling and creaking, the stone wall split down the middle and opened. Ahead of her was a smooth, unadorned stone corridor.

"Why does it look so boring down here? I guess even Opus gets artist's block sometimes…"

The door behind her closed back up. She was now locked in, and the lines of the stone wall fit together so seamlessly, it was as if the door hadn't existed at all.

To the right was the set of stairs that served as the tower's main passageway. The tower itself was about two hundred meters, but once people started climbing it, the stairs began rotating until they seemed to spiral endlessly. The staircase would pause at certain intervals, enticing visitors to reach the top.

A formula nullifying all magic had been inscribed into the stairs of every floor except the top one to keep players from using a Flight spell to reach the summit. It was a type of trap that cruelly transported any player who stopped walking back outside the tower.

This was Skill Master Cayna's silver tower. A player could complete the trial by reaching the top after climbing for twenty-four hours without rest. Failure to do so meant being dropped outside and having to start all over again.

To the left was a large reception hall where she greeted visitors. As Cayna headed toward it, a baroque-style veranda and great blue sky spread before her. It seemed to be built like a type of open stage.

In actuality, it was supposed to be enclosed by thick walls and covered with a ceiling to keep out the wind and rain. The single remaining brick wall contained a mural. The clumsy-looking sun was drawn rather roughly. The eyes one might expect to be carved into place rolled around and took in Cayna's every movement.

"Well, well, well! Long time no see, Master. What brings YOU here after abandoning my magnificence for two hundred years?"

"...*Sigh.* Looks like you got a mouth on you now..."

Like the NPCs, the Guardians who managed the towers in the game were only supposed to stick to the script... She never expected it would do a complete one-eighty and turn into this punk delinquent character. She was struck speechless.

"Did anyone pass the trial while I was gone?"

"Nope. Nothin' but peace and quiet around here. I'm so bored, I think I'm gonna puke."

What's with the attitude? This Guardian can't move in the first place, so what did it think it could possibly do to pass the time?

"Oh yeaaaah. That Skargo guy dropped by about sixty years ago. He wanted to talk to ya, Master, but you decided to ignore all my calls. Um, hello?"

"Uh, about that... I've been a little busy..."

Whenever a visitor arrived, the Guardians were able to contact their masters through the rings to inform them—hence why Cayna could leave the tower for a stroll whenever she liked.

She herself had no memory of what had happened sixty years ago, let alone two hundred, and tried to keep her answers vague.

"...Hey!"

"Hmm? What is it?"

"That Skargo guy was here. Didja hear me?"

"Yeah, I heard you... Who's Skargo?"

"WHAT?!"

"Huh? Buh? Wha—?"

If this Guardian had limbs and a body, it would have slapped a hand to its forehead. It heaved an exasperated sigh and mumbled to no one in particular:

"The old hag's finally gone senile..."

"Pardon? What was that just now?"

The word *hag* didn't escape her attention, and Cayna immediately took out a staff from her Item Box.

Standing two meters tall, it was composed of three intricately twisted dragons facing three different directions. Their open maws each held a jewel; red, blue, and gold, respectively. It was a rare item known as the Arcal Staff, a heinous piece of equipment that could rain down the highest level of Flame, Frost, or Lightning Magic in a single strike. However, it could only be used once a day.

"Uh, hey, Master? Whatcha doin' with that staff?"

"I was thinking I could use it to beat my foul-mouthed Guardian into shape. Better yet, why don't I freeze you for the next two hundred years?"

"My bad. Forgive me, Master."

It wasn't the most heartfelt apology, but Cayna decided to let it go and put the staff away. Besides, since the entire tower was set up with special Artifacts, she wasn't sure if her magic would have any effect anyway.

"...So who's Skargo?"

"Wow, no love for him, either, huh? Poor guy. Don't go forgettin' he's your son. Hello?"

"...? Whaaa—? My *son*?!"

The Guardian looked at Cayna and sighed with a *"C'mon, seriously?"* as she let out a frantic cry. Tilting her head questioningly and murmuring "Son, Skargo, son, Skargo" as if it might strike a chord, she remained lost in thought for some time.

"Oh… Ohhhhhh!!"

Ten minutes later, she seemed to realize something and pressed a fist to her palm with a shout.

"The Foster System! I remember now!"

"…What the heck you goin' on about?"

The Admins officially called it the NPC Compensation Program, while players knew it as the Foster System. It was a ridiculous and unprecedented request from early designers that passed through the Admins that basically boiled down to *Coming up with all these NPC names is getting to be a pain.* This system offered to recruit players' sub-characters as NPCs.

Leadale included a feature where, for a small fee, you could create up to two characters.

Most players treated these as mules, characters who held items that weren't used often but were still too valuable to get rid of. Once you acquired your own base for use as storage, these mule characters would be reduced to nothing more than pitiful, forgotten ghosts.

The Foster System was a scheme for the Admins to buy up NPCs. There were also perks if your character had a decent set of skills. They might be appointed to an important position, and depending on where they were appointed, the player who contributed the character might get half their salary.

As a result, a lot of newbie players registered with the system with an eye toward monetary gain. Since these characters wouldn't disappear from the player's profile, newcomers and veterans alike used the system for a bit of peace of mind.

One requirement was that there be some connection between the contributed character and its player. Of the relationships people decided to go with, there were naturally a few outliers. They ranged from those who boasted "My little sister knows one hundred eight techniques" to those who declared the characters were their wives. Players who insisted on an "Ultimate Slave Harem" were dealt with.

There were widespread rumors that these NPCs might be used for quests at some point, but that didn't turn out to be the case.

The truth was, players had registered so many all in the name of money that the Admins couldn't handle them all.

Cayna had submitted a total of three sub-characters, two of which she'd purchased in-game. At the time, she had decided all three would be her children.

Skargo, the eldest of the three, was an elf and priest type who was highly skilled in the healing arts. He had probably gotten involved in the church.

Next was her daughter, Mai-Mai, Skargo's younger sister and also an elf. Her specialization in Attack Magic had helped her find employment in the game's Mage Guild.

Cayna's youngest, Kartatz was "adopted" even in the conventional sense. He was most likely employed as a skilled dwarf craftsman.

In the world of Leadale, elves lived about five hundred years and dwarves about three hundred, so she figured all three were still alive by this point. Each had been given an inferior copy of the Guardian Ring, so Skargo must have bypassed the trial and come here directly.

"So I'm an unmarried seventeen-year-old with children over two hundred years old…"

"Whazzat? Quit makin' no sense."

The Guardian looked as if it wanted to say more, but Cayna was unbothered. With an air of *Well, I guess it keeps things interesting, right?* she walked over to the edge of the stage.

As she placed her ring within a cavity in the floor and turned it, something clicked, and a stone sarcophagus big enough to easily hold an adult rose up.

Each tower was equipped with a large storeroom. Cayna opened the lid and checked through the contents. She could clearly tell what was inside, even though it seemed too dark to see. The Item Window opened on her right and displayed a large quantity of items in storage on the left.

This was no different from her usual game experience, but her mind was still full of questions. Even so, theorizing wasn't really Cayna's forte. Her less-than-stellar friend had been especially good at that, so she couldn't help but feel she should just defer if they ever crossed paths again.

The Guardian spoke to her as she carefully went over what to take with her, all the while wondering between responses if a friend like this Guardian would be any fun.

"Hey, Master. You didn't just come to pick stuff up, right?"

"Hmm. I knew it—I'm running low on plant ingredients... Right, I'll have to make that a top priority. By the way, do you know what's been going on lately?"

"Yeah, I heard a bunch of stuff from Skargo. About the seven nations turning into three and all that."

"Huh? Why do I have so many gag weapons? Was I holding them for someone? I wonder what became of everyone."

"Beats me. Half your friends were human, right? They gotta be six feet under by now."

"Well, yeah, that's true..."

Cayna sorted through her stores for quite a while, and the sun was at its zenith by the time she finished. She closed the sarcophagus lid and pushed it back into the floor.

Afterward, she approached the mural Guardian, pressed her hand to the wall, and transferred about 90 percent of her MP. Maintaining the world and the quests that went along with it was the Admins' job, but as a Skill Master, it was her duty to take care of the Guardian and the tower.

In addition to many other rewards, Cayna had acquired the highest MP level in *Leadale*'s history, so she always made sure the Guardian had a full supply of magic. That was why, even after two hundred years, it was still functioning somehow.

Even so, when she checked it just then, it was clearly on the verge of running dry. Cayna would have preferred to fill its tank, but even with her continuous MP renewal spell Passive Skill: MP Healing, doing so was bound to take all night. She had made a promise to Marelle and was set on returning to the village sometime that day.

As Cayna considered what she should do, the Guardian spoke up.

"Hey, Master, I got a favor to ask."

"Hmm? You don't say things like that very often. What is it?"

"Apparently, the other Guardians at the other towers have shut down. Can you check 'em out if you got time?"

"...Ah, guess they've been neglected, too. I understand. I'll look for them if I have time."

The Guardians of each tower could communicate among one another, but that ability was useless if some of them had fallen into disrepair. Since the rings worked with any tower, she would at least be able to avoid the traps, but she'd also have to dive underwater...

In that case, it meant Cayna would have to regularly patrol the thirteen towers. Despite being a pressing issue, though, it wasn't as if she knew where they all were. Since she couldn't access the World Map, for now she'd have to find a densely populated area and gather information.

This would more than likely come with its own large set of problems. Highly visible towers wouldn't be too much trouble, but there was no way she could search for those buried underground. Furthermore, the ocean was just as challenging but for a different reason. After all, the continent of Leadale was surrounded by water to the north, west, and south. If Cayna wanted to look for places the

Guardian Ring might react to, she'd probably have to float over the sea for hours on end. Either method required time she simply didn't have.

For the time being, she pointed southwest from the veranda and issued instructions to the Guardian.

"I'll be in that village over there for a while. Call me if anything happens."

"Got it. Thanks much, Master."

From the center of the stage, Cayna gave the Guardian the signal. A blueish-white pentagram appeared and began glowing beneath her feet. Before she knew it, Cayna was in the forest surrounding the silver tower. She looked up at it for a moment before turning on her heel and heading in the direction she had pointed out earlier.

"Hmm. Shoot… I should have put something down that would give me the option to teleport."

At the very least, thanks to the Distance Measurement spell Cayna had cast before she left, she could walk a straight line to the village that lay over forty kilometers away. Traveling the base of a mountain by foot meant a lot of circumventing and added quite a bit of distance. Even though she was walking on flat earth now, Cayna was still a bit worried whether she'd be back at the inn in time for dinner.

"Haaah… Heave… Haaah… Hooo…"

After a great deal of thought, she eventually decided to just run. Although Cayna specialized in magic, it was a chance for her to show off her full specs as a high elf. It was a shame no one was around to witness it.

She used an Active Skill, Travel Speed Up (duration: one minute), and chose the Magic Skills Agility Up and Movement Up. Cayna repeated this again and again as she tore down the road.

Since she was in a forest, the boost she got from the trees made the journey easier than it would have been in an open plain. Even so, she wasn't used to running, and the sky was turning dusky by the time she approached the village.

Cayna had been bedridden in her former life, and while she could still remember the sensation of running, actually doing it took some effort. She constantly fell down over nothing and got tripped up by her own legs. A few times, she almost ran into branches and tree trunks because she was busy looking at her own two feet. The only reason she made it out alive was because the trees took care to warn her of any imminent danger.

If her fellow guild members had seen such a sight, they surely would have said, *What are you, stupid?*

There was also the option of flying, but since Cayna had given her MP to the Guardian, she had less than 10 percent of her usual amount. Even if she tried, she probably wouldn't even last five minutes in the air.

At any rate, the village was only a few minutes on foot from the main road—but that wasn't taking into account her present body's athletic specs. Her stats weren't the problem. With the weakest character specs in the game, Cayna was ill-suited for sprinting at full speed. Even the forest couldn't fix that. On the way back to the main road, she took a number of breaks and healed her fatigue on multiple occasions.

And that's when it came.

Quenching her parched throat with the filled water canteen Lytt lent her, Cayna took a deep breath. *Better get going*, she thought as she stretched, feeling good as new, when the loud howling of a beast echoed nearby with a "*Graaaaaaaagh!*"

"Huh? What? Where's it coming from?!"

"From the main road, Cayna" came Kee's monotone reply.

Fearing she was under attack, Cayna had taken up a strange pose.

Embarrassed, she soon raced ahead, fearful that someone else was in trouble.

She cut through the forest and came upon a hunter sitting on the main road. It was the villager Marelle had smacked over the head with a tray for speaking out of line.

A bear towered before him on its hind legs, ready to strike.

While it was indeed a bear, it stood about four meters high and had twisting horns that extended toward the corners of its mouth. This was a horned bear. Back when Cayna played the game, horned bears were nicknamed "bore bears"—tough for newbies, chump change for midlevel players.

The horned bear stiffened as soon as it saw Cayna.

This was thanks to her Active Skills, which readied her for a fight. Intimidate (sharply decreases an enemy's ability to escape), Glare (slows an enemy's movements), and Warrior Smile (has a 22 percent chance of nullifying the enemy's defenses) had automatically kicked in, and the poor horned bear had no place to run.

In any case, Cayna hadn't once considered fighting with a weapon when she decided to rush into the fray. The only thing on her mind was *I have to save that villager!*

With a running start, Cayna leaped into the air to knock the horned bear out of the way. She threw a beautifully executed flying kick right into the horned bear's gut.

"HYAAAA!!"

"GWAGH?!"

The second she made impact, Weapon Skill: Charge automatically activated. Cayna was insanely powerful and high-level despite being one of the weaker races. Her kick bent the horned bear's massive body in half and sent it flying. It then crash-landed in the forest along the roadside. The fierce cracking of toppled trees could be heard as the monster disappeared into the wooded depths.

The hunter, unsurprisingly, had broken into a cold, paralyzed sweat at the sight of Cayna's flying kick. Silence momentarily fell over them.

Cayna reacted first and rushed over to the hunter.

"Are you all right?! You're not hurt, are you?!"

"Y-Yeah…I'm okay. Wow, miss… You're pretty incredible, aren't you…?"

"A-ah, um… Yeah! Ten, no, twenty of those bears are nothing for me! Ha-ha-ha!"

Since monsters like that really weren't the least bit of a threat, this was no exaggeration.

Perhaps subdued by the way Cayna thrust out her chest and laughed uproariously, the hunter stood and offered his thanks.

"Thank you, miss. I was almost done for. I would love to give you something as a reward, but I'm afraid I don't have anything on me."

"There's no need. Isn't it natural to help others in trouble?"

"Y-yeah, that's true…"

"Well then, instead of a reward, I'd be happy if you called me 'Cayna' instead of 'miss.'"

"I see. Of course. My name's Lottor. Thank you again, Miss Cayna."

"It's no trouble. I'm glad you're safe."

With a sigh of relief, Cayna peeked into the dark forest that had swallowed up the bear. She was sure the enemy's HP bar had gone from yellow to red to zero the moment her kick connected. In other words, it had been a one-hit KO.

"What should I do with the bear?"

She was certain she'd read on the official website that its meat was delicious. Thinking maybe she could treat the villagers to a feast, Cayna stepped into the forest. Its horn and pelt would also make good material for weapons.

Lottor hurriedly followed after her.

"Hold on, what if it's still alive? Fighting a bear in the forest is asking for death."

"Don't worry, it's dead. Would you mind waiting just a moment?"

Cayna cast a Light spell on a silver coin and stepped farther into the forest.

The horned bear had smashed through a straight line of countless trees and was lying dead with bloody foam around its mouth. She grabbed it by the horns and tried to pick it up, only to realize it was much lighter than expected. She dragged it back to the main road. Lottor watched in amazement as the petite girl pulled along a horned bear three times her size with ease.

The sun had completely set by the time they arrived at the village, and an anxious Lytt had clung to Cayna in tears. She gave a scream when she saw the horned bear, but the giant prey sent the villagers' excitement through the roof. When the village elder declared it a blessing from the forest and called for a banquet that very night, the people cheered and set to work. Married and unmarried women alike gathered together and began dissecting it. The men, on the other hand, brought out the tables and chairs from the inn and set up a large bonfire in the village's central plaza.

Cayna had thought the inn was the place for large gatherings but then realized this plaza was actually pretty convenient for such an occasion.

The few children present laid out buckets of water around the bonfire just in case. Cayna didn't have much else to do, so she helped them out.

Lottor then approached and asked what they should do with the horned bear materials.

"Um, I don't really need anything. Please use them with the other villagers."

"Oh, no, we can't do that. Aren't you the one who slayed it, Miss Cayna? There's a pelt, horns, fangs, and claws."

The pelt could be worn as protection against the cold or crafted into a rug, the fangs could be used in place of nails, and the claws were already suitable as small knives. Cayna thought about it for a moment and decided to take only the horns so she could make a beginner's spear or something similar out of it. The rest would apparently be divided among the villagers.

Since Cayna was the guest of honor, she could only watch without lifting a finger until everything was ready. She was then handed a tankard filled to the brim with fruit wine.

"Go on, Miss Cayna."

"Uh, pardon?"

Not understanding what was going on, she looked around at the villagers. They all smiled as if she'd done something funny.

Refusing to just stand by, Marelle explained. "Since you're the guest of honor, go ahead and give a command."

I get it, Cayna realized. It was like a toast. She'd never actually given one, though, and only knew about them from TV and books.

After a moment's thought, she shouted, "To new friendships!" and raised her tankard high. The crowd responded with bright smiles, and the modest banquet finally began.

The skewered horned bear meat was the main course, but the women had lined the table with other dishes as well. One might have thought they could go on cooking forever, but once a certain amount was set out all at once, that was apparently it.

After their work was done, the women joined in the fun with drinking, eating, singing, and dancing. It seemed the party would end when the initial round of food and drink was gone.

Cayna slowly nursed the fruit wine she'd been given. Since there was a wide spectrum of resistance against status ailments, players like

Cayna didn't typically drink. However, she realized abstaining would be rude in such a situation and decided to push herself.

Thus, after only the smallest sip of fruit wine, Cayna's senses soon turned bubbly.

What did alcohol intolerance look like in high elves, who were considered royalty among the elven race? No one had warned her, and she had never bothered to ask for herself.

As the food dwindled, the villagers' focus turned to Cayna. Naturally, the hunter Lottor spread the word of her heroic valor. Cayna blushed and curled in on herself as she listened.

Not only that, but just as the villagers finished singing her praises, she took the tankard she'd been using to hide her embarrassment and began drinking with relish. Her thus-far-slightly-buzzed consciousness was quickly swept away. Her sudden silly expression astounded the villagers.

"Guess Cayna was a lightweight."

"You think she pushed herself?"

"She seemed to be of age, but...maybe she's younger than I thought?"

Naturally, a party is considered over when the main guest is smashed. The villagers started cheerfully cleaning up.

Cayna, who had fallen asleep before the banquet's end, was carried back to her room on Marelle's back.

CHAPTER 2
Magic, a Hunt, a Development, and a Well

When Cayna woke up with a headache the next morning, she vowed she would never drink again.

"Agh…"

With a fed-up expression that seemed to say, *Is this what it means to wreck yourself with alcohol?* she headed to the well to wash her face.

There, she found Lytt giving a "Heave-ho" as she drew water from the well. The girl noticed Cayna just as she was lifting up a small, filled pail.

Lytt alternated her gaze between the pail and Cayna. Deciding guests were the priority, she offered the small bucket of water, but Cayna refused.

"It's okay, Lytt. You're at work now, right? I can do it myself."

"Um, but…"

"Oh, and look at what you're wearing! Do you like it?"

"Yeah!"

Lytt had on a star-shaped hair accessory. The silver lamé sparkled and turned blue and green depending on how the light struck it. It was one of the items Cayna had taken out of storage the day before and gave +1 Defense as well as poison nullification. She thought it suited Lytt, so she had brought it back as a present.

It was the first item she had ever made with the Offline Mode Craft Skill: Accessory. Cayna had stored it away as a keepsake and had completely forgotten about it until rediscovering it yesterday.

It was incredibly rare for a village girl to own such an item, and the memory of how Lytt had danced with glee made Cayna smile. She patted Lytt's head as the girl nodded with a marvelous grin.

Cayna then approached the well and swiftly pulled the rope to draw water. She looked into the relatively cool, clear water and murmured, "Actually, I want warm water," as she held her hand out over the bucket.

Magic Skill: Additional Warm Water: Start

An instant later, the invisible light that poured from her outstretched hand slightly heated the water in the bucket. Lytt's eyes widened as steam rose from the pail, and she gave a hearty round of applause as Cayna dipped the towel she'd brought with her into the water.

Marelle, who had come out to complain about what was taking her daughter so long, appeared befuddled by how relaxed the two of them were.

"Oh? So magic can do things like that, too?"

"I'm sorry. I interrupted Lytt's work…"

Not wanting Lytt to get in trouble, Cayna had bowed her head low. Marelle merely responded with astonishment.

Cayna had become an overnight sensation in the village. The people greeted her warmly whenever they crossed paths and would even offer her a literal piece of their pie. There weren't many young women in town, so the older citizens began regarding her as a sort of adoptive granddaughter. Cayna had no intention of revealing her character's true age by this point and accepted the role without question. She soon began chatting with the elderly at the hospital and wasn't particularly bothered by the all-too-familiar setting.

"Hmm, seems pretty handy. You think people like us can use it, too?"

"The Warm Water spell? Um, you'll need to learn the Iyah and Iyahra for Fire Magic and the Ohta for Water Magic, so…"

"Okay, okay, I get it! At this age, I don't have that kinda time to study magic."

As Cayna counted the different forms of magic on her fingers, Marelle waved her own hand dismissively.

Even if Cayna offered them skills using a scroll, she had no idea if the villagers could actually learn spells. Watching Cayna sink deeper into thought with a serious "Hmm," Marelle patted her shoulder with a wry smile and went to leave.

Just then, Lottor walked in the open door with something in one hand.

"Good morning, Miss Cayna. I've brought the bear horns you asked me for yesterday."

"Oh, are you sure? Won't it be a valuable source of income for the village?"

"No worries. You're the one who took the monster down, right? That means this belongs to you."

A village like this on the outskirts of the Kingdom of Felskeilo and dependent on the flow of outside trade throughout Leadale didn't have much to offer. Thus, caravans would routinely come by once every several months and sell everything from grain to game and replenish daily necessities.

"Hmm. All right, in that case, why don't I take down another one for you?"

"Oh, no, no, no. You're not even a villager, Miss Cayna. There's no need for you to do such a thing."

"But you've all been so kind. I want to show my appreciation."

The two horns he handed to her were tied together with rope. Cayna stared at them as she made her suggestion, and Marelle placed a hand on the girl's head.

"You don't have worry about us so much. After all, you're our guest. It's not like we're bein' nice because we want a reward."

"That's right! Miss Cayna, didn't you say yesterday that it's only natural to help others in need?"

"...But I'd feel guilty if I accepted such kindness yet did nothing in return..."

This desire to repay others was a self-indulgence born of Keina's inability to do anything for herself after the accident.

Her uncle and cousin. The doctors and nurses. The other admitted children as well as elderly patients. They would come to see her when she wasn't playing the game and help ease the pain of losing her parents and facing such trying circumstances. However, she no longer had the chance to repay them.

"Well, go ahead and do whatever you like. We're all pretty happy with life here."

"Hear, hear! It looks like wisdom really does come with a... Gwagh!"

"Get back to work, you! Quit dawdling around!"

Marelle angrily chased Lottor out with a tray before turning around with a big smile and patting Cayna on the back as if to say, *Don't sweat it.* She then headed back inside.

Cayna shifted her gaze between Marelle's back and that of Lottor, who had been forcefully sent on a hunt. She followed the latter.

He noticed her as he was covering himself with leaves outside the village.

"What are you doing, Lottor?"

"M-Miss Cayna?! Don't sneak up on me like that! Ya nearly gave me a heart attack!"

"Ha-ha, I'm sorry about that."

Once he could breathe again, Lottor resumed patting himself down with leaves. Cayna stared at him with keen interest. It seemed to be some sort of ancestral method of effectively masking human scent.

She figured she ought to follow suit and cast Deodorize to erase her own scent. Afterward, Cayna sniffed the air but couldn't tell if there was much of a difference and simply angled her head curiously. She resumed following Lottor.

As a hunter, it was his job to venture out every two or three days and use traps to hunt small birds and animals. He also knew his way around the forest and had to stop Cayna from traveling down the game trails her eyes expertly spotted.

"Huh? But this is a game trail, isn't it?"

"It belongs to some type of carnivore. If we go down that way, it'll probably pick up our scent and follow us to the village. We should take this narrow path."

The lush area he indicated was so overgrown with weeds and field grass that it was impossible to tell if there was a path at all, but Cayna's keen high-elf senses told her where to go. She half-dubiously continued trailing Lottor, and they indeed came upon a road that was just barely passable.

Her elven sensitivities were genuine, but this sixth sense of hers had never come this naturally before. However, if this truly was reality and not just a game, she had no choice but to get used to it. Even if the adjustment happened slowly over time, Cayna wasn't yet a full-fledged high elf. There were still parts of her that didn't know the first thing about this society and were decidedly "un-elf-like."

As Cayna followed Lottor, one thing was soon made clear.

She had no idea how to navigate a forest.

As they came out upon an area where the trees grew sparse and she went to take a step toward a wide space densely scattered with fallen leaves, Lottor issued a warning.

"Miss Cayna, you don't know what's hiding in there. I think we should go around it."

"Oh, really? All right."

Insisting that it was better to have more targets if they hoped to catch anything, he headed toward a choir of birdsong. He then stated there were so many that he and Cayna wouldn't stand a chance and reluctantly backed away.

Back when she was playing the game, none of those details mattered. Cutting straight through the forest and mowing down any enemies that stood in her way was all part of the experience.

Now that Lottor was here, it was only natural that she follow his lead. She also felt slightly guilty for saying such silly things and sticking so close to him. She hoped she could repay him by helping out somehow.

Finally, Lottor was able to collect a few birds from the traps he had laid a few days prior. After Lottor reset the traps, their forest stroll came to an end.

"Miss Cayna, are you really an elf?"

"Ah-ha-ha... I was mostly on the battlefield, so I never did much hunting."

She had used the stories from the manga and novels she read a long time ago to fool his suspicious gaze, but it wasn't long before she had a chance to show off her battle skills— Just as they were heading home, a horned bear appeared.

The scent of leaves wouldn't help them with this one. The horned bear rose up on its hind legs to take a swing at Lottor, but Cayna sent it flying an impressive distance with a quickly cast Wind spell.

The horned bear went tumbling onto the main road. By the

time it shook its head, stood up, and checked its surroundings, it was too late.

With a big help from a running start and some Wind Magic, Cayna had already unleashed her beautiful flying form. The kick, powered by an extra burst of Weapon Skill: Charge and a boost of indiscriminate force, exploded in time with an inexplicable shout of "SUPER DANGEROUS DESTROYER KICK!!"

Cayna's face grew beet red when she realized Lottor was there to hear her triumphant battle cry—a moment she would pretend never happened.

Dragging the bear down the road, she hurried down the path to the village with Lottor, making every effort to hide her red ears the entire way.

The villagers gladly welcomed another helping of valuable food and resources. However, since the caravans would soon be arriving, they would butcher and safely store it so it could later be used for bartering.

Cayna planned on giving them the whole bear since she didn't have much use for it, but they once again insisted "At least take this!" and offered her the horns. She didn't feel quite right about accepting the kind offer, but two horns could be used to make a pronged spear, while the other two could be used as a catalyst to summon a familiar. Strength-wise, it would be about level 20 and weak enough that Cayna could take it down with a snap of her fingers.

She had no idea what level the people of this world were at, but she figured she might as well help wherever she could.

The following day was a boring one that consisted of absolutely nothing. Tossing around the horns as if they were beanbags, Cayna strolled about the village, wondering if there was anything she could do. The town had nothing but houses and fields, so her only option was to sit on a boulder by the roadside and watch the villagers tend to their work. There weren't any attractions of any sort, so the tranquil scenery was pretty much the only excitement the village had going for it. Coming here, one couldn't expect much more than collecting the eggs of the chickens who walked around as if they owned the place.

With this in mind, Cayna looked at the Map Window in the corner of her vision that showed her progress. Her movements over the past two days between the silver tower, the village, and the surrounding area were marked down like a satellite image taken from above.

"Kee?"

"I have created a map of the remote region. Let us expand our range and form a more detailed picture."

"Yeah, I guess that's about all we can do. That aside, doesn't this village feel familiar?"

The cluster of houses at the center of the village. The fields along the outer perimeter. Cayna felt as if she'd seen them somewhere before and pondered with an intense "Hmm." Soon enough, a memory welled up from deep inside her.

"Ah, this must be one of the Entry Points in Offline Mode."

The VRMMORPG game *Leadale* had both an Online Mode and an Offline Mode, and each had different Entry Points. In Online Mode, it was the royal capital of whatever nation you belonged to, and in Offline Mode, you were put in any random village. It was the player's job to turn their little hamlet into a fortress by completing the villagers' requests. Those who completed the scenario and acquired fifteen magic spells and thirty skills carved a pathway to quest success.

In *World of Leadale*, aside from the seven basic types of magic, you couldn't earn a single skill without completing quests. Only those who obtained four thousand skills and completed the prerequisite quest could be Skill Masters.

However, there was a hidden disadvantage. If even one of your skills was gained through a scroll, you were disqualified from becoming a Skill Master. On that note, it wasn't an exaggeration to say the title itself was a trap set by the Admins. Naturally, a skill cannot be voided once obtained. Even if you try to start that prerequisite quest, it won't initiate because the skill has already been acquired.

Game addicts like Cayna who had been around since beta testing knew about this, but those who only jumped into the world after the game got off the ground didn't and missed their chance for the title.

Incidentally, the Admins scrubbed anything about this truth as soon as it hit the Internet. Thus, aside from those who joined in the game's earliest stages, not many knew about it. Veteran players wailed that they should channel their efforts into more productive avenues.

In that case, why not help this village progress like the ones in Offline Mode? she wondered idly.

"That might end up being a bit of a pain, though…"

The field workers called out to Cayna as she mumbled deep in thought.

"Hey there, Miss Cayna. Got some business here in the fields?"

"…Huh? Ah, um, I was just wondering how I could help the village out."

Upon hearing this, the villagers looked at one another and burst into laughter.

"Wh-what's so funny?"

"Nah, don't take it personally, Miss Cayna. It's just that you're a guest at the inn."

"That's right. Taking care of the village is a *villager's* job!"

"You don't gotta worry about somethin' like that."

Obviously, she couldn't say much to their unanimous responses and jovial laughter. She ducked her head and quickly left. Soon after, she gazed up at the sky with crossed arms and mentally checked through her array of skills one by one.

They really did run the gamut. Some, like the Magic Skill: Warm Water she had used recently, were good for a single quest and pretty much useless afterward. There were also plenty she'd acquired in order to obtain certain high-level skills, only to never touch them again. Others were problematic if taken lightly. Craft Skill: Building: Castle was a good example of this.

Fewer than half of all skills were used consistently into the foreseeable future. Even Craft Skills that actually specialized in creating something numbered fewer than 2,500—as was the case with Weapon Skills, Active Skills, Passive Skills, and Special Skills. There were so many that even Cayna couldn't remember all the ones she had in her arsenal. She had to check her Skill List for each new situation and see what would fit.

She strolled around the outer edge of the village, passed through the wild fields that long ago served as a rest stop for carriages entering the village, and found herself at the back of the inn.

There, she yet again spotted Lytt drawing water from the well. Since Cayna was under strict orders from Marelle to stop doing her daughter's work, she could do nothing more than watch. Seeing that small body pull at the rope bucket with all she had was anxiety inducing.

As she thought that changing the structure of the well would be more effective than giving the girl a STR Up bangle, a flash of inspiration hit her.

While they were still in the process of transforming the village into a fortress, she could use her skills to create various accommodations within it. This included a possible water-drawing mechanism for the kitchen well. Its framework would be made with a wooden caterpillar tread. A simple hand pump was best in such a situation, but since they lacked the required metal, she'd have to forgo any automatic capabilities.

The final product would be a caterpillar-style machine cranked by hand and run by gears. It would be affixed with numerous containers and run water through a trough.

To create the device, she would need a small amount of metal and a large amount of wood. They were better off integrating it with the current well, so the installation itself would be easy.

"All right! I've gotta work, not worry. I'll go ask Marelle for permission."

The woman was bewildered when Cayna suddenly came flying in yelling, "I want to renovate the well!"

Cayna told her she wanted to create a mechanism that would help not only Lytt but all the villagers draw water more easily. She even explained with gestures, but Marelle still didn't understand.

Though confused at first, the woman could see Cayna was much more exuberant than she had been that morning, so she granted permission.

"I got the okay from Marelle! Yahoo!"

"Ah! Hold on, Cayna! Didn't you come in for lunch?!"

Cayna was jumping around like a fish that had just been given water and started to rush out, but Marelle's voice brought her back to her senses.

Each day at the inn included breakfast and dinner, but lunch was a separate fee. Having caused trouble, she handed over two of the coins from the stockpile she'd showed back on day one and said, "You can return the difference when I leave the village." This was met with "Make sure you eat a proper lunch, then."

Having acted strangely shamefully, Cayna finished her lunch with a crimson face.

After that, she circled around the well and glared at her Item Window. The cause of her troubles was the fact that she didn't have all the materials on hand, and what she did have wasn't enough to make what she wanted. It would require a great deal of wood, and in a farming village, such resources were needed for kindling. In that case, she'd have to figure something out on her own.

"Hmm. I guess cutting some down is my only option, huh?"

Based on how she'd felt in the forest yesterday, Cayna had some serious doubts over whether she could cut down the trees and shrubs against their will.

As she thought this, she came to a sudden realization.

"Ah, I know! I don't have to cut them down because some are already broken."

Cayna thought back to the brutal scene the bear had created after she'd sent it flying farther than expected. Deciding to strike while the iron was hot, she returned to the area from the day before.

There, she found the trees toppled across one another like a row of dominoes. One of the trees at the front was gone. The villagers must have taken it. A single trunk would probably suffice quantitatively, but she could surely find other uses for the others, too. Cayna didn't know when an opportunity like this would come again, so she decided to process the whole kit and caboodle.

Craft Skill: Wood Processing Level 3: Start

A fierce wind spun around Cayna, collected the branches from three fallen trees, and swept them away. The bark was then peeled into thin strips, and the round slices piled up right before her eyes with a loud *Thump! Thump! Thump!*

The forest filled with the sound of rustling as trees were tossed around by the wind, but finally, all grew quiet once more. Cayna stared at her startling progress in mute amazement. She then abruptly dropped her shoulders and gave a sigh.

"Sheesh, I knew Wind Magic was a must-have, but this really is something…"

One of the disadvantages of being a high elf was that she couldn't gather her own plant ingredients. She'd bought them at the store before or requested materials from fellow guild members, but her eyes now shrank to dots as she witnessed the process for the first time.

All Craft Skills required default magic such as Earth, Water, Fire, Wind, Ice, or Light. Players used Wind Magic to saw and process wood as Cayna had just done, but the game's display never showed anything like this. The corresponding effects paled in contrast. Compared with what she'd just witnessed, the display for this spell looked like nothing more than little tornadoes.

A single log slice was the size of a truck tire. She bundled a dozen together as one and ended up putting fourteen in the Item Box. An amount weighing the equivalent of a ten-ton truck vanished into thin air.

"...Don't think about it too hard, Cayna. You'll be done for if you start thinking. Yeah."

She put a palm to her forehead to soothe the headache brought on by trying to understand matters outside the laws of physics (even though she was the one who was breaking those laws). She then took out a gag weapon from the Item Box.

It was Tragic Night: Jason Blade, forged with Intimidate (for preventing enemies from running away) and Fear (for temporarily paralyzing an enemy's movements). At a glance, though, it was a regular old hatchet.

After scraping the extra bits of foliage off the fallen branches, she tied them together with rope and put them in the Item Box as well.

"I should go ahead and give these to Marelle."

Cayna didn't need to sleep outside anymore, so there was no need to carry kindling around with her.

Last, she opened her Skill Window and checked all the materials in order to assemble her large-scale items. She would process each part here so the finished product would be nearly put together by the time she returned to the inn. The wind kicked up once again, and stumps danced through the sky.

"It's all good. Totally fine," Cayna murmured as she sweat bullets and immersed herself in her work.

A week later, all the available villagers gathered at the well at the back of the inn. The circle, with the inn's very residents at the center, stared curiously at Cayna, who had installed the strange wooden contraption over their well.

Cayna had left the base alone and had two connected gears acting as an axis like on a tire wheel. Square boxes were placed along the attached caterpillar track at set intervals. It was about forty centimeters wide. Lastly, a hand-cranked gearbox was attached to the axis, and a trough collected the water dropped from the spinning boxes.

Cayna first turned the handle herself and checked to make sure there were no malfunctions. She then turned it over to Lytt. Surprised that she'd suddenly been given the honors without any explanation as to how it worked, the girl grew frazzled.

"Huh? Um, what should I do?"

"All you have to do is turn that handle to the right. Spin it with all you've got."

Lytt did as she was told and cranked the handle to the right. She was a bit timid at first but began turning it faster and faster. The caterpillar tread rattled as it went around, and the drawn water passed through the trough to the bucket. The water immediately filled up and began overflowing.

The spectating villagers cheered at this. They advanced with cries of "Me too! Me too!" and each happily took turns spinning the handle.

"Ohhh! I can get a ton of water without hardly any effort at all."

"I see! This certainly is useful! Comin' up with somethin' like this... You really are a marvel, Miss Cayna."

"Even my grandma can get water now!"

Even Marelle and her husband, Gatt, were nodding repeatedly with heartfelt thanks. The village elder walked up to Cayna as the villagers' glee sent her into a victory pose.

"Pardon me, Miss Cayna, but do you think you could do the same thing to the well at the center of town?"

"Yes, of course. I can make one right away."

There were three wells in the village, and the one behind the inn was allotted to those living in the southern sector.

The centermost well was for the northern sector, and the last was located on the outer edge of town by the fence. Apparently, that well had caved in and had been out of use for quite some time. It was possible to dig it back out, but the scent of water would likely attract monsters, so it remained blocked off.

"Time to add the finishing touches."

The villagers stepped back a bit, and two different techniques popped into her head. An instant later, an almost three-meter-tall pillar of flames rose up from beneath her, and sparks flew over Cayna's head.

The red light signaling an Effect Up status hovered around her like mist. The villagers unsurprisingly recoiled from this, but the mysterious sight quickly left them speechless.

Magic Skill: Flame-Type Addition: Boost: Start

Magic Skill: Additional Preservation Level 9: Endless Night: Start

Golden particles released from her outstretched palm and sparkled as they clung to the water wheel. It shone gold for some time but disappeared when Cayna took a deep breath and returned to her usual self.

She'd first used a boost spell, which would make the subsequent spell 1.3 times more effective.

The second spell was magic that multiplied the caster's level by the magic level and converted it into an equivalent number of days. It created a coating that prevented the target from rusting, rotting, or breaking.

In other words, for 12,870 days, or around thirty-five years, the water wheel would remain good as new.

A water wheel was installed in the central well before the day's end, which inspired a new round of hurrahs among the villagers. It was then decided that yet another banquet ought to be held "in honor of Miss Cayna's great achievements."

They offered her alcohol as they had the day before, but she firmly refused. All grew still as the villagers' glares bore into her.

Needless to say, she unwillingly ended up drinking regardless…

The next day, she once more vowed to never drink again, but Marelle's reply of "What? C'mon now, you'll get used to it if you just keep at it" sent a shiver down her spine.

CHAPTER 3
A Journey, Common Sense, the Royal Capital, and a Game of Tag

"........"

A tense air traveled through the quiet forest. The intended target didn't move a muscle beneath the cover of fallen leaves.

On the hunter's left arm was a large bow nearly as tall as its wielder. Despite being unable to visually confirm the target lying beneath the leaves, the hunter took aim and moved forward ever so carefully.

A slow hissing sound was audible from somewhere. The moment the hunter approached, the giant, foliage-covered body pounced and recklessly pierced its prey with sharp fangs.

...Or at least, should have pierced it, had the hunter not completely slipped beneath the flying predator in that instant.

"Zan Arrow!"

With this final warning—however heartless—the soft skin of its belly was punctured, and this forest menace that had put every single one of the hunter's nerves on edge had been taken out.

"Phew, that got my heart goin'. I owe a lot to Lottor."

The sparking arrow that now quietly fizzled away had struck a snake that was around ten meters long. The patterning on this variety of python-like monster, a reverse boa, was opposite that of typical snakes. By appearing to lie dead on its back, it lulled prey into a false sense of security and struck as soon as the poor victim drew close. Its back, which was camouflaged to look like a regular snake's belly, was actually incredibly tough, so it was easier to fell the monster by aiming for its underside.

When she'd arrived to collect medicinal herbs, Cayna had heard whispers of "Be careful" and "So scary!" from among the trees and soon cast Active Skill: Survey around the area. That's when she found the long belly slithering through the leaves.

After confirming the arrow was truly gone, she rolled up her catch like a hose and bound it with rope. For the time being, she gathered only a modest amount of medicinal herbs, even though it hurt her conscience, and concluded that it really was okay to do so no matter where she went.

However, each time she picked one with a plea of "Just a little, okay?" the herbs would go, "Gyaaah?!" and adamantly voice their displeasure, so Cayna's heart felt rather crushed. The elven ability to hear the voices of plants wasn't without its disadvantages. It required steeling yourself to a certain degree.

"Come to think of it, I sure do have a lot of monsters here."

The reverse boa wasn't the only creature hanging from a rope. There was also the chameleon-like fowa lizard, which could take down enemies with teeth that had evolved into razor-sharp needles, and three leech birds, which looked like hummingbirds but drank blood instead of nectar. She had also taken down a horned bear and had already stripped its horns, pelt, and meat to put in the Item Box.

And so on and so forth. Cayna had gathered quite the bounty despite only venturing just a bit deeper into the forest. Spotting them had been easy. After all, Lottor had taught her how to avoid dangers in the forest. Once she'd taken this information and used it for the exact opposite of its intended purpose, finding monsters wasn't hard at all. Half the day wasn't even over yet, but she already had a huge haul.

Cayna thought it strange that a village so unaccustomed to fighting had been able to live peacefully thus far despite being this overrun with mankind's natural enemy. However, the reason came to her soon enough.

The fence surrounding the village seemed to be protected by a charm that warded off monsters. Charms weren't a skill one could carry around with them, though, so Cayna guessed it had been placed within the last two hundred years.

It had been well over nine days since Cayna had found herself waking up in the remote inn. She had been to the tower three times since then, and her store of magic was essentially full.

Furthermore, she planned on visiting the remaining locations of the other Guardians once she used the communication network to pinpoint their locations. However, her own Guardian informed Cayna that some of the towers' communications had apparently been suspended. Therefore, it was imperative she gather whatever information she could about them first.

The Skill Masters' rings all responded whenever a tower was nearby, and if she could reach one, she could use the ring's incantation to get inside.

But there was another problem that had to be dealt with.

Even though they were called towers, out of the thirteen in existence, only Cayna's actually looked like a tower. From what she'd heard, Opus's was a Western-style building, and the tower underwater was like a dragon palace. It frustrated her to no end that not one could have just been normal. Now finding them was going to be an absolute pain.

Using magic where no one would see her, Cayna decided to fly around and fill in the village and tower areas on her map. Searching was like a hexagon strategy game.

She also helped out in the village. Marelle had told her to do as she pleased, and Cayna did just that.

When she mentioned this to the Guardian of her silver tower, though, it tiredly muttered, **"Skill Masters shouldn't go sellin' themselves short."**

At any rate, what she *did* need was a bath. There was nothing of the sort in the village, and when she asked how people normally cleaned themselves, the answer was that most wiped their bodies with a damp towel.

When she requested it of Marelle at the inn, the woman brought out a basin of lukewarm warm she could bathe in for an additional fee. But even though Cayna had no trouble affording it, she would start feeling bad if she made it a habit. After all, it wasn't as if Marelle could heat up the water with a single spell the way Cayna could.

And thus, the idea of creating a public bathhouse for the village popped into her mind.

First, she had to decide on a location. In terms of a space suitable for such an undertaking, the central plaza was a viable candidate. However, the villagers used it for a variety of purposes, so building it there was unlikely to work out.

As Cayna walked through the town, she noticed there were a number of empty houses and thought maybe she could ask for one.

When she hurried over to the village elder to ask his permission and also raised the matter of a well, he cheerfully told her to use whatever land and well she pleased.

A hot spring created with Magic Skills didn't require a water source. After all, there were plenty of skills that made excellent substitutes.

First, she had to move every single bit of furniture from the empty house to her Item Box and use her skills to bring the empty house under her control. The high-elf skill Territory Control was just the ticket. Cayna could use it, since she was elf royalty according to her backstory.

Next, she cleared away half the walls and floor of the building and chose the area that might otherwise have been a backyard garden as the perfect place to dig a hole deep enough for people to sit.

To turn it into a bathtub, she compressed and solidified the dirt so the hole wouldn't turn into a quagmire after the water was added. She did this by summoning Earth Spirits. As Cayna was busy processing the wood for the tub, several water-bottle-sized pawns flitted about and hardened the earth.

This may have looked like a fairy-tale scene, but at level 220, the Earth Spirits were actually forces to be reckoned with. Any normal person in this world would be unable to handle them.

Cayna set a special boulder in the very center of the large hole and began laying the tub with wood to surround it. This was one of the standard Building Skill blueprints, and she packed in as much detail as she could.

Finally, using the boulder as a center point, she split the inside and outside of the house down the middle and surrounded the entire area with a gourd-shaped fence. As soon as she cast a spell that would keep it going the same as a well, it was complete.

She thought procuring the wood materials would be an ordeal but decided to be realistic and use magic to cut them down.

Still, it was a deplorable practice that she refused to show anyone.

First, Cayna went around bowing her head to the local trees, saying, "I'm sorry for cutting you down." Then, she would cast sound-proofing magic on herself and magically chop them down. This way she wouldn't have to hear the condemned trees' screams or the enraged outcries of the others as she picked up their fallen brethren. She felt terribly guilty and had the unpleasant feeling she wouldn't be able to visit the woods for quite some time...

The unique boulder installed at the center of the bath was a charm known as a magic rhymestone. Within the game, it was a material that could absorb magical energy from the air around it and endlessly spawn dungeon monsters. Cayna had been keeping it in storage in her tower.

Although it was disguised as a rock, she had gathered a number of magic rhymestones together and configured them to produce several effects. Spring Water ensured there was a constant flow of water that possessed beauty and healing properties, Purification filtered out any impurities, and Insulation kept the water at a constant temperature. Further still, she cast magic that would prevent it from requiring maintenance for forty years. It would need basic cleaning, however.

Once the project was finished and she deemed it operable, she showed the villagers. They needed an initial lesson on how to wash before entering the bath but unanimously took a liking to it afterward.

Although she was unable to provide soap (there was no skill for that), Cayna had instilled the importance of bathing in the villagers. It was particularly well received among the elderly women. The locals decided they would take turns maintaining it. Apparently, Cayna and the villagers could use it for free while visitors would be charged a fee.

As the day's hunt came to an end and Cayna lined up her haul before Marelle, Lottor came in and stared at her bounty in mute amazement.

"You caught this much *again*? What're we supposed to do?! Even the whole village can't finish it all."

"What?! You mean this is all edible?! The birds I understand, but even the lizard and snake?!"

Marelle's statement shocked Cayna. She personally would never dream of eating any of these.

"Hey now, why so much? And what's with all the variety...?"

Lottor's shoulders dropped at the six animals plus a heaping pile of frozen meat strung up at the back of the inn. His face seemed to be saying, *Is this a plot to crush my hunter pride?*

"What's this meat here? It's white and cold..."

"That's a horned bear. It was so big that I decided to cut it up ahead of time, but I didn't want to carry the raw meat back, so I froze it with magic *(and put it in my Item Box)*. Oh, here are the pelt and horns."

Some monster or pesky animal kept jumping out at her every time she took a step in the forest, so she'd just ended up flying the rest of the way home. But even the sky had found ways to annoy her, as hawks soon swooped in to attack. She had no other choice but to take them down, but the ridiculous encounter rate was a serious problem.

Back in the *Leadale* game, Active monsters couldn't attack you if your level was higher than theirs. But when you didn't pay attention to your Active Skills outside of battle, you'd get sick of encountering animals who instead attacked on instinct.

Butchering the bear had been pretty rough. She'd watched how they did the first one back at the banquet and vaguely remembered the steps involved. Cayna had been reluctant, but she'd powered through the stench of blood and the incredibly tedious process. Despite throwing up midway, she'd chopped up the meat and put it on ice with Magic: Freeze. At some point, she would secretly ask Lottor to teach her the process from step one. Either way, Cayna had no choice but to accept the inevitable and just get used to it if she was going to live in this world.

"By the way, I think it's about time for me to leave this village soon," Cayna said, sitting up straight. "I'll wait until after the caravans arrive, though."

Marelle and Lottor fell into silence.

"That so? We'll miss ya…"

"Well, you are an adventurer, Miss Cayna. Can't stay in one place for too long…"

As a solemn air fell over them, Lytt walked over with a curious expression. She had come to draw water, yet Cayna, her mother, and Lottor were looking at one another as if someone had died. Naturally, she had questions.

"What's wrong?" she asked.

"Ah, Lytt. Um, well…"

Cayna tried to respond, but Marelle stopped her. She met Cayna's gaze and shook her head.

"It's fine, Cayna. Don't say anything. You can do it the day of."

"Huh? But…"

"We're tradespeople. Meetings and partings are a part of life. She has to learn to get used to it."

Lytt looked at Cayna, who had been trying to tell her something before Marelle cut her off. Deciding on her own that it was probably grown-up talk, she turned the handle as usual and drew water.

Cayna had been unable to broach the subject ever since, but their hour of parting came surprisingly fast.

The next afternoon, five horse-drawn caravans arrived. It was almost exactly noon when she heard them.

The neighing of horses. The rough beat of hooves. The rattle of caravan wheels as they rolled along the ground. The bustling sound of a large group of approaching people.

Their arrival simultaneously filled the villagers with anticipation. To Cayna, the noise had an *Oh, lots of people are here* feeling to it, but Marelle heard differently.

"Hmm? They sound a little frantic out there, huh?"

"Oh? You think so?"

"Those guys ain't the type to get worked up over nothing. Maybe something happened on the road?"

Curious, Cayna looked over at the dining hall entrance. Just then, a man came flying in. Dressed in leather armor and equipped with a long spear, he dashed over to the counter in a panic.

"Madam! Alcohol! Also, hot or cold water!"

"Geez, someone's in a rush. What in the world happened?"

The man was clearly in an odd state of panic. Cayna was in the middle of eating lunch at the counter and observed him as she ate her bread.

After Marelle brought out a bottle of alcohol from the back, she called Lytt over and told her to show them how the well worked. The man took the bottle and ran back outside, nearly tripping in his hurry.

Concerned by the way he clicked his tongue and muttered, "Shit," Cayna gobbled up the rest of her lunch and followed him.

A sight she'd never seen before unfolded as she stepped outside.

Two box carriages drawn by four horses each and three covered wagons drawn by two horses each were sitting there. The merchants who seemed to have ridden in the carriages were lined up in the wild fields at the corner of the village and unharnessing their horses one by one. They unloaded their luggage as they made preparations and set up shop. She watched in wonder as the alighted passengers came together and erected a market in the blink of an eye.

Just then, a harried voice yelled from a separate group of just under ten armed travelers. From the rough tone, Cayna could tell there was no time to waste. The shouting continued as they made a circle around one area.

"Hey! Hang in there!"

"Kenison?! Hey! Answer if you can hear me!"

"Hurry up with those herbs!"

"Dammit! The blood won't stop!"

Cayna saw this was no trivial matter.

"...Is someone injured?" she asked.

"Mm, yes."

As she began moving toward them, an unfamiliar voice unrelated to the group called out near Cayna. Before she knew it, a bespectacled dog-person known as a kobold was standing next to her in brown, baggy robes that dragged along the earth. He looked like a cute Welsh corgi sort of breed, but the voice was undeniably that of a learned man.

"It seems they ran into an ogre on their way here. The guards managed to fight it off somehow but not without major injury. I'm afraid it doesn't look good."

Cayna could sense his concern, but the *All is lost* attitude put a crease in her brow.

"...Are you saying nothing more can be done?"

"With those wounds, I'm afraid to say..."

She glared at the kobold, who did nothing more than shake his head dismissively. She then raced toward the group with a shout.

"Move it!"

"H-hey! Miss, what in the world are you...?!"

She pushed her way through the huddle of mercenaries and came upon a young man lying on a blanket. The side of his leather armor was torn open and wrapped with a bandage. The wound had been dyed crimson with blood, which was still trickling through.

Most girls seeing so much blood would have run away by this point. Unfortunately, Cayna had experienced a deeper hell than this before.

She used Search to check his vitals and saw the man's HP bar steadily dropping. Once it changed from yellow to red, she realized what was happening and muttered, "Poison!" The mercenaries tried to remove the girl who had just barged into their circle after seeing their comrade inching closer toward death by the second.

Cayna's next move astounded not only them but everyone else in the area as well.

Special Skill: Load: Double Spell: Begin Count

Two blue rings suddenly appeared in midair. From the side, they appeared to cross at her shoulders and began spinning rapidly with Cayna at the center. The blue light became a sphere of latticework around her, and the numeral 10 floated at the cross point of both shoulders. It was a Special Skill that cut the delay time for casting magic in half and allowed her to use multiple spell effects at once. It would only last for ten seconds, but with Cayna's magic, this would suffice.

9

Magic Skill: Poison Purification Pa Nil: Ready Set

Magic Skill: Simple Substance Recovery Dewl Level 9: Ready Set

"Heal!"

The faint blue light enveloped the man, whose face had gone from pale to deathly white. Glowing, firefly-like drops soon appeared in the air one after the other and seeped into the man as if they were shooting stars in a planetarium.

"What?!"

"Two spells at once?!"

"Only three people in the whole country can do that!"

The mercenaries and merchants murmured with dumbfounded amazement as they stood frozen solid with shock at the unbelievable scene.

*   *   *

6

Magic   Skill: Continued   Healing   Dulite: Ready Set

Magic Skill: Range Recovery La Duula: Ready Set

"Hurry up and activate!"

Two layers of magic pentagram circles fixated over the man's head. Their glitter turned to rain and poured endlessly into his body. The subsequent magic turned to white semitransparent waves that fanned out across the area. It affected not only the mercenaries but the merchants and village onlookers as well. Everything from the smallest scratch to battle injuries healed in an instant. A crowd soon gathered, and everyone was too astonished to utter anything more than "Ohhhh…" as they watched.

3

2

1

End Count: Effect Finished

With a high-pitched sound, the blue lattice rings broke apart and disappeared. Cayna took a deep breath. The mercenaries who had been staring at her realized that color had returned to the young man's face, and his flank had stopped bleeding. Their disbelieving expressions slowly turned to joy, and cheers rose up at the survival of their comrade.

The villagers were hardly surprised that Cayna had pulled it off, but the merchants stood motionless with slack-jawed expressions.

"*Phew.* Glad that all worked out."

Filled with a sense of accomplishment at a job well done, Cayna gave herself a pat on the shoulder, even though something like this wasn't enough to wear her out. She then went to get up and leave.

As she turned her back on them, the middle-aged man who had come rushing into the inn called out to her.

"I'm sorry for the trouble, miss. We're deeply grateful to you for saving our comrade's life. Thank you."

"I'm just glad I made it in time. The magic circles will stay over him for a while, but it's safe to move him."

Upon the man's instruction, several people moved the formerly injured youth onto a stretcher and brought him inside the inn. The mercenaries thanked Cayna profusely, and she grew red with embarrassment.

The kobold who had called out to her before clapped as he approached.

"My, that certainly was a rare sight to see. You strike me as an accomplished mage. Might I ask your name? I am Elineh, the one who coordinated this caravan."

"I'm Cayna. I'm just your average rural shut-in, so don't mind me."

Since it would be awkward to explain her whole situation to these people, she decided to paint herself as a clueless retiree who had holed herself away in the forest. Cayna only knew the programmed world of the game but felt there was a good chance she could get away with not knowing the current state of the world if she was brushed off as just some country bumpkin.

Still, to think there would be kobold merchants.

Cayna had often seem them running around the game world as NPCs doing maid work and such and hadn't thought much of it.

Elineh, on the other hand, was usually greeted with preconceived notions of *This is a kobold?* so he was particularly pleased by her lack of reaction.

"Should you require anything for travel in a remote region, please do visit our caravans."

Judging she was of moderate talent, Elineh deemed this a good opportunity to promote himself and bowed his head.

*   *   *

A short time later, life was once again bustling in the previously tense central plaza. Vendors sold the vegetables and grains they had harvested from the field, and buyers bartered over the price of daily necessities. The mercenary guards headed to the inn for a drink while still leaving a part of their forces behind.

With Lytt by her side, Cayna sat and watched as Lottor exchanged the wild game that he (mostly Cayna) had caught for money. The merchant ogled in astonishment while flicking an abacus.

"Three horned bear pelts... That's quite a challenge for even the average adventurer. And isn't this a reverse boa skin?! Leech bird feathers?! No village hunter could ever take such monsters down. What sort of tricks are you playing, Lottor?"

Lottor crossed his arms and puffed his chest out proudly with a big "Oh-ho-ho!" He then swiftly pointed at Cayna next to him, who was having a pleasant chat with Lytt.

"This is all Miss Cayna's catch!"

"Wooow! *Clap, clap.*"

"Hee-hee!"

Lottor's and Lytt's praise made Cayna openly blush. The merchant, however, was thoroughly confused.

"O-out of curiosity, how did you do it?"

Because of the magic she cast a short while earlier, the merchant now mistook Cayna for a priest. The lack of sword cuts or magical burn marks on the pelts had raised speculation.

Cayna and Lottor stared at each other for a moment before answering in perfect unison, ""Kicked 'em to death.""

"The first kick was impressive enough, but that second one was really out of this world!" gushed Lottor.

"Don't mention it, really. Please forget what I said—it was just youthful enthusiasm!"

When she had been out with Lottor, Cayna had gotten carried away and accidentally let out a loud, strange yell; the embarrassing flub made her go red in the face. It had been absolutely no different from the first kick, a mere automatic Charge skill. When he went around that night regaling the inn with tales of her heroic figure, Marelle had yelled, "You're upsetting her!" and taken him down with a throw of her tray.

As opposed to their lively conversation, the merchant was stunned by the absurdity of it all.

"I am glad to see you are enjoying yourself."

With the inn full of mercenaries, Marelle had called Lytt over to give her a hand. Cayna was left perusing the wares alone when Elineh called out to her.

"I witnessed what you did a short while ago. It was a wondrous spectacle the likes of which this world has never seen."

Was he talking about the time she used the horned bear horns to make a three-prong trident and had it appraised by the weapon shop? They were so moved that after negotiations she was able to sell two for sixty coins.

Or was he talking about the time another merchant had shouted, "Who made this?!" and wanted to know every detail about her well mechanism?

If that wasn't it, maybe he meant the public bath?

Unsure what he was referring to, Cayna chose to give a round-about answer.

"I saw that sort of thing a lot two hundred years ago *(...through quests)*."

"Oh my, two hundred years ago. I see. But now you've decided to leave your forest?"

"That's right. A lot has happened."

"Is that so... Well then, is there anything you were hoping to purchase?"

Cayna wasn't really used to dealing with inquisitive types, so she chose her words carefully. Her parties had almost always been made up of only trusted friends since the very beginning, so she didn't do well with people like him. He was like the smooth-talking nurses who asked questions to try to suss her out.

"Actually, I'd like a map."

"I see. Yes, even maps look quite different than they did two hundred years ago. I trust you understand it will cost a modest sum?"

"I'd also like you to tell me about the royal capital and other subjects as well. Ah, will you need an information fee?"

"Goodness, no. Please consider your earlier magic display a form of payment."

"Can I really make money by putting on a show?"

"At the very least, that will depend on whether there are others in this world who can dual cast, yes?"

Elineh's amused manner of speaking made Cayna worry she had been a bit too hasty in disclosing her personal history.

"Looking for someone, hmm?"

The sun had long since set, and the inn's tavern was several times more bustling than usual as villagers, the merchants and their families, and the mercenary guards all crowded in. Cayna sat in her usual spot at the counter as she did at mealtimes.

Next to her, Elineh sat on a stool he brought with him and told her all about Felskeilo's royal capital.

For instance, the noble and commoner sectors were separated by the Ejidd River. Since it was situated halfway between the southern nation of Otaloquess and the northern nation of Helshper, the capital was a central distribution point that was said to provide anything. He also told her about the annual fighting competition.

Halfway through, Cayna murmured, "I wonder if that kid is there?" but the question Elineh threw back at her was the start of her troubles.

"May I ask whom you speak of? Perhaps I may know of them."

Oh yeah, what did I go with again? she wondered. After creating the characters, leveling them up a bit, and submitting them into the Foster System, Cayna hadn't really bothered to keep in touch, so she had completely forgotten what they looked like. If you asked anyone in the entire world, they'd say she was shockingly heartless.

"Um, he's an elf…"

"Ah, an elf. Is that so?"

"A priest, and—"

"Yes, I see. A prie… Eh?"

As Elineh spoke, the mercenaries' attention was caught. They froze.

Elf. Male. Priest. Even in the capital, few people fit this description. They all thought to themselves, *No, it can't be.*

However…

"His name's Skargo—"

""""""WHAAAAAAAAAAT?!""""""

Everyone listening—besides the villagers, of course—grew frenzied and let out a simultaneous cry of shock.

"Didja say Lord Skargo?!"

"Are you really acquainted with *the* Lord Skargo?!"

"Never thought I'd hear such awesome news in a backwoods place like this."

"Such a little miss knowing someone so almighty… What kind of relationship do they have?"

"Hey now, don't go overlookin' Miss Cayna. Don'cha know how mad talented she is?!"

"What kind of skills would a village girl possibly have?!"

The villagers and merchants at the other end of the counter suddenly started commenting and arguing with one another. Cayna looked at Marelle, who picked up a tray with a bright smile. Cayna pretended not to notice.

Actually, Cayna may have noticed something tray-shaped go flying out of the corner of her eye, but she was pretty sure that was just her imagination.

"Huh, so he's that famous..."

"You're way off, miss. Aside from the king and prime minister, High Priest Skargo has more influence than anyone else. He's not someone you can write off with a *huh*."

"That's right! He's a walking dictionary who's been around since the great upheaval two hundred years ago! A work of art! And number three in this entire nation! No one alive can resist his charms!"

"...You did say 'High Priest,' right?"

As far as Cayna could remember, all the game's most important figures:

> Had unrestricted access to the royal castles.
> Were NPCs.
> Appeared in cutscenes.
> Gave quests.

This much confirmed it. Something was definitely off, and Cayna began to chuckle.

"...Hey now," the mercenaries cut in as they watched her.

Elineh's instinct whispered not to ask any further questions, but curiosity won out.

"If you'll allow me, may I ask what connection you share?"

"Well, it's not really anything worth hiding—"

Just as the onlookers were returning to their food and drink with sighs of "They're friends at best" and "Geez, why'd she gotta surprise us like that?" Cayna dropped the truth bomb.

Naturally, she never realized it was a bomb at all.

"He's my son."

"GWAGHBWAGH?!!!"

The contents of every single mouth there went spewing without exception.

The villagers. Marelle and Lytt. Lottor and Luine with frozen, wide eyes and open mouths. The mercenaries were soaked in the alcohol they spurt out, and the merchant families had dropped their plates and utensils. Elineh had nearly fallen from his stool.

"...C-Cayna..."

"Yes? What is it, Marelle?"

"Y-you...have a child at your age?!"

A child?!

When Marelle put it into words, that was the moment the true age of the fifteen- to seventeen-year-old girl before them was shadowed by doubt. No statement could have been more mismatched.

"Ah, um, I have two more *(sub-characters)* as well..."

""""""WHAAAAAAAAAA—?!"""""""

She'd been interested in experimenting with specialized skills and thus had created and submitted two more foster children. These were the female elf Mai-Mai, who knew about eighty Attack Magic skills, and the dwarf Kartatz, who specialized in using his construction talent to build fortresses and castles.

The latter was an "adopted child" in the truest sense. Officially, if parents in *World of Leadale* were of different races, they couldn't give birth to a mixed-race child. It was set so they would take after one parent or the other. Even in this current reality, the laws seemed to be no different.

She was more than a little relieved to see that no one doubted that the child of a high elf like Cayna was an elf.

Incidentally, their three names came from some snails she'd found one rainy day at the hospital.

"At any rate, I'm glad Skargo is doing well."

Cayna may have been relieved, but astonishment, upset, confusion, and insanity swept through the tavern.

"......Huh?" Elineh repeated with a confused expression. He ruminated over what he'd just heard.

It was the morning after his first night in the rural village, and now he was enjoying breakfast with this self-proclaimed "drifter," Cayna, who had rocked the inn with her confession the night before.

Everyone—the mercenaries, Elineh, the merchants, and their families—were eating a morning meal of hearty stew. Naturally, it was packed with plenty of meat. This particular variety came from the horned bear, also known as "frontier beef."

How funny it was that there was more than enough in stock and they could eat their fill without worry.

Leaving that aside for the present, the real issue was the girl in front of him.

"I shall ask once more. You wish to go with us to the royal capital... Is that right?"

"Yes. I could go by myself, but I don't know the roads very well. Can I ask this of you?"

He wondered how anyone could possibly get lost on a straight road but eventually accepted her proposal without any strong objection. His gaze then moved past her shoulder.

"At present, I do not see any issues and gladly welcome you. I cannot say the same for the young miss over there, however."

"Huh? ...Oh."

Following Elineh's gaze, Cayna turned around and broke into a sweat when she noticed Lytt holding a tray and on the verge of tears.

The thought of abandoning the girl weighed on her conscience, so after informing Marelle, she took Lytt to the back of the inn.

"You're leaving, Miss Cayna..."

"Y-yeah. I can't stay in the village forever."

Cayna almost thought she could see the girl's dewy, upturned eyes whittling away at her HP bar. She crouched down to Lytt's eye level, took hold of both her hands, and spoke.

"Don't worry. It's only a temporary good-bye."

"Really?"

"That's right. I promise I'll come see you again."

Even so, Lytt couldn't hide her sorrow. Cayna held her tight as she whispered in her ear.

"I'll tell you something incredible as proof of our promise."

"Huh?"

"You can't tell anyone. Not Marelle, not Gatt. Not even Luine."

"O-okay...I understand. It'll be our secret."

"Do you know the silver tower by the mountains?"

"Yeah, Mom says a terrible witch lives there."

"To tell the truth, I'm the bad, bad witch in that tower."

"Huh? WHAT?!"

Lytt tore herself from Cayna, though not very forcefully. She stared at her in utter disbelief before murmuring, "But Miss Cayna isn't a bad person."

Happy to hear these words, Cayna took the girl into her arms again.

"It's a total secret, so I'll come back now and again to make sure you haven't told anyone, okay?"

"Uh-huh. After all, if you never come back, I'm going to tell *everyone.*"

"Right. It'd be terrible if I returned to my tower and couldn't show my face here again."

The villagers hiding in the shadows softly cried as they watched the two soul sisters smile at each other.

Two days later, the caravan and Cayna were ready to depart on both their journeys, and the villagers all gathered around to see them off.

"See you again!"

"Come back soon!"

"Bring your son next time!"

As she watched the people bid them farewell, Cayna felt like a young country girl returning to the big city after visiting home.

"Looks like someone's popular."

"I owe a lot to everyone, after all."

"Seems like the other way around to me."

As they watched Cayna wave both hands and say her good-byes to everyone, Elineh and the leader of the mercenaries were both convinced the girl was dense when it came to others' affection.

"Come to think of it, I forgot to introduce myself. I'm Arbiter, the leader of the Flame Spear mercenaries. Nice havin' you with us on the ride to the capital," a youthful man walking alongside the caravan said to her as she dangled her legs off the edge of the coachman's seat.

Each member of the group then introduced themselves. Cayna's eyes darted about in confusion as she failed to remember them all. After the one-sided introduction, Elineh led her inside the carriage.

It was then that Elineh and Arbiter looked at each other and nodded solemnly. Their hearts were now both mutually burning with a single duty:

We cannot let this young lady into the royal capital with such a disastrous sense of money.

Their reasons were twofold:

Example 1:

Elineh thought back to when he sold Cayna a map. He had assumed he'd be able to have quite an interesting bout of bartering with such an esteemed personage.

"A map of Felskeilo is worth about eight silver coins, don't you agree?" he began.

Even Arbiter, who was listening right next to them, had thought, *Hey, aren't you overcharging?*

However, the customer produced eight coins without question and gave them to Elineh.

"Ah, I see. Eight coins, right? Here you are."

Dumbfounded by her cluelessness, the two simply stared at the silver coins. Needless to say, Elineh threw in a map of another country.

Example 2:

Cayna had just cheered Lytt up after the girl overheard her request to join Elineh on his trip to the capital. In his opinion, having a mage as capable as Cayna was fortuitous enough. In fact, he desired it himself.

Even so, his merchant's soul compelled him to tell her, "As our guest, there will be a transportation fee. Including food and miscellaneous expenses, it will be ten silver coins."

However, when she didn't question anything and immediately tried to pay like a fool, the two hurriedly stopped her.

"What are you thinking?!"

"He's right. Hold on there, miss. You gotta be savvier!"

"Huh? Isn't that the current market price?"

At that point, both merchants realized: *It's hopeless. She lost her sense of money two hundred years ago.*

And thus, it was decided that Arbiter would teach her basic adventuring knowledge, and Elineh would teach her financial sense. Really, though, it was more like they bowed their heads and pleaded to teach her.

They hadn't been able to prove anything based on her actions in the village, but if such a financially clueless elf was released into the world, there was a possibility she'd crash the general market in an instant.

There in the carriage, a cloth was laid out inside a suitably small wooden crate. Mr. Elineh's economics class began.

On top lay three coins. Starting farthest to the right, they were bronze, silver, and gold.

"See here, Lady Cayna. First, we have this brown coin. Fifty of these will equal one silver coin, and one hundred silver coins will equal one gold coin."

The bronze one had some type of unfamiliar bird carved onto it. The silver had a flower, but the gold had a building. It seemed like some sort of guild that might be in charge of regulating currency. Elineh then took out a colorless, clear coin that shone delicately and put it next to the gold one. It was carved with an emblem that felt very similar to something Cayna had seen in her homeland.

"This is a crystal coin. It is engraved with the image of the god who was charged with assembling the world and is worth fifteen gold coins."

Cayna took it in her hands, looked at it, and suddenly cast a spell.

Magic Skill: Analysis

"What?"

She then took a transparent stick seemingly out of nowhere and cast Craft Skill: Duplication. A sudden torrent of light swept through the carriage, and as soon as it abruptly ended, Cayna had another crystal coin in her hand.

"Aha. I thought I'd seen this before. It's a family crest." She turned over the crystal coin she had made and stared at the crest one might find on a family altar.

Elineh, who had just witnessed all this, dropped his gaze and shuddered.

The creation of crystal coins was a closely guarded secret. He'd heard the process was known to only a small number of dwarves. Seeing it crafted so easily right before his very eyes left him dumbfounded.

Nevertheless, he pulled himself together.

"Lady Cayna! It is illegal to make money of your own accord!"

"Oh, I'm sorry."

Elineh wasn't sure what he would have done if she hadn't bowed her head and capitulated so easily.

The caravan arrived at an open area along the main road to stop while it was still light out and began setting up camp for the night. According to Elineh, there were a number of such suitable lodgings along the route, and many others gathered at this particular location to rest until morning.

In charge of setup were some of the merchants along with the mercenaries.

Nearby was a small yet clean river running with drinkable water.

Arbiter approached Cayna as she sat on the wheel of a covered wagon and muttered to herself while staring into space.

"One bronze coin, two, three, four... I wonder if sooner or later Okiku will come out from her well saying, *You're short one!*"

"It looks like he really put you through the ringer. Learn anything?"

"Yes...but I didn't think Elineh would be such a tough teacher."

Arbiter patted an exhausted Cayna on the back and beamed at her. "Well, did you at least learn the value of money?"

"By this point, if I said I still didn't understand, I bet I'd end up with *two* teachers."

Her complaining made him roar with laughter.

Apparently, an adult could live well off ten bronze coins a day, though most of it was food expenses. A night at Marelle's inn was twenty bronze coins. If you stayed ten days, it would cost two hundred coins. Convert that to silver, and it was four silver coins.

Logically, this meant twenty silver coins was a dizzying amount. After all, it was equal to a thousand bronze coins and fifty days at the inn.

"With that in mind, the spear was thirty silver coins, but I'm not sure it's worth so much..."

"No way. As soon as you showed me, I could tell that was well-made." Arbiter carried a single spear on his back. The azure tip was in the shape of a flickering flame. "Don't you think the weapon shops in the capital would buy it for more than thirty-five silver?"

"I'm not very good at telling if an appraisal is fair or too much."

"You can't use weapons, since you're a mage, but the weapons you created as a skilled artisan are worth two gold easy."

Cayna casually went along with Arbiter and made sure he knew she was listening while he folded his arms and nodded fervently.

Either way, she didn't get why a single silver coin in this reality was the lowest form of gil in the world of the game. So long as you knew the right skill for a particular type of weapon or armor, a skilled artisan could craft their own equipment just by paying careful attention to the materials. The only weapons you *couldn't* craft were the gag items distributed during events. These included the Supreme King of Fools Armor, the Hungry Like the Wolf Sword, Tragic Night: Jason Blade, and Shut Yer Yap Shield. The effects of each one were iffy on their own, and they mostly catered to collectors.

"Hey, come to think of it, you're an aspiring adventurer, right?"

"Well, I have to make money somehow. I'm not sure how I feel wandering around jobless…"

"Why not ask the High Priest for a little help?"

"I could never let myself be tied to my son's purse strings. I'd be a failure as a mother."

"Pretty sure lots of parents and children are like that, though…" Arbiter decided to chalk it up to the differences between elves and humans and continued. "Honestly, becoming an adventurer ain't all that hard. You go to an Adventurers Guild, sign up, and get a registration card. That's pretty much it."

He reached into his breast pocket and showed Cayna what looked like a credit card. It was about one millimeter thick and entirely crimson. Written in rainbow lettering was Arbiter's name, race, occupation, and mercenary group.

"They normally come in white, but groups like ours can choose a color. Anyone who has this is an adventurer. You'll have to pay two silver coins to get it reissued if you lose it, so be careful."

Cayna nodded with a "Yes, I see."

The VRMMORG *Leadale* was very much a Japanese creation; almost the entire game had been developed domestically. Perhaps that was why this world used kanji, hiragana, katakana, Romaji, and English. Furthermore, the in-game writing looked shaky, as if the letters of the alphabet had been tilted ninety degrees.

Simply put, it was as if someone had written on a piece of paper with an ink-soaked brush, then turned it sideways to let all the ink drip down. With a bit of effort, this was fine enough for everyday language. Sometimes, however, it looked more like ancient Chinese script.

Arbiter's card was written entirely in katakana, which Cayna found difficult to read.

Arbiter

Human

Soldier

The Flame Spear Mercenaries

I guess all these cards are written just in katakana, she then realized.

"Adventurer Guilds look the same anywhere. After all, the walls are completely covered in requests. Just pick one you like and take it to the reception desk. You only have a limited amount of time to complete it, so watch out for that. If you take on a request and can't deliver on your promise, you'll have to pay a breach-of-contract fee… I guess that about sums it up."

She'd never heard of there being a "breach of contract" fee or anything before, but Cayna thought it didn't differ all that much from the game. What she had to watch out for most at the moment was that this reality was different from the game. If she died, there'd be no Continue screen. She was better off assuming she couldn't come back to life and reappear in the main guild the way her character used to.

As Arbiter gave her detailed pointers and answered her questions, the sun began setting. One of the mercenaries ran over to tell them dinner was ready.

As the young man turned around to head back toward everyone, Arbiter's voice stopped him in his tracks. Arbiter tilted his chin toward Cayna.

"Kenison, this girl saved your life. Make sure you thank her."

"Huh? Oh, right. Come to think of it, I'm glad you're feeling better."

"You forgot?!" Arbiter said, snapping back at Cayna's *Now that you mention it* attitude.

The young man observed their banter enviously, then straightened himself up and bowed his head.

"Lady Cayna, thank you for doing everything you could to save me the other day!"

"L-L-L-L-Lady Cayna?! That really isn't necessary! Just call me Cayna!"

"Okay then, I'll call you Miss Cayna."

"Ngh... I still think that's overkill."

Cayna's red face and embarrassed blustering sent Arbiter into a fit of laughter. He continued his stream of "Ha-ha-ha!" as he headed back toward the crowd of people and the scent of delicious food.

His expression blank, Kenison watched his leader depart. He then shifted his gaze between Arbiter and Cayna, who appeared equally vexed.

"You're incredible, Miss Cayna. It's the first time I've seen the boss laugh at a time like this."

"Isn't life more fun when people are around? I don't think suddenly laughing at someone's face should count, though."

"No, no, he's usually way more irritable when we set up camp. The rest of us always get yelled at."

"It's part of being human. Doesn't everyone want to survive?"

"You're missin' the point."

Cayna didn't know what he was trying to say, and Kenison hung his head in total failure.

He wanted to get across that Arbiter was normally a strict leader who never hesitated for a second to tell off newbies like Kenison for dawdling if it meant ensuring the safety of a client. However, Cayna didn't see that side of him. Nor did she see how he ended up getting in trouble later after another mercenary came to get them.

As the curtain of night fell, Elineh came to Arbiter as he performed his rounds.

"You said there is something worrying you?"

"Yeah. It's the ogres we ran into on the way to the village. They're stubborn bastards and will probably come at us again."

At first, two ogres had carefully targeted the carriages. Four goblins had joined in as well, with the mercenaries taking two of them. One ogre had found an opening and approached the caravan while three people, including Arbiter, fought the other. Kenison was wounded when he recklessly tried to draw its attention, and the memory was still fresh. If Elineh hadn't immediately used one of the magic items from his wares, it was very likely that Kenison wouldn't have gotten away with his life.

"For now, what if we tighten security and ask that girl to lend a helping hand?"

"You mean Lady Cayna? She's just a normal guest at the moment…"

Of course, whether they had a skilled mage as backup would significantly influence their strategy.

In the true spirit of *Speak of the devil and he shall appear*, Cayna suddenly did just that. She held a decent number of dry twigs in her hand.

"Ah, there you are, Arbiter."

"Lady Cayna, what are you carrying? Does your bed not suit you?"

"Oh, the hammock? Nope, it's totally fine. I was surprised you have them. It's my first time sleeping in one."

The carriages were filled with mostly luggage and left no space for people to sleep. Elineh was small enough that he could just barely fit in the leftover spaces, but someone like Cayna didn't have that option. It was decided she would sleep in a hammock between two carriages and wrap herself up in a blanket. Staying off the ground was also a preventative measure against poisonous bugs and snakes. Regardless, she seemed to be enjoying herself.

Cayna put down the branches she had collected and produced small tubes from seemingly out of nowhere.

She had simply taken it out of her Item Box, but anyone who didn't know better would think they'd just popped into existence. She gave the two tubes to Arbiter.

"Here you go. I made these as temporary measures. Please use them if you find yourself in trouble, okay?"

Arbiter heard a light splashing when he shook the thin bamboo tubes, confirming the liquid inside. Cayna smiled at his strange expression and proceeded to explain.

"It's a potion. I'm not too skilled, and it's rather poorly made, but I've passed them out to everyone."

"Thanks for goin' out of your way for it. But didn't this cost a lot?"

"Not to worry. It is made from common plants that grew around the village, so there's nothing special about it at all. I promise you it's effective."

After being so casually handed such a gift, he would be astounded when he had it appraised in an appropriate outlet at a later point in time. The item, already out of production, was a precious commodity valued at twenty silver per unit.

This hadn't been Cayna's intention, of course. Her level-1,200 common sense had told her it should have been a "micro-potion," but in this world, the results were that of a Super High Potion.

"Well then, what do you intend to do with those dried branches?"

"I figured I'd use these to help with the night patrol. Wait just a second."

As she said this, Cayna grouped together the twigs on the ground, took out a wand, and tapped the earth. Moments later, a magic circle emitting a faint light appeared beneath the pile.

Magic Skill: Load: Create Wood Golem Level 1

"...Wait just one darn second."

"I'm quite certain you will never cease to amaze me."

The tangle of branches twisted together as if alive and changed shape before combining together to form an odd cylindrical doll. It was about one meter tall, and the gnarled roots that brought it to life retained their original form to serve as feet. The arms were as creaky as one might expect twigs to be. Its emotionless visage had two cavities for eyes, no nose, and a small mouthlike hole.

It was so ghastly that, should one come across it unexpectedly along a night road, ten out of ten people would scream and run away.

"Bohhh."

This seemed to be the sound it made. The doll placed its arms below its belly and leaned forward.

...The behavior was extremely hard to follow, but it seemed as if it was trying to pull off some sort of butler greeting.

As its creator, Cayna wasn't particularly bothered by its hideousness. Her expression was just slightly strained.

"U-um, let's see. If anyone bad approaches the camp, take them down, okay?"

"Bohhh."

As Cayna haltingly gave the order, its twiggy arms gave a dry creak of understanding. It scampered off into the forest, which was quickly falling into darkness. If someone didn't know better, they'd see it as some demonic vanguard.

Arbiter thought that later on they should also instruct it not to attack any friendly night patrol it might come across.

Silence fell.

"...Is—is that thing really okay?" he finally asked.

"...I—I think so. Maybe you'd like a round with it, Arbiter? It's super strong, twice that of a bear."

"Gah, seriously...?"

With Special Skill: Search, one could see that a horned bear was between levels 35 and 40. Since the wood golem was created at the lowest possible level (Level 1 × 10 Percent of User Level), it was a force to be reckoned with at a level 220 minimum. A bear didn't stand a chance against it.

Since it was made of wood, that did make it weak against fire. However, none of the monsters in the area used fire attacks, so it was unlikely to be an issue.

"So what were you two talking about?"

"Just the damn pains that put Kenison in your debt in the first place."

"Oh, you mean those ogres?"

"They're crafty and got one hell of a stubborn streak... Wait, did you just say 'those'?" It almost slipped his notice in the natural course of conversation, and Arbiter threw the question back at the easygoing Cayna.

"Lady Cayna, could it possibly be that you have defeated them already?"

"Yeah, was that bad? I wanted a go at them as revenge for Kenison."

"Crazy how you did that..."

"Ah yes, well. Good show."

They thought it best not to question Cayna's vague response too deeply. They'd heard more than enough fantastical stories for the time being.

The truth was, she'd chased the ogres around and around and around with Summoning Magic: Lightning Spirit after she found them hiding in the forest near the village while she was out searching for medicinal herbs. There was no question she'd driven them away, either. After all, they had prostrated themselves before her and begged for their lives. Cayna made them vow in broken speech never to come near the village again, filled their hearts with fear like a numbing curse, and sent them packing.

Cayna had also protected the village with temporary counter-measures, like the gargoyle on the roof of the inn that was invisible from below. She had simply instructed Lytt, who knew her true identity, to seek shelter there if anything happened.

Suddenly exhausted from hearing about Cayna's incident with the ogres, the two men quickly bid her good night and thanked their lucky stars for the goddess who had wandered into their midst. She seemed a bit lacking in common sense and normalcy, but they were grateful nonetheless.

Cayna would spend ten more days with the caravan before arriving in Felskeilo's royal capital.

The inspection prior to enter the city ate up some time, but that was largely to be expected.

The royal capital of Felskeilo covered a vast area and was divided by the Ejidd River and its sandbar. The river flowed through the center of the continent, and its plentiful bounty was so vital to people's livelihoods that they couldn't survive without it.

The southeast side of the river where Cayna and the others had arrived served as both the business and residential sector for commoners. It made up about 60 percent of the city and was home to a melting pot of races. One could even see the houses of the poor lined up outside its walls. Come nightfall, however, monsters roamed the lands beyond the walls where the military didn't patrol, making this section quite a risky place to live.

The sandbar was large enough to fit three baseball stadiums

and contained the church and the Royal Academy, among other institutions.

Across the way on the opposite bank was the capital's western sector, situated in front of a hill. There stood the noble residences and the unbroken view of the royal castle that towered high above them. The river by the capital was calm and smooth; most crossings were by small boat or large galley. There were a few tourist vessels as well.

For those in a rush, it was recommended that one travel by dragonfly. The ancestor of all dragonflies, it was known as the laigayanma and could grow up to eight meters long. The larvae were as much of a threat to the river as alligators, but tamed adults were often used as aerial modes of transportation and tourism. There were one or two other people on staff who would assist the dragonfly's master, also known as the insect tamer.

However, flying above the castle and aristocratic district was absolutely forbidden. Any trespassers would be shot down without a second thought, which meant everyone had to exercise great caution. Furthermore, this capital that now spanned across the river was once a major battlefield between the White Kingdom and the Green Kingdom. The sandbar had a special Point where one could grab special battle items.

"Uwaaaah, oh geez, oh wow... I can't believe there's a city in a place like this. What are these people thinking? Aghhhh. Is this really okay...?"

Elineh had informed her beforehand. But as they say, *A picture is worth a thousand words*, and as Cayna looked out upon the city, it was unclear if her feelings were that of exasperation, shock, or interest. She *was* sure she'd have a headache later, though.

Taking in her reaction, Elineh and Arbiter both gave satisfied nods.

"What do you think? The city of Felskeilo is praised for its beauty."

"Whaddaya think? Amazin', yeah? Shocking, right? Totally knocks your socks off, don't it? Heh-heeeh."

The mercenary leader was bizarrely excited. In a small voice, his subordinates warned Cayna, "This is the boss's hometown, so he's always like this," "You'll learn to ignore him after a while," and "You can just look the other way."

These words alone told her they saw their leader's triumphant grin as a bad habit they really wished he would correct.

As Cayna internally fretted over the state of the city, the carriage continued on its path. She would soon say her good-byes to Elineh and the caravan. They bypassed the carriage rest stop near the admission gate and came to a place that would lead out onto the main road.

"Thank you very much for allowing me to join you."

Cayna lightly disembarked from the bed of the carriage and bowed to Elineh and Arbiter.

"Well then, Lady Cayna. If you have the time, please visit our caravan whenever you like. I shall be sure to depend on you as a guard."

"Hey now, Master Elineh, what about our long-term contract?" asked Arbiter.

"Lady Cayna will, of course, take priority."

"You sly dog. Miss, come see us if you got nowhere to go. We'll welcome ya."

"A-a-ha-ha-ha-ha… I'm honored. To think you'd both be so eager to keep a customer."

"What, no romantic spark? That's cold."

"No, no, nothing like that. I just mean I'll gladly take you up on your offer when I've done all I have to."

"You may join us right now if you like."

"Ah, thank you but—"

"I jest. Well then, Lady Cayna, it has been an enjoyable journey. I hope we may travel together again."

"Yes, thank you for everything."

"Later, miss. Hey, hold on! Kenison!"

Elineh bowed and turned on his heel, and after Arbiter gave his own farewells, he called out to one of his comrades. Kenison came running over like a loyal dog.

"Yes, boss?"

"Escort Miss Cayna to the Adventurers Guild."

"Yessir."

Upon relaying these orders, the leader returned to the rest of his group and waved farewell.

Led by Kenison, Cayna continued down the main road jostling with every race imaginable. They soon came to a building that appeared to be three white towers placed together.

"Here's the Guild, miss."

"Thank you for guiding me here, Kenison."

"No, no! I'm the one who should be thankin' you, miss. I'll always treasure this life o' mine you saved."

"I'm glad to hear it. I'm sure we'll meet under better circumstances next time. Please give everyone my best."

"Will do! Well then, I'll be goin' now."

Cayna watched him disappear into the crowd, then dropped her shoulders with a heavy sigh.

"I'm really the one who should be saying thanks. Can't say whether it's for the rare compliments or stiff shoulders, though..."

Cracking her neck, she passed under the Guild's doorway.

She came upon the sight of a round, chair-less table anchored to the floor and several brawny, tough-looking adventurers. Farther in was a row of two or three counters similar to the lottery booths commonly found in Japan.

As Cayna approached the one closest to her, a red-haired woman who looked to be around her late twenties greeted her with a bright smile.

"Welcome to the Adventurers Guild. How may I help you today?"

"I'd like to register as an adventurer."

"I see; you'd like to be a member. Well then, please first write your name, race, and occupation on this form."

She's pretty no-nonsense about her job, Cayna thought.

Based on the employee's slightly probing attitude, she guessed the woman was simultaneously checking to see if she had what it took to be an adventurer. Once Cayna read over the application, she scribbled in her answers and soon returned it. After a bit of thought, she decided to make her occupation a mage.

Cayna curiously noted that she had been given a standard pencil, even though she was sure quill pens were the default in most fantasy settings. To be fair, she would have been at a loss on how to use one if that had been the case.

"Thank you, I shall take care of this for you... Oh?" The young woman looked over the form, and her eyes grew large as she stared at a certain point.

"Does something look off?"

"No, it's just that we don't see very many high elves."

"Oh? There aren't any others?"

"At the very least, you are the first I have met since starting this job."

Upon hearing this, Cayna's immediate thought was *Shoot*. If she was a rare race, she'd most likely have to worry about the danger of being bought and sold.

This concern was apparently evident across her face. The woman quickly eased up, and her genuine smile allayed Cayna's fears.

"Not to worry. Regulations in the royal capital have cracked down on slavery. Moreover, if the High Priest got word of such an incident befalling a high elf, there'd be no end of troubles."

In exchange for the form, she handed Cayna a placard-like board with *"Four"* written in the local language.

What's that son of mine terrorizing the general public for...?

"Your card will be finished by tomorrow. Please pick it up at any time. Shall I give you a summary of what to know when working for the Guild?"

"Ah, no, I think I'll be okay. The leader of the Flame Spears already explained things to me."

"My, so Mr. Arbiter recommended us to you. You should have said so sooner."

This *I'm SO sorry* apology seemed to be in regard to the woman's initial probing stare. Cayna told her something to the effect of "Don't worry about it" and left the counter. She looked at a wall nearby.

There, she saw countless papers half the size of a postcard plastered tight across a space that was about two meters high and four meters long. She idly stared at them all, each one written with a basic request, remuneration, and the client's name.

Let's see what we have here. "Please capture a monster for me." "Arena Management Committee"? ... "Emergency Guard Wanted" but it's an escort for an investigation? "Won't you help us find Shangri-la?" What is this? ... "Please look into my husband's affair." Is that part of an adventurer's job? ...Sheesh, what's going on here?

Among these, the one paper that suddenly caught her eye simply said, *"Please give me a potion. Will pay two silver coins."*

Without a moment's delay, she opened up her Item Box and checked the contents.

Huh? I guess the Super High Potions I gave to Arbiter were the last ones... I have potions I made a long time ago, but maybe I can get two-hundred-year-old items appraised?

Of the dozen she'd gathered together, Cayna took out a glass vial of red liquid. (A little over three milliliters' worth.) She shook the vial to make sure it hadn't solidified and brought it to the counter along with her application.

"Excuse me."

"Yes? Oh, Miss Cayna. Is something the matter?"

"I'm kind of jumping the gun a bit since I don't have my card yet, but do you think I could fulfill this potion request?"

The receptionist accepted the flyer and potion and stared at the vial. She appeared to be using Skill: Tool Appraisal. With a deep, slow nod, she politely stowed it away and stamped the request form.

"Yes, that is fine. However, while I cannot appraise the item fully, it is quite valuable, is it not?"

"It's been sitting around for a long, long time, so I'm just hoping it's still effective."

"The liquid is still translucent, so that's highly likely. Well then, here you are. Your payment of two silver coins."

"Thank you."

Cayna held the coins tight in her hand before covertly stowing them in her Item Box. She thanked the woman at the counter and left the Guild. Just as when she entered, people of various races intermingled as they passed her by.

"All right, I guess I should go to the inn first... I'm sure Elineh said to turn left when you left the Guild... How many buildings down was it again?"

The Guild's district seemed to be packed with lodgings. Any of the signs she saw in either direction could be for inns. They all had pictures of nightgowns and doorways, which was at least some consolation, since the letters were nearly illegible. Cayna thought someone really needed to fix that.

There actually was a skill that allowed you to understand an unfamiliar language, but the downside was that using it gave you a terrible headache.

Avoiding the crowds of people, she reached the end of the street and came across a sign depicting a dog holding a bone. With a single nod, she entered the building.

The interior was reminiscent of Marelle's remote village inn, and the tables and chairs were invitingly placed in a way that utilized the space. Unlike Marelle's establishment, however, this spot wasn't hurting for customers; in fact, it was packed.

Looking out over the crowd, you're be hard-pressed to find anyone purely human.

Short dog-faced kobolds. Slender werecats whose cat eyes were the same shade as their hair. Bipedal dragon-like dragoids, dwarves, elves, and many others.

The supposed proprietress of the inn, a plump werecat of about forty in an apron, greeted Cayna with inquiring eyes.

"First time here, right? Stayin' the night? Or you want something to eat?"

"Both, please. I was looking for some long-term lodging, and Elineh recommended this place."

The wary proprietress quickly changed her tune at Cayna's statement and patted her chest with an openly relieved smile. Still, Cayna couldn't help but think that perhaps the role of proprietress wasn't the right fit for someone of her portly build.

"A recommendation from a customer, y'say? Don't scare me like that."

"Are humans not allowed here?"

"Well, there are still many out there who don't look kindly on us."

"No need to worry. After all, I'm not human, either."

Cayna brushed her hair back a bit to show her pointed ears. A high elf's ears were not as long as a normal elf's. The demon race had them as well, but they still didn't match those of the elves. Between the three races, an elf's ears were the longest, followed by demons, and then high elves.

She didn't ask what race Cayna was, but this display alone set the proprietress at ease. She guided her to a seat at the counter. As the were-woman gave her the hotel register, she asked the necessary details.

"One night's stay is thirty bronze. Does that work for you? I know it seems a bit high."

"All right, I'd like to pay for five days, then."

Cayna handed over three silver coins. Now that she had a place to stay for the time being, she enjoyed a long-overdue opportunity to enjoy conversing with various races, then ate the proprietress's cooking with relish before deciding to hit the hay early.

The next day, the proprietress was astounded by her new guest's exuberant vigor. Cayna quickly filled up on breakfast and headed out to see the sights of the capital.

In short, she was like an overexcited student on a school trip. That said, Cayna had never known a typical school life, so there was no question this was an entirely new state of mind for her. Unfortunately, there was no one there to stop her and no one who could.

"First, let's start...over there!"

Although it stood in the shadow of another building, Cayna's eye caught sight of a brilliant, towering church across the way. However, she stopped by a market full of rarities on the way and grew distracted.

After perusing the small gadgets, textiles, and accessories among the vendors without buying anything, she visited the cooking-ingredient stands that made up a majority of the venue.

"Ooh, kirina grass. I should probably buy some, since I'm here."

The round bulb with the white daffodil-like flower was an ingredient used in potions, and according to the vendor, it could also be used to bring out the rich flavor in meat. It was treated similarly to garlic. She needed both the bulb and the stalk, so she requested that it be left as is and made the purchase.

To prevent odor, you didn't need a large quantity of kirina grass for a single recipe unless you worked at a restaurant. Cayna had never cooked before, however, so she had no idea. With hardly a moment's hesitation, she bought up the shop's entire stock and dumbfounded the vendor.

Next, she went in search of the colt bird. Its meat was said to be both delicious and spicy even without seasoning, though no one knew the reason. There was a theory that its prey was the source, but no one had yet begun any official research.

In any case, Cayna wasn't after its meat. She bought the hearts, which had been tossed away as trash post-dissection, for dirt cheap. Needless to say, the shop owner was bewildered at the sight.

She could make a simple potion by combining the two ingredients, so she thought it best to always have several on hand. Cayna used to have to gather everything by herself, so she was absolutely ecstatic to see how easy this was now.

After watching the laigayanma that occasionally whipped by overhead and purchasing some grilled meat kabobs, Cayna headed for the harbor along the Ejidd River.

A pier stretched across the residential district beside the river. Boats were tied to it at random intervals and made it difficult to tell where the water met the shore.

Nevertheless, among them were small sailing vessels that commoners shared for both daily life and tourism. The harbor seemed to be building upon one extension after the other at the narrowest part of the river.

Even so, the opposite bank to the sandbar was still about three hundred meters away. There was always the option of using magic to walk on water, but since she'd come all this way, she decided to take a shared boat to the other side.

From where she currently stood, the bank of the sandbar across the way looked to be about the size of an island. To the right, a white building that looked like the dome of Saint Peter's Basilica stood imposingly. Based on the conversations of passersby, Cayna understood it was a church, but she personally thought it looked more like a sheet cake topped with piles and piles of cream.

A lovely green park sat at the center of the sandbar, and to the left were two buildings that looked like monasteries of some sort. She could tell the corridors connecting the second and third floors to each other twisted like some sort of trompe l'oeil. This was the Royal Academy, which accepted students regardless of race or class as long as they had the right qualifications.

Furthermore, to the left of it was another building that had a gymnasium-like quality. This was apparently a workshop that specialized in crafting medium and large vessels.

All the above information was everything she had gleaned about the harbor from the inn the night before.

She paid two bronze coins for a round-trip ticket and stepped aboard a sailboat that was the width of about twenty people across. Several boats of the same size made round trips ten times per day, so she was told she could take the same boat back.

This sailboat was actually a simple vessel made up of three boats slapped together and affixed with a mast and sail.

The river's surface was a deep blue and not very clear, while the bank itself was a dull, muddy brown. In past wars, enemies would hide beneath the surface and sink anyone who tried to pass. There were humorous tales of how allies sometimes accidentally electrocuted one another during an assault. Cayna herself had several memories of dressing as a member of the Red Kingdom and hiding in the river's depths.

The water wasn't so cloudy back then, she thought a bit sadly.

Cayna reminisced further until the boat steadily reached the shore and the passengers began to disembark. Several youths were heading toward the Academy, while the elderly passengers were making their way toward the church.

She leisurely took in the sights before passing through the church's large open doors and stepping into the hall.

"…This place is like a mishmash of historical eras."

The Grecian marble pillars to the Byzantine and Gothic architecture—Cayna was stunned by how far this Japanese-made MMO had come.

Standing before a row of beautiful stained cathedral glass windows crafted in yet another style was a young sister who seemed to be preparing a tour for incoming visitors. Just as Cayna thought there was no harm in asking, an elderly sister approached her.

"May I help you with anything?" the old woman asked.

"Um, I heard someone named Skargo might be here."

"Ah, the High Priest? Yes, he is indeed present, but…"

"Do you think I could meet with him?"

Cayna clasped her hands entreatingly and grimaced when she saw the sister look up and sigh.

"The High Priest is quite busy. If you have not made a prior appointment, I'm afraid it is simply not possible."

"Hmm, no dice, huh? Oh well. I can't ruin that kid's life with my selfishness."

"? 'That kid'?"

"Well then, I'll be on my way."

The perplexed sister saw the elven girl off. With a disappointed expression that at the same time seemed to indicate she was enjoying herself, Cayna bowed and bid farewell with a "Ciao."

After a quick retreat out of the church, she made her way to the harborside factory district with her sights set on the Royal Academy building.

"Might as well check the place out while I'm here."

The factory was open, and it seemed it was okay to go inside as long as you stayed out of the way. It was probably worth mentioning, though, that wood and hammers would occasionally go flying.

This was what she remembered from the conversation she'd had with a passionate, aspiring dragoid craftsman staying at the same inn. He seemed to be an architecture student at the Academy who moonlighted as an adventurer.

"At any rate…I wonder where the Collection Point went?"

"There is a possibility it is on top of a building somewhere."

"That's probably still safer than out in the open…"

It was fine that Kee answered her sometimes, but to any outsider, she looked like a weirdo mumbling to herself. He was speaking at a normal volume, and Cayna quietly sighed with the realization she had a habit of whispering before checking her surroundings.

In essence, Cayna belonged to the Black and Purple nations of the north and therefore didn't know much about the actual situation here in the capital. Back in the game, she'd pretty much just heard the latest scoop from the Guild and watched the broadcast of each nation's battle situation unfold from the lounge area.

For each Collection Point, you had to insert a special item and defeat the monster that appeared. These special items were more like an assortment of rare item materials.

Pickup parties would get together in hopes of beating the monsters that appeared and collecting the items they dropped. The type of monsters at these Collection Points were not fixed, either; they could be birds, fish, and other various creatures. Based on what Cayna had heard from a friend in another guild, it sounded like a real challenge.

Even so, for nations like the Black Kingdom of Lypras, it was a lot better than slaying monsters that suddenly appeared in the dark of night over and over again.

After more than forty minutes of the craze, everyone in the guild was at a loss and asking themselves *What now?*

This time, Cayna's biggest anxiety was the safety of the royal capital itself. The monsters that appeared here wouldn't be level 100 or 200. After all, the players who could deal with them were usually around level 300 or 400. Cayna was concerned that the adventurers in this area weren't strong enough.

For example, she hated to say it, but even an impressive-looking soldier like Arbiter didn't reach level 100. The Search skill adventurers currently used apparently didn't display any specific amount of strength; Arbiter himself had confirmed this. Incidentally, whenever he looked at Cayna, it said *"Unknown."* That was only natural, of course.

In any case, if any monster should happen to appear, Cayna thought she at least wanted to be in the capital when it did.

She continued along the outer edge of the sandbar and soon arrived at what looked like a massive gymnasium or maybe even a railyard; this was the factory directly connected with the river.

When Cayna peeked in from the corner of the entranceway and looked inside, she saw the hull of a ship already on the water connected with the freeboard above the waterline. It was twice the size of the cruise ships one often sees anchored in a harbor.

"…What, an observer? It's dangerous, so don't get too close."

She had apparently leaned in to get a better look without realizing, and the strong, shirtless young man carrying a load of lumber gave her fair warning.

"Ah-ha-ha, sorry about that."

"Not many women check this place out. I'm guessin' you're not hopin' to be the boss's new pupil, right?"

"Huh? Boss? Pupil?"

The man gestured over at the ship with his chin. When she looked up at it, she saw a dwarf shouting out orders left and right.

"Whaddaya think you're doin'?! I told you that's wrong! And you, moron! What do you think *you're* doing?! Do you need me to explain the procedure multiple times?! Quit bein' lazy! Hurry up and get moving!"

At any rate, all she could hear was angry yelling.

With a dry laugh, the man turned back to Cayna and warned her that she'd be struck by the boss's wrath if she got too close. He was about to return to work when...

"You too, dumbass. Don't go whinin' to people who come to check out what we do."

As soon as he heard the deep, rough voice behind him, the young man literally leaped into the air.

A rugged dwarf with a gray head of hair and gray beard stood there glaring. The man hurriedly ran back inside as if seeking to escape, all while still gripping the lumber.

The dwarf watched him scurry away, then scratched the back of his head as he turned to Cayna.

"Sorry 'bout that, miss. They're a rough bunch... Huh?"

"Hmm? ...Oh?"

The dwarf looked as if he was about to say something when he suddenly froze. As Cayna watched him break out in a sweat, she thought for a minute and took a good look at him. It then hit her.

"Oh!" she exclaimed. "There you are, Kartatz! Long time no see! How ya been?"

"...M-M-M-M-M-M......M. M-M? M...Mum?!"

CHAPTER 3

Cayna face-planted with a *thonk!* onto the ground in the most dramatic, unexpected fashion.

"A-a-a-a-are you all right, Mum?! Did something happen?"

"N-no, I'm fine. How do I put it? I just *really* wasn't expecting to be called that…"

She took his hand and stood up, then looked at the dwarf again. She could definitely tell he was the same sub-character she had made, though he seemed a bit past his prime. It warmed Cayna's heart to see that he had followed his heart and forged his own path.

She didn't have any memories of being around other children, but Cayna patted Kartatz's head as if he were a small child in the hospital that she'd met and grown attached to—not that her real body would have allowed her to do so.

Kartatz's face flushed scarlet, and he brushed her hand away before turning around with his arms crossed.

"D-d-d-d-don't just suddenly pat my head! I-I'm not a little kid!"

"Hee-hee, you sure turned out to be a funny one. So cute!"

"D-don't call a man my age 'cute'! It's creepy!"

Behind them, curious onlookers crowded in the entrance as they watched this pleasant banter unfold. They were all craftsmen and pupils.

"H-hey. Who's that girl?"

"Sh-she looks like she's having a lot of fun with the boss…"

"Oh, she's patting his head…"

"They must be real close if he ain't hitting her."

"D-do you think spring has finally come for the boss?!"

"C'mon, just how old do ya think he is? That ship's long sailed."

"A-a younger lover! I-I'm so jealous…"

"Oh man, this ain't good…"

"WHAT THE HELL D'YA THINK YOU'RE DOIN'?!"

""""""""S-SORRYYYY!!""""""""""

The whispering pupils grew awkward around the pleasantly giggling Cayna as Kartatz yelled at the gathering at the top of his lungs. Laughing as she watched them leave in twos and threes, the dwarf murmured that she hadn't changed one bit.

"…Whaaat?! You left the tower and became an adventurer?!"

"Yep! Gonna go pick up my card later today. It's crazy; a lot's changed in the past two hundred years."

"Mum, if you're becoming an adventurer, does that mean you're gonna decimate some country?"

With a *blah, blah, blah* and *yada, yada, yada*, she had explained to him the events thus far.

Her son's earnest yet suddenly disturbing response prompted Cayna to almost instinctively slam the top of his head as she would with Opus. Kartatz fell to the ground face-first in an instant.

"Huh? What's wrong, Kartatz?"

"Don't you 'What's wrong?' me! Didn't you think your insane power might crush my skull?! Don't go whippin' out some dangerous weapon while keeping your anger bottled up!"

"Come to think of it, I visited the church before coming here, but a sister turned me away."

"There you go changin' the subject to avoid facing your actions… Wait, you went to see Big Bro?! Yeah, right. Of course ya would."

"Also, do you know where Mai-Mai is?"

"She's a professor at the Academy next door. They don't care about normal folk, though. Even if you go, you're gonna get stopped at the gate."

"Hmm. I see. Got it, Kartatz."

Kartatz hurriedly followed his mother as she stepped back and turned on her heel. He grabbed her arm to stop her, and Cayna looked at him inquisitively.

"I-I'm sorry, Mum. Did I say something wrong just now?"

Her curt answer must have given him the wrong impression. She looked at his rugged, flustered face and once again patted his head reassuringly.

"Don't worry, I promise I don't hate you or anything. But I'll be heading back for the day. I'm staying at an inn that serves nonhumans only, so come over if you need me for anything."

"R-right. And I said quit rubbing my head! But yeah, I'll make sure my sibs know."

"Thanks! Please do."

Kartatz watched his mother skip away and heaved a big sigh. He felt eyes on the back on his head, and when he turned around, he locked gazes with the group of workers who stared at him from the shadows with tearful reproach.

"......... Grrr."

"......... Eek!"

Needless to say, a thundering voice immediately resounded across the entire sandbar.

Cayna quickly returned to the Adventurers Guild and exchanged the placard for her card. It read *"Cayna | High Elf | Mage"* on a white background, and she was absolutely thrilled to finally have it in her hands.

It was close to the same joy she'd felt when she first logged into the VRMMO *World of Leadale* and took those steps onto the field as an adventurer, though her only memories of the actual moment were of her soon-to-be-unavoidable pain of Opus showing up in the same exact place and sending a flying kick her way. Of course, she fondly recalled the memory of answering in kind.

After taking a quick look at the requests on the board, she found two that said, *"Guard Wanted, Female Elf | Elineh"* and *"Recruiting new members; female elves who can use magic preferred | Arbiter"* and gave a wry smile.

"Those two know exactly what they're doing..."

Suddenly hit with hollow exhaustion, she gave up staring at the solicitations and headed out onto the main road.

...Just then, someone nearby greeted her.

"Why, hello there, miss."

"Ah... Do you mean me?"

When someone calls out, it's only natural to turn around and see if they mean you or someone else.

Upon doing so, Cayna saw a male and female pair standing before her.

"Did you call me just now?"

"Yes, that I did. You're an adventurer, I take it?"

The one who responded to Cayna's question with a satisfied nod was a fully armored knight in his fifties with white stubble and hair that was beginning to pepper. However, his armor was more stained than white and appeared to be vintage. Unlike the knights who patrolled the town, he had a normal long sword in a tarnished sheath at his side.

Accompanying him was a girl who looked to be about Cayna's age. She had silver hair and wore a robe over her leather armor. An azure ball floated over the tip of her spear. She'd been staring at Cayna ever since the man spoke to her, but the moment they locked eyes, she waved both arms in a panic and turned bright red before hiding behind him.

He crossed his arms at this and gave a hearty laugh. Then he approached Cayna.

"I'm Agaido. Come on now, don't hide. Introduce yourself!"

Looking downward as she moved to stand next to him, the girl gave a small bow.

"U-um, I'm Lonti."

"…Oh, okay. Um, I'm Cayna?"

She had no idea why they'd flagged her down. Cayna answered in a way that went along with whatever they were saying, Agaido in particular. Back in the hospital, the golden rule for staying comfortable was to "always let the elderly person dominate the conversation."

"From what I can tell, you are very capable, yes? Maybe you could lend us a helping hand?"

"I don't know what you need help with, but is it some sort of request? Unfortunately, I only just became an adventurer, so I'm not sure I could even show you around the city…"

"Fear not. We're locals who know our way around. What we're asking is tougher than that."

"Tougher? Do you mean like defeating monsters or taking out thieves?"

"You see, there's someone I'm looking for."

Just when she'd thought his request was going to be particularly dire, the man's quick, casual response sent her reeling with slight disappointment.

Noticing her reaction, Agaido waved his hands and corrected himself.

"Don't be fooled—our target is incredibly cunning. You can't let your guard down."

"Ah, so it's some sort of heinous criminal? And you're saying you want me to capture them?"

"Hmm. Yes, I guess you can look at it that way. Will you do it?"

"I don't mind. That is, if you're willing to offer a financial reward."

If this had been the Cayna back in the remote village, she wouldn't have even mentioned compensation. Ever since Professor Elineh and Sergeant Arbiter's lessons, the mantra of *Demand payment, even if only a single bronze coin more* had been drilled into her head repeatedly.

"If you're lookin' for a payday, leave it to me. As soon as this job's done, I'll make sure you're swimming in coins."

"All right, that's a promise. I accept!"

The two gave each other a thumbs-up, and Cayna firmly shook hands with the old knight. Lonti was undeniably a mere bystander here.

"...That said, this city is surprisingly large...," started Cayna.

"It looks like the target frequents this side of the capital pretty often. We'll manage it somehow if we split up."

"I see, so the three of us will each be going our own way?"

Looking out over masses of people would be annoying, but Agaido pointed at everyone, including himself.

"No, I'll be searchin' by myself. Lonti, you know the target's face, so why don't you go with Lady Cayna?"

"I-I'm going with C-Cayna?"

"Lady Cayna doesn't know what our target looks like, right? Okay, keep an eye on my partner here, will ya?"

"Yes, of course. I'm always happy to respect my clients' wishes."

Cayna watched as Agaido raised a single arm and disappeared into the crowd. She then turned back to Lonti, who immediately stepped back with an "Eek!"

Cayna wondered if her face was really that scary and quickly grew worried.

"Um, do elves bother you?"

"A-aghhh?! I-I'm sorry! It's not that I find you scary or anyfin!"

Cayna giggled as Lonti grimaced and stumbled over her words. It was kind of like when she interacted with the kids at the hospital, and she held out her hand to Lonti.

The girl shifted her gaze between Cayna's smile and outstretched hand as if they were something truly bizarre.

"It's my first day as an adventurer. I'm Cayna, a high elf. It's nice to meet you."

Lonti's cheeks instantly flushed bright red, and she timidly put her hand in Cayna's.

"I'm Lonti Arbalest, a first-year in adventurer history at the Royal Academy. It-it's nice to meet you, too."

They looked at each other and smiled for a moment, but then red-faced Lonti turned her gaze downward.

…However, she seemed to notice something and raised her head with a gasp.

"Ah! Are you a high elf, Cayna?! What is elven royalty doing in a place like this?!"

"Well, there's always an exception to the rule, right? That aside, let's get going, or we'll lose daylight."

She had spent the entire morning sightseeing, so only afternoon remained. There would be even more people once night fell, which wasn't very helpful during a manhunt. The two set off in the opposite direction from Agaido and for some reason held hands like a pair of innocent lovers.

"By the way, what kind of person are we looking for exactly?"

"Ah, p-please excuse me. Um, he's a red-haired boy who is a little younger than me."

"That's pretty vague…"

After a bit of thought, they moved from the main road to a side street that was one over. The two maneuvered around obstacles and made their way through the narrow, complicated road that served as a back entrance to shops and houses.

Cayna thought it'd be just as commonplace as the parks in her old town if it were made into a children's playground. The capital had never seemed like that sort of place up until now when she was finally walking through it. That was why she figured these backstreets would be the perfect hiding spot for a kid.

For some time, she and Lonti looked in places a child might hide and quickly raced through the alley.

"It's not like he would go around wandering around every nook and cranny, so where might he be…?"

"Huh? You entered this backstreet without a plan?"

"I've just been thinkin' that all kids have some sort of seekwit hideout."

"Some sort of…what…?"

Just as Kee picked up something that might be useful in their search with his Acquisition Skill, a scream came from the main road. The two hurriedly turned around and left the back road.

There, bystanders were all looking up and shouting things like "Look out!" and "Kyaaa!" as if the world were ending.

The reason was just overhead.

A rope was strung between two houses across the main road. It looked like the kind used to hang laundry.

In the very center, a kitten was clinging for dear life, and a boy was crawling on the line like a caterpillar in an attempt to save it.

"I guess there's going to be a crowd of onlookers watching a heart-racing rescue attempt no matter where you go…," Cayna said in a murmur as she joined that very crowd and looked up. The people let out an occasional word of encouragement as they watched the red-haired boy's strenuous efforts.

Prepared to run in as backup at any time, Cayna came to a sudden realization.

Huh? A red-haired boy?

She had a bad feeling and tried to hold back Lonti, but it was already too late.

"A-AGHHH?!"

The distraught yell that suddenly followed practically ripped through the air. Lonti's shriek startled the kitten clinging desperately to the rope. Its grip loosened, and the kitten tumbled toward the ground.

The boy dove after it and somehow caught the kitten midair, and the crowd watching from below let out a scream that signaled an imminent tragedy. There were even some who covered their faces with both hands as if to say, *I can't take anymore!*

Having predicted the worst ahead of time and prepared for it, Cayna remained perfectly calm and cast the spell she had prepared beforehand on the boy.

Magic Skill: Load: Float

"What?!"

She ignored the astonished cry next to her.

The round boy holding the kitten tightly was shocked to realize he was hovering in midair. No longer bound by gravity, he floated as if he were as light as a feather and lightly touched the ground.

Soon enough, the bystanders let out a round of clapping and applause and rushed in on Cayna and the boy. Turning around to face them all, Cayna gave her thanks with a bow of the head. Children who looked even younger than the boy holding the kitten raced toward him with anxious expressions, and he was immediately surrounded.

"Are you okay, Captain?"

"Yeah, I'm feelin' awesome."

The red-haired boy eased his friends' concerns with a thank-you, then saw Lonti standing next to Cayna. Embarrassed, he took a step away from them.

"L-Lonti…"

"I finally found you, Prin…I mean, Young Master."

With this alone, Cayna understood everything and nodded with a smirk. It had a sense of *I see—so this is the kind of Event I ran into.*

I've done four thousand quests yet never had one like this.

Unaware of Cayna's internal understanding, the red-haired boy foisted the kitten on Lonti before yelling, "Let's go!" and racing off with the other children.

"Ah! Wait! Wh-what am I supposed to do with this?"

"Wow, that was fast. They're already long gone."

"Hey, Cayna! Please stop acting impressed and go catch them!"

"Yes, yes, right away. For now, we should probably link up."

"What?!"

Before Lonti could object to anything, they flew over the wall of onlookers with Active Skill: Leap and chased after the boy's group.

Cayna knew what he looked like now, and if push came to shove, she thought she could freely use any type of magic to catch him. She first called upon a Wind Spirit with Summoning Magic and had it pursue them.

Meanwhile, the boys being chased went into the maze of back-streets and took a break. The fact that they realized Cayna was approaching was only a coincidence. As they took a breath and faced forward, they locked eyes with her.

Since she didn't have the same deep knowledge of the back roads, running through various obstacles would only slow her down…so she walked on the walls.

""""WHAT THE HECK?!"""" they shouted in unison.

Cayna completely ignored this as she cracked her knuckles and grinned darkly. Since she was in profile, it was a little awkward. In fact, it was rather unsettling. How could someone have walked on walls to chase after them, and where had she come from?

"'Kay, time for my client's request. You guys ready to part with ten or twenty of your limbs?"

""""People don't even have that many!""""

As she hounded the boys, who searched for another escape route, Cayna really did have a problem.

How should I catch them?

She had a crazy array of skills, but not many could be used to capture without causing injury. Magic Skill: Paralysis Net could immobilize an opponent, but it also injured them. Even if she attacked with the smallest amount of force, her targets were still children. It would carbonize them in an instant.

There was also the option of summoning a large spider and having it cast a web.

...However, since the spider itself was about four meters long, there was a possibility she might be arrested by soldiers if people thought she was the one causing trouble and potentially a messenger of the Demon King.

There wasn't much helping it, so she decided to treat it like a game of tag and chase them until they were too tired to move. A bit of exercise seemed like fun, and she started off with a bit of persuasion.

"Hey! You can't escape, Primo! Be a good boy and turn yourself in!"

"Who the heck you callin' Primo?!"

"Lonti just called you Young Master Primo, right?!"

"You're the worst, Lonti!"

Walking on walls and literally leaping over obstacles, the barely armored adventurer girl used unimaginable methods to close in on the boys, who knew these streets like the backs of their hands.

The red-haired boy leading the group finally decided to use the ace up his sleeve. It was his greatest weapon, which he'd used to shake off countless soldiers.

He switched directions, moved farther into the residential district, and escaped into the redevelopment zone, where homes now devoid of people stood. It was known as a backstreet trash dump.

Weaving through the narrow gaps between houses, he timed his attack. To the left and right sat wooden crates and piles of scrap wood. When the female adventurer approached, they would get her in one go.

BWAAAAAAM!!!

A thundering noise resounded, dust flew, and the street was quickly buried in crates and lumber.

"Yeah!"

"We did it!"

"How's that?!"

…The friends let out rounds of cheers.

Wiping the sweat from his forehead, the redhead was about to thank his friends but was shocked to hear someone calmly say, "Watch out for this dangerous pile, 'kay?" from the other side of the rubble. He turned around.

Weapon Skill: Rabbit Stream

BOOOOOOOOM!!

The crates and lumber that had formed a mountain only a moment ago were blown to pieces and soaring through the sky an instant later.

A human form appeared beyond the curtain of dust that kicked up. A sword that glowed a faint blue cut through it from top to bottom, and the female adventurer appeared with a fearless smile. Fragments of wreckage belatedly rained down on them.

"H-hey, wait, where did you get that sword?!"

"S-she's a monster…"

"Hey, you, have some manners! What part of me is monstrous?"

"Let's get outta here!"

"Sheesh, you're a tenacious bunch…"

Cayna had been positive they would lose the will to fight by this point but was disappointed to see she was completely mistaken.

Putting away the Rune Blade, which increased the user's power when pumped with MP, she sent the same Wind Spirit she'd recently called upon to go on ahead and get after them.

The pursuer and the pursued once again raced through the city. The boys came out upstream of the river-facing capital and went along the pier as if it were a giant jungle gym before slipping into the canal below. Prior to the city's expansion, this area was originally where one of the river's tributaries converged. Now it was merely a canal that discharged everyday wastewater into the river.

The boys jumped into the boat hidden there and began rowing as hard as they could. Small boats had rowing competitions during the capital's festivals, and every year their group put up a good fight even against the adults. They used their impressive might and experience from the competitions to swiftly depart the riverbank.

As they passed beyond the sandbar and turned around to declare "Whaddaya think of that?! Serves you right!" their faces froze.

After all, they were watching Cayna approach them while walking on water with no trouble at all.

This also stirred up wide-eyed bystanders on the pier who were curious as to what was going on.

"DON'T THINK YOU CAN ESCAPE ME! HURRY UP AND TURN YOURSELVES IN!" she shouted into a yellow megaphone that she seemed to have procured out of thin air.

The boys frantically turned back around and began paddling as if their lives depended on it. They didn't even care how they looked anymore.

Scratching her cheek with an "Eh, it is what it is," Cayna broke into a jog and maintained a reasonable distance as she began closing in on the small boat.

In the end, the boys ran out of steam and motivation after about four laps. With every single one of them exhausted, apprehending their redheaded leader was a cinch.

The sky had faded to a dusky orange when Cayna picked up the boy by the collar, bound him with rope, and handed him off to Lonti and Agaido.

The two had apparently witnessed the whole ordeal, but only Lonti stood there openmouthed.

"Ha-ha-ha, you're pretty amazing!" Agaido said, but he didn't comment much beyond that. "Here's that reward I promised."

He handed Cayna a bag stuffed with bronze coins, and she eyed it curiously. She'd never seen so many before.

"What's all this?"

"See, I kind of had a bet with the bystanders during your river race just now. Splitting it fifty-fifty sounds good, right?"

"Sheesh, nothing gets past you…"

The restrained redhead lay limply on the ground, trembling slightly.

"The hell's your problem?! Do you know who you're messing with?!"

"I have a pretty good idea, but 'Primo' is fine. I don't want to get involved any more than that."

"Oh, so you know the circumstances surrounding our young master, then?" asked Agaido.

"Well, yeah. Lonti called him Prin earlier. He's a prince who ran away from his stuffy life in the castle, right? It's a classic scenario anyone could figure out. That's why I didn't believe for a second we were catching a regular brat."

"Dammit, Lonti! It's all your fault she's calling me Primo!!"

"*Sniffle…* I'm so sorry!"

Cayna put the purse away into her Item Box and confirmed that the request was now complete. With a satisfied smile, Agaido gave her a round golden button that looked as if it could be worn on a coat.

"Um, what's this for?"

"If you run into any trouble while in the capital, you can just show that."

"Uh, I have a feeling that'll only cause some other sort of trouble."

"Ha-ha-ha, well then. Thanks for taking on our request, miss."

"I'm sorry for the trouble, Cayna," said Lonti. "Thank you very much for today."

With a vigorous gesture unsuited to his age, the man hoisted the caterpillar-like boy onto his shoulders, his laughter audible even as he boarded the small, luxurious sailboat that sat at the edge of the river. After a deep bow, Lonti soon followed.

"What kind of alien ninja is that guy...?"

Cayna watched the boat begin sailing lazily along the river, then she turned around and decided to head back to the inn.

She had yet to learn just how peaceful life had been until then.

Bam!

As soon as she passed through the inn door, Cayna was greeted by cheers and full tankards. The twitching in her face was almost a natural reaction by this point.

"Welcome back! You sure are late!"

The proprietress's brown cat ears pinged, and she happily offered Cayna a large tankard of spirits. When she finally accepted, there was cry of "Chug, chug, chug!"

Unsure what exactly everyone was celebrating, she turned to the proprietress for help.

"You did something pretty amazing on the river, right? Everyone's talking about it, but we don't really get how it happened. They're saying they know they'll understand if they hear it from you. Ah, that drink is a gift from us, of course."

...So they basically just want me to be the late-night entertainment?

Cayna realized what was going on an instant later, and she blanched. The tankard in her hand was the primary cause of this. In the meantime, the cheers continued, and she put the drink to her lips in reckless abandon.

Incidentally, she had no memories of that night.

◆

Let us turn to the Royal Academy.

It was an institution that sat in the center of the sandbar on the Ejidd River in Felskeilo's royal capital. Race, age, and gender had no bearing on enrollment. So long as you had the proper talent, the Academy's gates would welcome you with open arms.

Now, let us turn the clock back to around when Cayna reunited with Kartatz.

In an alchemy classroom, a female student was called upon. The reason had to do with part of a lesson where she was to create and present a potion. While it was problematic enough that she had submitted it late, the potion itself was the bigger focus.

The alchemy teacher was Lopus Harvey. He had disheveled hair, and his once-white professor robes were dirty and worn. His bangs covered half his face, and he had an obvious five-o'clock shadow. He didn't look like the type of person anyone would expect to be teaching at the prestigious Royal Academy, but he was a fine alchemist.

Clearly lacking any motivation, the man rested his elbows on his desk and looked up at the female student standing nearby.

"Hey, I know this is the potion I had you make…but did you really make it?"

"Y-yes…"

He picked up the vial of red liquid she had submitted and looked at her suspiciously.

"Are you sure? If you did, I can recommend you to the royal palace, but…"

"What?! Really?!" The girl's face immediately lit up at the opportunity to advance in the world.

However, Lopus's lackadaisical attitude never wavered. He shook the potion around and continued.

"So you had someone make this, right? Do you even know the recipe?"

"Ah, y-yes. You take a kaju root and..."

"Nope, nice try. This ain't made with cheap ingredients like that. It's an Artifact made through a process unknown to anyone."

Lopus's sharp eyes glinted through the hair obscuring his visage, and the girl drew back, face pale.

"...So who made this?"

They were back at square one, and while Lopus was still as laid-back as usual, his interrogation gave him a different energy. Finally, the girl tearfully bowed her head.

"I-I'm sorry! I couldn't get the ingredients together and put in a request to the Adventurers Guild to have it made!"

"I see. Got it. I'll give you another assignment later. You can go."

He shooed her away with his hand. The girl bowed her head once again and left the classroom as if seeking escape. She didn't even wipe her teary eyes.

Lopus was looking at the red liquid in the vial before him when a knock came at the door. He looked up.

"Helloooo! I'm coming in, okay?"

A quintessential blond, blue-eyed elf walked in. Her braided hair fell down to her waist, and she wore a red robe that was long enough to hide her feet.

She was the headmaster of the Royal Academy, Mai-Mai Harvey. And although they didn't look the least bit compatible, she was Lopus's wife.

"Ah, it's you... Don't see you around the Alchemy Department very often."

"Well, I just saw a girl run past me crying. Not only does it make you look like an idiot, people will start saying you're abusive, y'know."

Mai-Mai gleefully approached Lopus as she conducted her teasing cross-examination, but he ignored her and instead handed over the vial of red liquid.

"You're no fun... What's this?"

"A potion that was submitted as an assignment."

"Hmm, who made it? It doesn't look like something even you could make."

Mai-Mai peered at the contents as she swirled the liquid around and understood in an instant.

"You know, don't you? Probably an adventurer."

"Ohhh, right, an adven... *Whaaa—?!*"

Mai-Mai's brain sorted out what she'd just been told, and she was left speechless by the absurdity of an object thought impossible in this world.

Watching her, Lopus gave an exaggerated sigh before taking the red vial from his wife's hand and putting it on the desk. Its ability to fluster a former Imperial Mage spoke of its true value.

"If something like this made its way around the world, markets would fall into major chaos. For now, I'll head over to the Guild tomorrow and warn the person who made it."

"It takes a lot to get someone as lazy as you to move. Bring them back if you can."

Lopus sighed in exasperation at her casual comment.

"What, you wanna make 'em a teacher or something?"

"First comes the interview. Then I suppose we'll have to wait for the results."

Mai-Mai waved lightly as she went to leave but stopped and turned around.

"Ah, sorry, but I have dinner plans with my big brother and the others today. Can you tell everyone not to wait up for me?"

"Yeah, got it. But the High Priest sure does whatever the heck he feels like…"

Mai-Mai sidled up to Lopus, gave him a quick peck on the cheek, and excused herself with a cheerful wave. At the door, she turned to give her beloved husband a wink.

"Apparently, my dopey little brother has something urgent to talk about."

Mai-Mai's destination after leaving the Academy was a shop on the sandbar's north shore.

It was a high-class restaurant for nobles known as The White-Tailed Black Rabbit. The siblings sometimes used it as a place to come together and catch up on the latest. This time, she'd received a letter from Kartatz that said, *"It's an emergency!"* and called a sudden meeting.

"…And that's what happened."

"Wh-wh-wh-whaaaaaat?!"

"I see… That's what Mother Dear is up to…"

Kartatz told his two siblings all about his sudden encounter with Cayna that afternoon. Upon hearing the news, his sister, Mai-Mai, stopped eating and closed in on him with an enraged expression. She shook him furiously.

"WHY. DIDN'T. YOU. CALL. ME. RIGHT. THEN?!"

"Hmm. Perhaps I should invite her to the church and extend my warmest greetings?" muttered the tall, beautiful Skargo, who was the eldest of the three siblings. Every movement and gesture was accompanied by a glowing light, the sounds of twinkling and sparkling, and a rose backdrop. With lemon-colored hair and shining green eyes, he pondered in melancholy as slender fingers pressed against his lips.

Incidentally, these were not misheard sounds or hallucinations. Of the insane number of skills available, this was the number one thing that people hated on in the message boards and made them doubt the Admins' sanity. This was Special Skill: Oscar—Roses Scatter with Beauty. It was a completely aesthetic effect that the user could cast at any time.

Nevertheless, being purposefully reminded of their mother, Cayna, wasn't without its problems…

Mai-Mai stopped shaking Kartatz and shrugged at her older brother's comment.

"Maybe we shouldn't bother? And what was the point of her hiding away in the forest because she got sick of people anyway?"

Skargo nodded at her assessment and combed through his hair with a *whoosh!* His two younger siblings were great at selective hearing and didn't press the issue further.

"Still, to think Mother would be an adventurer… Hang on. Was she the one who made that potion?"

"Huh? I told you—Mum said this was her first day."

"Wellll, a potion made through a lost process kinda fell into our hands."

"Hmph. I do wish Mother Dear had informed me she would be visiting."

"She said she got turned away at the door. Apparently, she went to the church before seeing me."

At Kartatz's explanation, Skargo prodded his forehead, and his almond eyes shone with a cacophony of twinkling as they gave a sidelong glance. He thought for a moment.

"Failing to notify me of her arrival is most terrible sacrilege against my most honorable mother."

A black mist slowly rolled in behind him with a *rrrr*, a dark, seething smile crossed his lips, and his eyes glinted with an unnerving *shinng!*

Mai-Mai lightly smacked him and cut this display short.

"Skargo, don't be so quick to make threats like that! Mother would give you a good scolding if she knew. She's kind and would never endorse such a thing."

He murmured, "I suppose you're right," and the black mist dissipated with a *fwoosh*. He ran a comb through his long hair, and it cascaded over his shoulder with a *swoosh*.

"Well then, if Mother Dear is going to be settling down in the royal capital, the question is what to do about our positions in society, correct?" Skargo asked.

"Are you unhappy with somethin' in your job, Big Bro?"

"But of course. To me, Mother Dear is the only heaven in existence. Every occupation should have her at their center. Yes, of that there is no doubt!"

A huge wave roared with a *splash!* behind him, and his siblings heaved a collective sigh. Even after two hundred years, it was clear that his "Mother Dear" supremacism hadn't faded. In fact, it had only gotten worse.

At this point, there was only one way to stop the man.

"Guess we gotta get Mother to scold him."

"Our High Priest just might sink the country…"

CHAPTER 4
A Daughter, an Academy, a Tower, and a Summoned Beast

Cayna sat uncomfortably for breakfast, trying to quell the nonstop throbbing in her head. She looked so obviously unwell that fellow guests gave her medicine for hangovers. No matter how much of a Skill Master Cayna was, when she drank, it hit *hard*. After all, Passive Skill: Poison Resistance could only get her so far.

And that came as a result of vehement opposition from a majority of players in the game world of *Leadale*.

Players were allowed to kill one another solely during wartime. It netted you just a negligible amount of experience points, but low-level players nonetheless went wild over it. As a result, they formed factions and targeted higher players, such as Limit Breakers.

Skills that started as Status Ailment Nullification became Status Ailment Resistance. These were later updated as different variations, like Poison Resistance, Paralysis Resistance, and Silence Resistance.

The high-level players had thought this was going too far, but the lower ones that made up a majority of users had praised it.

For someone like Cayna, who specialized in magic, there were several times when she got caught up in a strategic battle and failed because she was outnumbered. She personally would casually think, *Guess no one's perfect*, but others didn't seem to share her opinion. There was one point at which high-level players, like Limit Breakers and Skill Masters, conspired together and formed their own country. When they eventually became undefeatable, the message boards and official site exploded.

It was most likely this turn of events that led to Cayna's current lightweight tendencies. When she was still an avatar, whether she was protected against poison depended on probability and the game's programming. Now that her avatar was her own physical body, she had a feeling that the mentality of "twenty-one and over" and "underage drinking," as well as a number of other factors, had likely weakened her Poison Resistance. Not to mention that Marelle had told her, "Hangovers are a part of enjoying a few good drinks," and forbid her from using Poison Purification. Cayna loyally obeyed this command and endured the aftereffects.

Cayna did as she was told because she saw Marelle as a mother figure in this world.

Hmm, what'd I come here for again? I said I'd look for the towers, right? But will anyone even know what I mean by Guardian Towers?

She'd visited the market early in the morning, bought some kirina grass and colt bird hearts, then ate breakfast at the inn before setting out for the Guild.

Several people she ran into on the way would make comments like "Oh, you're the girl who walked on water!" She wished dearly that they wouldn't.

What am I, a pond skater?

It was magic that couldn't be easily shoved under the rug, so there wasn't much helping it. The more people there are, the faster rumors spread. It had turned into a game of telephone, and there was bound to be plenty of misinformation, but…

Instead of collecting information in town, wouldn't people like Elineh's caravan, who travel to different places, have detailed knowledge of remote areas? I'll go back to that carriage rest stop and ask.

She switched directions just before the Guild and headed to the carriage lodgings and found that Elineh and his caravan hadn't left yet. As Cayna grew near the members she recognized, Elineh immediately came out and got the conversation going.

"I heard what happened, Lady Cayna. It seems you have parted the river, correct?"

"Who in the world told you that?!"

"It was a joke."

Realizing he'd been toying with her, Cayna fell to her knees. Waterfalls poured from her eyes as she inched over to Elineh.

"ELINEEEEEEH!"

"Yes, yes. I understand, so please cheer up."

"Sniff…"

The thought that her benefactor believed she would resort to such brute force brought Cayna to tears. She wiped her eyes and faced Elineh again.

"Now then, what could be the matter?" he asked. "It doesn't seem like you've come seeking employment as a guard…"

Skirting around her title of Skill Master, she asked him if he had any information on structures similar to that of the silver tower near the remote village (which, come to think of it, she had never asked the name of).

"I see. So, Lady Cayna, you intend to find these towers?"

"Well, that's the ultimate goal anyway. After all, there's nothing else right now that really strikes me."

"There does seem to be a beautiful castle floating in the middle of a lake in the northern Kingdom of Helshper that no one is able to enter…but I cannot think of much else otherwise."

155

"The north, huh?"

The countries to the north included the former Purple Kingdom of Helbehr to the northeast of the former White Kingdom and the old Black Kingdom of Lypras to the west. Every month, the three nations would participate in the furious battle that took place in the Black Kingdom.

Cayna and her insufferable companion belonged to the Black Kingdom in particular, so the country's landscape was full of craters, devastated by the powerful magic and Weapon Skills her fellow Skill Masters used in their firefights. She remembered how different things looked after each battle.

It didn't have any lasting impact in the world of the game, but if something like that happened now, this capital would turn into more than ruins in an instant and become a wasteland.

Unsurprisingly, there didn't appear to be anyone as twisted as the twenty-four Limit Breakers and thirteen Skill Masters to do such a thing (though she did think there were a lot of strange characters).

When she considered this, Cayna realized how much of a challenge it would be to use her own power. After all, if she waved it about carelessly, she might all too easily kill people.

"Lady Cayna?"

"Oh, yes… I'm sorry."

"Were you thinking of the past? If it's not too much trouble, I would like to ask what the world was once like."

"Ah, well, I'd say it was a brutal era of constant warfare."

Elineh departed after promising to let her know if he discovered anything else about the tower. He told her that the information was free of charge this time, but if he did learn anything, she'd have to pay a fee next time. Merely refraining from talk of money from the outset was a kindness on his part.

Thinking this over, she headed for her initial destination: the Guild.

As she went to check out the requests on the wall, the same woman who was at the reception counter the other day greeted her.

"Ah, Cayna. Would you mind coming over here for a minute?"

"Of course."

Cayna went up to the counter and was handed a small gilt-edged piece of paper that looked like a certificate. It was written in the local language, which would be a pain to decipher, so Cayna decided to just ask.

"What is this?"

"You've been summoned to the Academy. Maybe it's a personal request of some sort? It seems to be related to your potion from the other day."

"By 'Academy,' you mean the one on the sandbar?"

"Yes, the Royal Academy. The invitation doesn't give a fixed date, but one can only assume they mean at your earliest convenience."

At any rate, going to the Academy would give her the chance to visit Mai-Mai, so Cayna didn't see a problem with visiting. Cayna had only ever been to elementary school, so she was a bit excited to experience the different world this new school would open up for her.

When she went to the harbor to cross to the sandbar, many people curiously asked her, "Aren't you going to walk across the river today?" but she had no intention of being the spectacle she'd been the other day and gave a vague reply of "Uh, maybe later." She pretended not to hear the particularly stubborn ones and crossed to the sandbar on the commuter boat. Cayna was a bit shocked to find she'd already attained notoriety around the harbor.

When she showed her summons to the guard at the Academy, they said something to a crystal ball in the guardroom, and the gates opened. Someone would be coming to lead her in, so she was asked to wait for a while.

After several quiet minutes, a familiar face came quickly pattering out of the building.

"I—I apologize for the wait. Thank you for responding to our summ... Cayna?!"

"Hey there, Lonti. Feels like we saw each other only yesterday. So you're a student here?"

Unlike the day before, Lonti wore green robes and didn't have her wand with her. The girl steadied herself and bowed her head.

"Thank you very much for yesterday. The knights were quite surprised at how quick you were."

"That Primo really is hopeless. If I see him in town again, can I catch him with no questions asked?"

"Y-yes, please do. More importantly, what have you been summoned for?"

"Hmm, that's what I've come to ask, too. At any rate, do you think you could show me around?"

"Of course. I was told to first bring you to the headmaster's office. Right this way."

Cayna followed Lonti and entered the school. Along the way, Lonti explained a number of points about the Academy.

First, she said she belonged to the Vocational Magic Department and had registered with the Adventurers Guild as a part of her classes. There were also other departments like the Holy Department, where one could study healing and purification magic, and the Alchemy Department, where one could learn how to compound medicines. Anyone could enter the Academy so long as they had the necessary magical prowess. (The tuition was minimal, and the country would guarantee the funds for you.)

"'Compound'? Not synthesis?"

"Hmm? It's common practice to grind and mix materials together when creating medicines. Do high elves use a different method?"

"...Ah, I see. Player-only skills haven't been passed down to NPCs."

"...Pardon?"

Cayna couldn't say for sure without the whole picture, but it appeared that skills once used by players no longer existed in this world. In that case, perhaps the reason Lonti had been so surprised when Cayna used Float the day before was because she hadn't used a chant.

"This is the headmaster's office," said Lonti.

While Cayna had been ruminating, Lonti had led her to an impressive door that was different from the rest. Cayna knocked, and a woman bid them enter. Lonti opened the door and stepped inside.

Trailing behind her, Cayna's eyes met those of a female elf in red robes. She sat at a stately desk with a large glass window behind her.

Before Cayna could even notice who she was, there was a sudden *swoosh* of soft cloth, and the high elf was caught in a tight embrace.

"...Um, you're Mai-Mai...right?"

"Ahhhh, it's been sooooo long, Mother!"

"WHAAAAAAAAAAAAAAAAAAAT?!"

As soon as the first voice cooed above Cayna's head, Lonti gave a cry of astonishment.

She's so tall and soft and slim. Why do I have to be so small? wondered Cayna.

No matter how messed up the character creation process was, her original body had been all skin and bones, so there was nothing she could do about her appearance.

Now that Mai-Mai was within reach, Cayna pinched her cheek and forcibly peeled her away.

"Uwaaaagh, you're so mean, Mother! We haven't seen each other in two hundred years!"

"What do you think you're doing, acting like this in public? You're the headmaster! …Hey, Lonti, you okay?"

"…Yes."

Cayna waved her hand over Lonti's distant eyes to bring the girl back to herself. Fortunately, it seemed as though her soul hadn't completely left her body, so it didn't take long. However, she immediately pressed Cayna for answers.

"U-u-u-um, uh, are you the headmaster's mother, Cayna?!"

"That's right. After all, I'm over two hundred years old." (A huge lie.)

"Yaaaay, Mother!"

Speechless and dumbfounded, Lonti watched as the headmaster of the Academy clung to Cayna from behind like a large child (puppy ears and tail included).

Unsure of what to do at this point, Cayna chose not to fight back and instead produced a small amount of lightning in her hand.

As soon as Mai-Mai saw this, she quickly leaped back, straightened herself up, and cleared her throat with a cough. After reassuming her normal appearance, she turned to Lonti.

"My apologies, Miss Arbalest. You may return to class."

"Ah, yes… Please e-excuse me…"

Possibly hovering between illusion and reality, Lonti gave a bow and excused herself from the office.

Mai-Mai was about to hug her mother from behind again but froze when she noticed Cayna's dark aura (the skills Might and Glare, respectively).

"Hey, Mai-Mai?"

"Y-yes?! Wh-what is it, M-Mother…?"

"Why *exactly* was I called here, I wonder? Was it so you could give me a hug?"

"N-no, I j-just wanted to discuss something with you!"

"I won't tell you not to be so clingy, but save it for when we're in private. You have a position to uphold, don't you?"

"*Sniff.* Yes, I understand."

Cayna tried giving her daughter a proper motherly warning but sensed she'd been slightly off the mark. After all, she had rather vague memories of her own mother.

Despondent from the rejection, Mai-Mai returned to her desk and removed from a drawer a glass vial filled with red liquid. It was the High Potion Cayna had given the Guild the day before as part of a request. Taking it with her, Mai-Mai instructed her mother to "Please follow me" and exited the headmaster's office. Cayna felt sorry for sending the elf into a depression and thought perhaps she'd been too harsh.

"Mai-Mai?"

"Y-yes? What is it, Mother…?"

"Do you know about the other Guardian Towers?"

"…U-um, they are similar to your own silver tower, correct?"

"Right, those are the ones. There are twelve others in this world."

Mai-Mai thought for a moment before shaking her head and responding, "I've never heard of the others."

"I see," said Cayna. "Got it. Thanks."

Mai-Mai hadn't heard of the towers, even though she'd been around when the game had lots of players.

Back in the day, Cayna had used her sub-characters as more than just storage space. They'd also been NPC personnel to whom she'd given a certain degree of movement and had walk alongside her. It was commonplace to have sub-characters trail behind you like little ducklings so they could gain battle experience and level up.

Cayna had done exactly that with her three sub-characters, all of whom were likely at level 300. Since their skills and magic abilities took the longest to level up, she had thought it would be nicer to have them all at the same level rather than radically different. Cayna had clear memories of approaching other towers and calling upon monsters with Summoning Magic while she helped them gain experience points.

However, Mai-Mai apparently had no recollection of this. Cayna decided to put that out of her mind for now, since she had no way of looking into it. She would have to check with Skargo and Kartatz later.

As Cayna stewed over this conundrum, she was led to was seemed to be a class that was in session. Her daughter opened the door without the least bit of hesitation and stepped inside while announcing, "Look who I brought!"

Several wide desks were lined up inside, and the strong scent of herbs wafted across the room. About twenty students were grinding and mixing ingredients. They did no more than glance at Mai-Mai's sudden arrival and hardly took their eyes off their work.

The person she had called out to was a shabby-looking male teacher standing at his desk. He ordered the students to keep working and followed Mai-Mai out to the hall where Cayna was waiting.

"You're kidding, right? You brought this little lady here?"

"Why the heck does everyone call me that...?"

Cayna sighed at the fact that even this shaggy-haired, unshaven, wayward-looking man had called her "little lady."

Noticing Cayna's irritated expression, Mai-Mai tried to calm her down with a "Now, now."

"Not so fast, Lopus. Don't say things like that. This is my mother, after all."

"Come...again?"

This sudden truth robbed Lopus of all words.

"Anyway, this is Lopus Harvey. He's an alchemy teacher as well as my husband."

"......What?"

Cayna wanted to somehow use special effects to show an ice floe behind her, but she managed to keep herself in check.

Squirming and flailing over her own statement, Mai-Mai blushed and squealed, "Eek, I said it!" Hearts and music notes fluttered everywhere while her mother and husband looked at each other and sighed.

"I am so sorry. I'm afraid I haven't always done the best job raising her. It must be hard for you."

"No... I've learned a lot from her carefree ways, so I wouldn't say that's totally true."

The two exchanged glances once again and awkward smiles.

"You're a good man, Lopus. Take care of her for many days to come."

"It looks like *miss* isn't the right term here. May I call you Lady Cayna? I'd feel pretty awkward calling you Mother."

"Hey, you're ignoring me! And what're you two shaking hands for?! What's with those tepid expressions?!"

Mai-Mai ground her teeth in frustration without realizing she was the very reason her mother and husband had hit it off.

Completely ignoring Mai-Mai's sobbing as she cried them a river, the two got to the subject at hand. Lopus took the vial of red liquid from his wife and handed it to Cayna.

"Now, about this...," he began.

"Someone requested a potion, and I submitted it," said Cayna. "Was that a bad move?"

"If something like this started circulating, it would completely change how people view existing compounds. Don't go flaunting it."

This confirmed her suspicions; the process of creating medicine was different in this world. From the glimpses of what she'd seen in the classroom, her skills would make their laborious process unnecessary.

"...Mai-Mai."

"Yes! What is it, Mother?"

Cayna sighed as her daughter beamed and came rushing over like Pavlov's dog at the mere mention of her name.

"You know Potion Creation I, don't you?" Cayna asked her.

"Huh? No, you never taught me that."

"What? Well, does Kartatz have it?"

"Who knows? My stup…I mean, I've never seen Kartatz make anything like that."

Just as Cayna thought her memory might be off, Lopus amusedly poked into the mother-daughter conversation.

"Hey, Lady Cayna. Do you think you could show us how it's made?"

"What?"

Without waiting for an answer, Lopus walked back into the classroom, left the door open, and urged Cayna forward with a "C'mon!"

Cayna turned around and asked Mai-Mai if this was such a good idea, but her question fell on deaf ears as her daughter pushed her into the classroom.

"If Lopus says it's fine, then it's fine."

The students were used to the officially recognized "Idiot Couple" coming and going, but they looked suspicious as a girl their age walked in with them.

In addition to the tools used for making compounds, there were several vials filled with brown liquid on the desks. The main lesson of the day had apparently ended, but Lopus told his students they could turn in their finished products later and invited Cayna to the teacher's desk.

"We'll be doing a demonstration now, so you should all pay close attention."

Hold on, Lopus! Didn't you say it'd be bad for the market if this got around?

Of course, no one could hear her internal commentary.

Not in the least bothered by the reproachful stares, Lopus lined up the classroom materials on his desk. Before they began, he first pulled Cayna over and introduced her.

"This is Lady Cayna, a mage. She's also our headmaster's mother."

This blunt announcement turned all who heard to stone. Then, after a beat, the students let out a unanimous cry of "WHAAAAAAT?!"

Lopus quieted the class with a wave of his hand. Cayna was surprised by the students' trained reaction to such a gesture.

"Go ahead, Lady Cayna."

"Hold on a sec, these ingredients aren't even the ones in my recipe... What's this?"

"It's kaju root and kirina grass bulbs. Do you need more?"

Cayna determined that this process was fundamentally different from what she was used to based on the ingredients and mixing utensils on the desk before her. She defiantly turned to look at the confused students.

She took out three round stalks of kirina grass and the frozen colt bird hearts. After she explained what was in her hand, she cast the skill Potion Creation II.

Commotion stirred within the classroom in an instant.

Blue dots pulled from the air converged directly in front of Cayna, and a watery sphere immediately swallowed up the ingredients in her hand like a spinning blade. The colors shifted from blue to red to all the colors of the rainbow as the ingredients fused together.

Finally, extra liquid separated and formed a ring around a red compressed ball that could fit in the palm of your hand. It was like a shining blue-and-red disco ball and released a mysterious energy as if it were a single life force.

The moment the students gasped at the fantastical sight, there was a loud *crack*, and the sphere broke apart. Both they and Lopus were left speechless at the shocking phenomenon they had just witnessed. Mai-Mai alone happily murmured, "That's Mother for you."

The only thing that remained in Cayna's hand was a glass vial of red liquid that looked exactly like Lopus's.

"And that is how you create a potion," she said simply, tossing the finished product to Lopus.

He safely caught it and compared the potions he was holding. After confirming they were indeed the same, he raised his hand.

"...Mind answering a question?"

"Depends."

"Where did the vial come from?"

A heartbreaking silence descended, and a stream of sweat fell down Cayna's forehead.

He had no way of knowing this, but this was an issue that drew criticism even in the game. Most items made through the Craft Skill system fit perfectly in their containers. Since these containers usually disappeared once you used up the contents, disposing of them wasn't too much of a problem.

However, as in any world, there were those who made it their job to pick a fight about these things. Players split into two camps—those who wanted separate containers and those who were fine with the current setup—and bickered over the topic constantly. Needless to say, since the Admins didn't get involved, it was a topic of debate that kept cropping up whenever you least expected it.

Of course, Cayna hadn't really cared one way or the other, so now that she was being questioned, she couldn't give a proper answer.

"That's just the way it is! ...Them's the rules!"

She said only as much as she had to and quickly excused herself from the classroom.

"Huh? Ah, wait! Wh-where are you going, Mother?"

"Home."

"What?!"

Baffled by Cayna's sudden displeasure and the way she gave up on the whole affair with a single word, Mai-Mai dashed after her.

Lopus had a few questions of his own as well, but he understood his mother-in-law's hurry and gave a small laugh. After all, he knew even the wisest have their unexpected quirks.

"But we barely got to see each other!" cried Mai-Mai.

"You can just come visit me, then!"

"Don't be like that!"

Lopus's shoulders trembled until the mother-daughter conversation faded from the hallway.

The next day when Cayna showed up at the Guild, the red-haired girl once again called her to the counter and handed over a summons.

"It looks like this time they want you to be a teacher at the Academy no matter what. That's really impressive."

The woman said this with admiration, but the only thing that popped into Cayna's mind was her daughter's happy-go-lucky smile.

Magic Skill: Load: Curse: Type: B

Cayna backed away from the counter and muttered a spell under her breath. An instant later, a black skull appeared over the summons form, and a purple flame turned it to ash.

This skill had been distributed for Halloween and was intended to surprise the target.

It was one of three types of rewards for a simple quest.

For Type A, a human-sized pumpkin holding a lantern would follow the target for an hour.

For Type C, the curse would temporarily render the target despondent, put them in a white kimono, and make them pretend to be a ghost.

Type B, the most devious of all, deployed a small firecracker to the target. Five seconds later, it would explode in a colorful array of five firework displays. They caused absolutely no bodily harm, but it was a nasty trick that set off another seemingly endless wave of explosions whenever it touched something inorganic. If it exploded in a room as tightly packed as the headmaster's office, there was no doubt it'd be a blast-o-palooza.

"Why's my kid such a weirdo?"

Cayna was happy Mai-Mai adored her, but she wasn't sure how she felt about the constant need for attention. Little did Cayna know that it was her eldest son who was the real problem child.

That night, she heard a tale from the dragoid she befriended who was staying at the same inn.

"Apparently, there were a bunch of explosions going off in the headmaster's office today."

"Wow, sounds dangerous."

"Everyone at the Academy is wondering what happened, and rumors are flying. For better or worse, though, no one was injured."

"Wooow."

No one seemed to suspect anything despite her sarcastic replies.

◆

Ten days had passed since Cayna had arrived at the royal capital, though she'd only started her work at the Adventurers Guild the day after she visited the Academy.

The problem was that there were countless requests on the board. Since Guild members weren't separated by a ranking system, it was up to each person to determine whether they could handle a quest.

Cayna was definitely suited for the tougher tasks. However, the Guild preferred that requests like plant harvesting be left for the newbies—nothing Cayna wasn't capable of, but listening to the plants' pained cries was a less-than-pleasant option.

Thus, she decided to leave it to the young receptionist who screened the requests.

"Excuse me, Almana. I have a favor to ask of you."

"Oh, good morning, Miss Cayna. How can I help you?"

"Please choose a request for me!"

"Pardon?"

Almana wasn't the only one shocked. Cayna had thrown every adventurer present for a loop.

In other words, they were all thinking, *What are you even saying?*

After she said it, Cayna realized how strange she must have sounded. She looked at their reactions and corrected herself.

"A-ah! S-sorry! It's not like I can't read it or don't know my own strength! I'm just looking for work that isn't all that destructive! U-um! Um, uh…"

The receptionist Almana watched Cayna's desperate panicking and couldn't help but break into a smile.

"Understood, Miss Cayna. There's no need to fret. I shall provide counsel."

"O-okay! Thank you very much!"

Almana's smile suddenly reminded Cayna of her cousin. They didn't see each other much before the accident, but she saw Cayna and talked with her almost every day while she was in the hospital. She was like a real older sister, and Cayna worried that her cousin had fallen into grief after her death.

Cayna tried to prove herself in this world because she didn't want to worry the people she met here. Almana smiled at this bold display, and Cayna blushed.

An in-depth conversation at the counter would disturb others, so Almana led her into a small room with nothing more than a table and two three-person sofas. It seemed to be used for discussing personal requests.

"Well then, Miss Cayna. Since you are a mage, you specialize in magic, correct?"

Almana took out a book as thick as an encyclopedia and opened it on the table. It was like a smaller version of the request board. These were the forms officially submitted by clients.

"Do you know the force of your strongest magic spell?"

"Um, it could probably…blow away a house."

"Oh my."

This was, of course, a big fat lie. It just sounded like the most plausible answer.

If Cayna had told the truth, Almana would have either burst into laughter or doubted her actual strength. Even without an Amplification Ring or anything like that, it wasn't too farfetched to say she could scorch half the city if she unleashed her greatest magic power. That was how much Cayna stood out in this modern world.

"Can you use anything other than Attack Magic?"

"Other things… Well, I can make a rock golem, stuff like that."

For some reason, it was becoming an ongoing pattern where every time Cayna was about to answer truthfully, she thought better of it and gave a vague answer instead. In this case as well, any single golem she created would be leagues stronger than any knight. Cayna was just now starting to get a feel for how nerve-racking it was to constantly lie about her powers.

"Well then, in that case…how about this?" offered Almana.

Almana placed a request in front of Cayna that read *"Dye Hunting."* It really didn't make much sense at all. In Cayna's mind, she pictured adventurers running around with nets trying to catch paints coming out of tubes.

She stared with a puzzled expression as Almana explained further.

"The aim is to capture a monster that is used as an ingredient in a special dye."

Cayna wanted to say, *Why didn't they just write that?!* but she resisted the urge. After all, this was the kind of scenario that called for shorthand. Any adventurer who took requests regularly would have been able to tell what it meant.

Next, Cayna was told how to find the company that made this particular dye, and she decided to pay them a visit with the request from the board in hand.

The building was a small one that specialized in dyed products, but the president of the company, a plump middle-aged man, told her the location was nothing more than an office. The real factory was along the riverbank.

A team of adventurers had apparently devoted themselves to fulfilling the company's request earlier, but they were injured in the process and disbanded. Consequently, the company was having difficulty procuring the dye as of late.

The staff had their doubts about this young girl who offered to take on the request single-handedly. Even so, you can't make an omelet without breaking a few eggs, and the company president with whom she spoke bowed his head and said, "We appreciate your help."

The clients seemed to be at their wit's end. Even Cayna started to worry if this was really such a good idea.

She would find the monster they needed for their dye along a dry riverbed upstream of the capital. The president himself offered to guide her there. In this world, it was dangerous for the average person to go beyond the protection of the walls, but no one ever thought something even stronger than the monsters that lived there would be escorting *him*.

As the president led her along while flinching at every leaf rustling in the wind and fish jumping in the river, there it was before them.

At first glance, it looked a lot like the round-leaved sundews that live in marshes and dissolve insects for sustenance.

Of course, no sundew in the world stood five meters tall.

The creature's organs, which used a sticky liquid to capture bugs, were grotesque tentacle mouths that looked like a cross between horror-movie monster and plant. It wriggled its long stalks and seemed to grab anything that drew close. In fact, Cayna and the president were currently watching it easily catch a laigayanma calmly passing by. The mouths attached to the multiple stalks started tearing the creature to pieces.

"…So how do people usually collect the material?" Cayna asked.

"Ah yes. Let me think. I believe the adventurers normally procured us one or two leaves."

It seemed their usual team would divert the mouths and just cut off a few leaves. Cayna looked around but couldn't determine if any more of these monsters were nearby.

"I see. So is this the only one here?"

"No, there should be quite a few living along the riverbank."

"Understood. In that case, it won't be a problem if I take it by the roots."

"…Pardon?"

She had the speechless, slack-jawed president step back, then picked up a single pebble from the riverbed. Tightly gripping it in her hand, Cayna focused her magic and cast a spell.

Magic Skill: Load: Create Rock Golem Level 1

The pebble she threw stopped in midair, and the surrounding river rocks began forming a large pile that then absorbed the pebble.

The pile began twisting and turning until it slowly gained a humanlike form. Arms popped out, it grew legs, and a slightly bulging head surfaced. Its eyes were two hollow cavities, one of which emitted a bright-red gleam as the rock golem gave the first cry of its transient life.

"MOH!!"

"It talked?!"

The president looked up at the rock golem in bewilderment. Apparently, normal rock golems couldn't say a single word. The president's reaction was new to someone like Cayna, who was used to seeing these creatures while playing the game *Leadale*. A golem strik-ing a cool, daunting pose and yelling would just be weird. Probably.

She'd made this golem to be the lowest possible level, but it was still over level 100.

Its height was half that of the sundew monster, but its abilities were clearly overkill.

It lumbered over and firmly grasped the stalk's roots, all while completely ignoring the biting tentacles that twisted around it. With a terrifying gleam in its red eyes, the golem uprooted the sundew from the slippery bank.

"Is this enough? …Uh, sir?"

When Cayna confidently turned around to report the good news, she found the president frozen stiff and wide-eyed.

When people see something so far beyond their expectations, they lose the ability to move. She slapped the president across his face to try to snap him out of his stupor and once again asked if they had enough ingredients. The president nodded stiffly.

She decided to have the rock golem carry the monster back. However, it was clear that a strange hunk of rock standing nearly two meters tall and carrying a grass monster would draw crowds of curi-ous onlookers. Soon enough, they'd be surrounded by guards and unable to pass through the gate.

When the president pointed this out to her, Cayna released the rock golem and returned it to pebbles. She considered putting the sundew monster in her Item Box, but she thought maybe showing something like that wasn't such a good idea and reduced it with magic instead.

Whistling innocently, the two of them passed through the gate and made their way to the factory where Cayna would return it to normal size.

The employees had heard from the president that they'd gathered the monster ingredients and were glad to be able to return to work.

Looking at the daisylike ingredient she took out of her bag, the workers heaved a disappointed sigh as if to say, *This is it?* However, an instant later, the monster grew into a giant grassy hydra that had people scrambling for safety and falling over.

"Now we'll be able to get going again. Thanks!"

"No, no, I was simply doing my job."

The president's face shone with a lively craftsman's spirit as he thanked Cayna and signed the request as a final formality. She waved at the employees peeking at her from the shadows, and her first job thus came to an end.

Next up was a rare direct request from Agaido when he ambushed her in front of the Guild.

"I'm actually the prime minister of this country."

"Wow, how about that."

"You really couldn't care less, huh…?"

"What kind of country would have a jock prime minister? You're no Mito Koumon, neither."

"'Jock'? 'Mito Koumon'? You say the strangest things sometimes."

"So anyway, what's this request about?"

Apparently, Agaido wanted to do something over in the redevelopment zone but was having troubling making it happen due to lack of funds and whatnot. If nothing was done with the area, it might attract people like Primo who posed a hazard to public safety, so he was wondering if she could help fix it somehow.

"…By the way, why did you choose me of all people?"

"I heard the stories. You're the mother of the headmaster of the Academy and High Priest Skargo, right? I also heard you used some ancient spell at the school. There's been lots of other reports comin' in, too."

"I'm not gonna get too much into it, but if this request involves me becoming some political tool, then I couldn't give you a bigger no."

"The High Priest is already dead set against that. That's a fine boy you got there."

"I guess it's because I haven't seen him yet..."

At any rate, Cayna took on the request and weighed her next steps. Initially, she considered clearing the land and using her unique high-elf powers to turn it into a forest. However, even if she prepared the spell, the range would extend far beyond the redevelopment zone, so she gave up that idea.

In the end, she dug into the depths of her memories and used a news program she'd seen in the hospital called "Building a Castle to Rebuild a Village." She took apart all the dilapidated houses and used the lumber as materials for her Craft Skill: Building: Castle spell.

In almost an instant, an eight-meter-tall Japanese-style castle was constructed over the empty plot. Cayna felt a little bad for the kids who'd just lost their playground, but when it came to town planning, switching out the old with the new was commonplace. They'd simply have to give up and accept it. Plus, she figured it'd now be much easier for the soldiers to catch Primo.

Actually, she ended up having to make the castle twice. The first time, she'd thought that putting a cave inside it would be good for tourism and casually knocked away a pillar, which sent the whole thing crumbling down. It was a huge mistake that wasted all the scrap wood. The current and final iteration was a size smaller due to the materials available.

The next day, the patrolling soldiers discovered the castle, and the resulting clamor turned the capital on its head. Based on investigations conducted by soldiers and officials, the crime rate dropped to zero. Onlookers and vendors soon gathered, and it developed into a pseudo-sightseeing hotspot where one could buy "Mysterious Building Dumplings," various "Mysterious Building" grilled foods, and "Mysterious Building" miniatures.

It's said that its success continued for long after, but that is a tale for another time.

Cayna's ecstatic client happily paid a sum of twenty bronze coins for the job.

Cayna also walked on walls to make some roof repairs, and the crowds of spectators that formed as a result made it difficult to pass through the streets, thus angering the soldiers.

A personal request came in that said, *"My boat has capsized. Please help me pick up my scattered luggage that has fallen to the bottom of the lake."* This seemed to come from someone who had seen her walking on water.

To solve their dilemma, Cayna walked over the lake's surface to where the boat had capsized and summoned a Water Spirit to collect all the belongings from the bottom.

However, since the summoner herself didn't know exactly what the items were, it ended up hauling *everything* onto the shore.

Cayna also had no idea how long this had all been at the bottom of the lake. It would be fairly obvious to figure out what these objects were had they fallen in recently, but many were rotted beyond any recognition. Among the rusty wreckage was something she initially thought was just a sturdy steel box, only to learn it contained a skeleton clutching a stone that was bound with chains.

Naturally, the guards and knights were called, and she was almost taken in for questioning but showed them the button Agaido had given her and managed to get out of trouble.

A few days later, even stern-faced adventurers recognized her as that clueless, bumbling little lady who was off-the-charts powerful.

They'd occasionally offer her advice, which would in turn lead to enjoying pleasant exchanges and conversations.

Of course, there were the usual disagreeable and jealous types, but Cayna ignored them as best she could. Cayna would hear interesting tidbits on occasion or word of a delicious food stand, so she made a habit of visiting the Adventurers Guild whenever she had free time.

Then, on one such day...

"Huh?"

"Hmm? What's up, missy?" a fellow adventurer asked Cayna as she stood at the request board with her head cocked askew.

She pointed to a request posted near the bottom.

"Didn't somebody accept this one earlier?" she asked.

The burly adventurer who had spoken to her called his friends over to look at it. Other adventurers who seemed to have time on their hands also chimed in, and information started flying left and right.

Cayna really enjoyed the vibe here. Members normally went their separate ways in other guilds, but the lively conversations made the Adventurers Guild quite a comfortable place to be.

"Ah, this. I heard someone failed and had to pay a penalty fee."

"They were a group of four who ain't regulars here. I figured they were outsiders."

"Anyone who takes on a job just for the pay is gonna run into trouble."

The request said, *"Please do something about a ghost. — Battle Arena Committee — Eight Silver Coins."*

"Hmm."

Cayna decided the job sounded kind of interesting, and she took it from the board.

"Whoa, you gonna go for it, miss?"

"Hey, if you meet the ghost, tell it I said hi."

"Well, be careful out there."

"I will, thanks."

The hardened men smiled pleasantly as Cayna took the paper and called over to Almana at the reception desk.

Cayna visited the Battle Arena the next day.

The arena wasn't located in the city center. Instead, it lay beyond the castle on the hill.

She took a moment to cross the river (entering and leaving the city via the river itself was prohibited), showed her request form to the guard who stood at the walled gate east of the aristocratic district, and made her way to her destination.

After circumventing the hill and plugging along on a twenty-minute hike, she arrived at the Battle Arena.

According to what she'd heard at the Guild, an annual combat tournament was held there. Fearless fighters would gather from all over, and the event generated more requests for guards and defense than any other time of year. It was also apparently used for the knights' mock battles, testing for the Academy, and the circus.

Cayna would be leaping for joy at the news of a tournament had it been part of a game, but since this was reality, she didn't really feel like watching people hurt one another.

When she showed her request form to the guard at the entrance, he actually gave a look that said he wasn't expecting much. Well, that would be anyone's reaction, really. One young girl had come to take on a task at which teams of four and five had failed.

Inside, the slender-faced supervisor named Max had the same reaction, but they were grasping at straws by this point.

"Please help us. We appreciate your assistance," he said with an earnest bow.

The ghost had suddenly appeared about ten days prior in the

corridors and on the stage. Those it constantly and silently shadowed would grow so disturbed that they either quit or skipped work without leave, and it was obstructing their operations. The apparition didn't have any one form, either; it could be an old man, a child, or anything at all. However, each one was vague, which only sparked greater fear.

After getting the gist of the situation, Cayna was given permission to stay two or three nights, and she decided to prepare for her meeting with this ghost.

First, although she understood the basic structure of the Battle Arena, she took a good look around inside as well. It was strikingly similar to the Roman Colosseum she had seen on TV. It was as if they'd restored the famous building in white marble. From what she'd heard, it had been here before the capital was founded, and its creator was a total mystery.

"They're really making good use of the arena's eeriness, aren't they?"

"That alone gives me a bad feeling."

She agreed with Kee's suspicion. This time they were facing the undead (?), and the long sword with the red jewel in the hilt she always carried on her was at her waist.

A salamander lived in the blade, a rare weapon known as the Eternal Flame capable of transforming into the shape of a lizard. It was a nifty kind of item you might see a hero use in an SFX movie to take down baddies. A bizarre gag weapon like this made you wonder why it even needed to look like a sword in the first place.

She then initiated every Active Skill that would help her find the enemy and slowly continued down the corridor. The Battle Arena administrators were too scared to enter, so Cayna was the only one around. Since surveying such a large facility was impossible, she called out one underling after the other with Summoning Magic and placed one in each area. These beings were connected to the very depths of her consciousness, so even if they were weak, they could serve as security cameras. It felt like a nine-way screen in her mind.

Of course, 24/7 surveillance wouldn't be necessary. Those she summoned could differentiate between an intruder, an employee, and a ghost.

Cayna pretty much finished her rounds before noon. She took foodstuffs out of her Item Box, started a fire in the center of the arena, and began cooking.

She burned scrap wood from her previous castle construction that wasn't fit to use, and her ingredients were colt birds she'd bought at the market and a root crop that was part carrot and part radish.

As to why she decided to cook in such a place, it was because she was laying out the bait. There was no doubt something doing a poor job of hiding itself was following her (although Kee had been the one who had noticed).

Cayna had laid several traps and thought she'd catch whatever it was if she just did nothing. She never needed a fire to begin with; a Cooking Skill would have perfectly sufficed.

After a short while, someone's anguished scream of *"GYAAAA!"* could be heard from afar.

Wagging its tail happily, a cerberus the size of a horse appeared in the contestant entrance with the intruder in its mouth. Incidentally, the person being held by the center head was Primo dressed in shabby commoner clothes.

"Y-yo, what's the deal with this thing?!"

"It's Summoning Magic. So?"

"I never heard of no magic like this!"

"That just means you still have a lot to learn. You're, ah, what's the word again? 'Unread'?"

Agaido treated Primo like a regular kid rather than a royal, and she and the prime minister had an understanding. If she found the wayward prince, Cayna could rough him up as long as she notified the guards to retrieve him.

Cerberwoof set Primo down, and the boy's stomach let out a loud growl. He seemed pretty famished, so Cayna handed him a bird leg fresh from the fire, which he took from her and began scarfing down ravenously. The way he acted like a schoolkid who'd forgotten his lunch made her doubt if he was actual royalty.

After he finished eating, it was interrogation time. When she asked why he was here, he answered, "'Cause I saw you cooking."

While she did think, *Nothing about this is particularly enticing...*, there was no way she could get the guards to leave their posts.

Normally, Cayna would report him to the guards, but the management was too scared of the ghost and wouldn't enter the arena. She decided she had no choice but to keep an eye on the boy until the job was finished. When she was about to order Cerberwoof to protect Primo, he insisted he would come along no matter what.

It didn't seem as if a specter could cause any bodily harm, but that was just her guess. Cayna had no idea what dangers awaited. She wanted him to stay someplace safe, but the safest place was right next to Cayna. It would be a major pain, but it wasn't as though she wanted him to meet his maker here. She settled on bringing him along.

While she was impressed by his fearless grit, she couldn't tell whether he was being courageous or reckless. Cayna thought it was better not to think too hard about it.

To make matters worse, the creatures she had summoned into the coliseum were running rampant. Although they weren't disobeying Cayna's commands, it was clear that each had a mind of its own. Any one of them could crush an average human in an instant.

"The heck even is this beast...?" asked Primo.

Cerberwoof followed Cayna's orders to keep watch over the boy and trotted behind the two with a three-part panting melody. It had a black body and three sets of blazing red eyes. Its breath went beyond warm and was sometimes scorching. Cayna snickered every time Primo turned around and got freaked out by its rows of sharp fangs.

Considering it was classified as a single system, summoning most likely had the greatest variety of all *Leadale*'s magic. Once you knew one Summoning Magic: Beast skill, you could independently register any beast-type monster you defeated. The one restriction was that for each monster type, you could only summon the very first one you'd defeated.

When Cayna caught the cerberus in the Underworld, it was level 480. There was still some trial and error involved, but it was learning to follow specific commands, even though it had only been able to "Fight" or "Go Back" in the game. Cayna could tell how convenient this creature was.

There was also Summoning Magic: Dragon, but the dragon that appeared when one gained the skill was the same color as one of the seven nations. You could choose from an intensity level of one to nine and then call upon it. Collectors would go out of their way to frequently visit the Skill Masters, and there also seemed to be those who learned to summon all nine varieties. This astounded hobbyists.

When summoning a dragon or spirit, the summoned target's level was calculated using the formula "intensity level × user level × 10 percent." In Cayna's case, the minimum was level 110, and the maximum was level 990.

As for Primo—no, the prince of this country…

He had zero trust in this adventurer girl named Cayna, whom the prime minister and High Priest spoke of so highly despite her only recent arrival in the royal capital. Even the old yet muscled prime minister, who was known for being both blunt and quick to violence, would say things like "That little lady certainly is interesting."

When it came to shaking off the guards, the prince outran them all.

Or at least he thought so, up until his easy capture via an unfathomable trick that allowed his captor to walk on water. Even in his dreams, he replayed that frustrating scene on an endless loop.

The High Priest had overheard Primo muttering snide comments to himself about this girl and had been deeply offended. For three hours, the prince had to listen to the High Priest's wishy-washy argument that far went beyond the mantra of "how great a mother's love is." The prince had paid the price for his actions, and his resentment had taken deeper root.

Thinking he could at the very least unmask her true nature, he'd tried following her and looking into her background, but the more he investigated, the less he understood.

First, there was the fact that she was a high elf. Even among the elves, they were known for being pure-blooded royalty who sat high above the rest and isolated themselves from the world. He had no idea why one would be trotting around as an adventurer. Rumor had it that high elves fought at the back line and only fired off single, powerful bursts of magic, but from what Primo could see, she had a host of techniques that included walking on water and going up walls.

Next, someone like her apparently had three kids: the High Priest, the headmaster of the Academy, and a dwarf who worked as a craftsman by the harbor. He realized half the country's major positions were held by her family members.

Furthermore, after snooping around for information at the Adventurers Guild, the prince learned that, although she didn't look it, she was an impressive soldier. That much he could believe after her sword blew his secret weapon to pieces.

Last, he couldn't stand the fact that Lonti, the one who had outed him as a royal, held a strange respect for her. This was merely jealously on his part, but he didn't seem to realize it.

It was all too good to be true.

It was for these personal reasons that he followed her through the city. However, just as he'd sneaked into the arena and started feeling hungry, a tantalizing smell had enticed him. No one would have ever guessed a giant three-headed dog would be silently hiding when he went to investigate the enticing aroma.

He let out a scream and turned to escape, but a crayfish the size of a carriage was standing behind him.

Its four pinchers were enough to terrify a child with no battle experience. His face grew white, and he froze. The three-headed dog had grabbed him by the nape of the neck.

Now, he was face-to-face with her.

The prince considered giving her a piece of his mind, but one fire-roasted chicken leg was enough for him to throw that chance away.

More than anything else, Primo lamented his own simple-mindedness.

"Grrrr."

"Awoo."

There was a terrifying pressure behind him, and he sensed that the three-headed dog was conversing with something. Primo told himself, *Don't turn around, don't turn around, don't turn around,* and he thought he sensed something heavy send vibrations along the ground. He turned around against his better judgement.

There it was, across from the black three-headed dog.

The enormous, towering creature practically grazed the ceiling, its scaly body a fiery crimson hue. Its vicious mouth looked as if it could swallow a person in a single bite. There was a flickering red light as the beast's fangs gnashed together—

Before he even realized what this creature was, his gaze met its golden reptilian eyes. An instant later, Primo fell unconscious.

Hearing something fall to the ground with a thud, Cayna turned around to find Primo sprawled on the ground.

"Huh? Hey, what's wrong?"

Cerberwoof's nose twitched as it sniffed the air, and just barely squeezed into the corridor behind it was a Red Dragon peering at Cayna as if to say, *How's it lookin'?*

That alone told her what was going on.

Summoning a low-level monster wasn't so bad, but high-level ones had the skills to match. To face her undead enemy, she had called upon several fire-type monsters.

She had sent out a level-700 dragon from her reserves for the time being, since the most powerful undead Cayna ever encountered in the game had been a dullahan that was over level 800. Apparently, this had been a bad idea. (Kee had advised that if she tried to summon a maximum level-990 monster, it'd be impossible to strike a good balance with the other creatures she'd sent out.)

Cayna ascertained that either Might (largely reduces an enemy's ability to evade), Pressure (dampens Battle Spirit), or Evil Eye (faint effect) had done Primo in. His face looked incredibly pale, and he seemed to be having a nightmare. There was no way she could leave him.

Using a Craft Skill, she created a plank with the wood she had previously obtained and added wheels to it, then had Cerberwoof take the dragon to the campground.

Night had fallen while they were wandering around, so Cayna decided to wait for morning in the center of the arena.

That aside, Cayna seriously questioned whether it was okay for Primo to be there. She figured the palace was probably in an uproar thinking he'd been kidnapped. If someone were to find them here, there was no question Cayna would be the prime suspect.

"Still, it doesn't look like this is the work of the undead…"

She tried invoking the highest-level Summoning spell, Create Undead, but nothing happened. That only confirmed that what they were facing wasn't undead.

In the game world of *Leadale*, this type of magic wasn't exactly forbidden, but it was extremely frowned upon. Everywhere in the fields outside the towns, there were so-called filth meters that acted as hidden parameters. These numbers indicated the likelihood of undead spawning during the night. If they hit even 50 percent, there was a possibility undead would appear.

However, that wasn't the case here. In other words, there were no impure creatures in the arena.

The creatures she had summoned were only active for a maximum of six hours at a time. Since she didn't know what was out there, she only re-summoned the cerberus and let the rest disappear naturally after their time had expired.

She tried combing through the arena with Manhunt and Search but found nothing. Not even a single hidden door. Skill Master or not, after coming this far without anything to show for it, she was at a complete loss and had no idea what to do next.

As she opened her Item Box to look for a tool with the idea that she could dig a hole and look for an underground cave, the rarely used Guardian Ring that she had stowed away began blinking. When Cayna hurriedly took it out, it gave a faint blue twinkle.

"…Wait, it can't be. This is one?!"

She leaped into action the second the realization hit her.

Leaving Primo with the cerberus, Cayna raised the ring and called out the passcode.

"One who protects in times of trouble! I

beseech you to rescue this depraved world from chaos!"

An instant later, countless shining stars appeared in the shape of a cross like a fountain beneath her feet and surrounded Cayna. In the blink of an eye, both she and the stars vanished.

The fainted prince awoke, perhaps stirred by the bright light, only to find the docile cerberus curled up near an open fire.

When the radiant light around her faded, Cayna's surroundings had completely changed.

She looked upon a perfect half-circle dome that was about fifty meters in diameter. Beneath her feet was a green utilitarian floor demarcated into lined grids. Above her was a video of clouds floating across a blue sky.

A sun that looked like a cutesy plush toy was floating in the center of it. If she had to call it anything, it was like something from one of those old geocentric miniature model sets.

In the center of the room was a white sculpted flowerpot like the kind you might buy at any home goods store. The pillar-shaped receptacle reached waist height, and in the packed soil at its center was a small brown maple leaf that was half wilted and just barely hanging on to life. Guessing that this was the Guardian's core, Cayna poured half of her own MP into it.

Life immediately returned to the leaf. Smoke spouted from the top and coagulated into a whitish human shape.

The figure had its right hand on its belly and was bent over. Seemingly unable to solidify, it hovered in wisps as it spoke.

"Warmest greetings. This is the Guardian Tower of the Ninth Skill Master, Sir Kyotaro. Might I ask the name of our guest?"

"I'm Cayna, the Third Skill Master. Where's your master?"

"I am terribly sorry, Lady Cayna. My master is absent at the moment. Or rather, he shall never return again."

"What?! What's that supposed to mean?!"

The Ninth Skill Master Kyotaro was a Limit Breaker like Cayna and a member of the dragoid race. He was in a different Guild from her and had even become a guildmaster. When it came to battle, he was a vanguard through and through, which was pretty much the complete opposite of her own fighting style.

On the day he halted his tower activities, he had apparently announced, *"This is my last day,"* and *"Our dreams will also soon come to an end. Thanks for everything; it was a lot of fun. It was too bad only twelve Skill Masters could get together one last time, but we'll probably meet again elsewhere."*

And with that, he left and never returned. The tower went into Sleep Mode afterward, but it had recently felt the presence of a Guardian Ring—Cayna's Guardian Ring—and thought it should at least try to send a message. However, its MP had run dry, which subsequently sparked the ghost sightings in the arena above.

Cayna, on the other hand, perceived the circumstances surrounding Kyotaro's final message.

"Only twelve other Skill Masters could get together." = His message took place after Keina Kagami's death.

"Our dreams will also soon come to an end." = The end of *Leadale*.

In other words, this world was not "future Leadale," but "the future Leadale after the players left." No matter how hard she searched, Cayna would never find a player from a long-lived race. This was the reality she faced.

"…Shoot, I'm really in trouble now…"

Truth be told, she'd been hoping to meet another such player. She could hear the cracks forming in her emotional foundation before it shattered into a million pieces. Every ounce of strength left her body, and she sat down.

She dropped her head and gave such a loud, elongated sigh that anyone who heard might have thought the life was being sucked out of her.

The white figure held out a Guardian Ring to her. Unlike Cayna's, it was sky blue. She felt as if she could gaze into its depths forever.

"Lady Cayna, my master no longer exists. I shall recognize you as the new master of this tower. Please take this."

Cayna continued staring at the ring mutely. The figure took her hand and closed it around the ring. It then stepped back and bowed.

"I await your orders, Master."

She looked between her two rings and thought of her own Guardian. This one couldn't have been more different from that mural of hers. Annoyed with the discrepancy between the two, she sighed and got to her feet. Being down in the dumps would get her nowhere, so she pulled herself together.

"Hmm. I can't think of anything in particular. At any rate, let the people above use the arena, okay?"

"Yes, understood. Do many people appear to be living in the area now?"

"Oh, right, it's been about two hundred years. Now the castle of a new country is right across from here."

"I see. Incidentally, it seems that a child in the arena above is making a fuss."

"Come to think of it, I forgot I left him there. I guess he's awake now..."

The shock of everything had completely driven Primo's situation from her mind. Or she just forgot he existed.

He was a cheeky, annoying brat, but she had no intention of telling a kid he should keep quiet, even when he had something to say.

After all, he was someone else's child. Surely his education would straighten him out.

Her mission here was practically done, so she had to switch modes and think about handing Primo over to the guards.

At any rate, after giving the core the MP she had replenished while they were talking, she decided to head home.

"Well, I'll be going now. I'll come again to fill you back up."

"Understood. I shall see you off, then. Do take care."

The scenery changed in an instant. Cayna found herself at the very edge of the arena in the nosebleed section. Looking down at the center stage, she instinctively tilted her head at the odd sight before her.

First off, Primo was still fine. He was cowering behind Cerberwoof with a panicked expression.

Next, there was the cerberus itself. It protected Primo with three sets of bared fangs and growled ferociously before each head howled in unison. This steadfast pup was following Cayna's commands spectacularly.

Last, there were three people in white armor with their swords drawn. They surrounded Cerberwoof and closed in on it with their deft swordplay, but they couldn't land so much as one measly little scratch.

"What the heck is going on?"

Cayna left the spectators' section and hopped down to the stage below. Upon hearing her feet hit the earth, Primo rushed over.

"Hey! Do something, will ya?!!"

"Wait a sec, what's going on here?!"

"My father sent these knights to come get me, but your little pet keeps getting in the way. It won't let them get close!"

Aha. It appeared even this world had spies and the like.

In all likelihood, Agaido had probably sent these knights to keep watch over Cayna.

However, once she ordered the cerberus to protect Primo, they couldn't follow her anymore.

"Cerberus! That's enough! Stop!"

As soon as it heard its owner's voice, the cerberus backed off the knights and ran over to Cayna. She stroked its neck lightly as it snuggled up to her. The fur was hard and stiff rather than fluffy.

The knights approached cautiously, swords still drawn. Cerberwoof and Cayna stepped aside to clear a path, and she pushed Primo in front of them.

"I apologize for my little pup's blunder. It's dangerous to sleep outside at night, so I had the poor thing protect the boy, but..."

"Are you the adventurer the prime minister spoke of?"

"Why are you letting such a dangerous monster roam about?! We're lucky nothing terrible happened!"

"Your actions are inexcusable. My apologies, but I must ask that you please come with us to the knights' guardroom."

Cayna could somehow tell that these guys were hopeless examples of stubborn red-tapeism.

"I'm sorry, but I'm in the middle of a request right now. Could we do this another day?"

"Are you, a mere adventurer, defying us?!"

Perhaps sensing the tension in the air, Cerberwoof recommenced growling. If Cayna let go of the leash, it would crush the knights' heads in less than an instant, and it'd be game over. Doing so seemed as if it'd come back to bite her in the future, however. Cayna didn't really care about personal grudges against her, but she didn't want to cause problems for the adventurer community.

As for Primo, he now stood behind the guards and goaded them on with "Yeah, tell her!"

"Sheesh, looks like authority's the only thing you'll answer to."

Sighing, Cayna opened her pouch and took out a button with a small bell attached.

She never thought she'd have to use it for a second time so soon after the first. When she asked Agaido later, he said that possessing it proved she had the support of the Arbalest Marquess. It was a little scary that he'd entrust her with such a thing after fulfilling only two requests.

Her children's reactions if they discovered their mother had gotten tossed in jail would be even scarier. It was no joke. She'd heard her eldest son was among the nation's top three officials, in which case, she had to use her authority to keep these knights from losing their jobs.

The button presented before them made the knights tremble in fear. After stopping them from kneeling and apologizing for their rudeness, she asked them to take Primo home. They quickly obliged and dragged the flailing prince out of the arena.

Cayna waited until they disappeared from sight, then sat down by the campfire. Cerberwoof settled behind her to prop her up.

"Agh, I'm beat! Thinkin' about all this stuff is just stupid!"

Letting out a single moan to air her grievances, Cayna took out a pillow and quickly decided to go to sleep. The request would be over by morning.

Feeling Cerberwoof's warmth as it nuzzled its nose against her with a happy whine, she drifted off.

The next day, Cayna cleaned up the campfire and sent Cerberwoof away. She reported to Max, the arena's supervisor, that the problem had been taken care of. Since they couldn't trust that information alone, it was decided she would receive payment after it had been confirmed that the ghost was truly gone.

In the end, the Adventurers Guild paid her eight gold coins three days later.

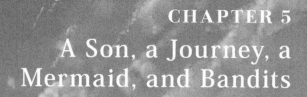

CHAPTER 5

A Son, a Journey, a Mermaid, and Bandits

The madness started in the church cathedral.

After his early morning recitation of scripture, Skargo tilted his head at his unexpected guest's senseless question.

"…Hmph. Looks like you still don't get it."

"What is it, Lord Agaido? Could you at least phrase your question in a way that is simple to understand?"

Skargo quickly glanced to the side with an impossibly sharp gleam in his eye, and it sent the misunderstanding sister who got caught in its path tumbling.

Agaido overlooked this with a wry smile and spoke with a self-important air as he stroked his mustache.

"I just received word from my spies. It seems Lady Cayna hasn't left her room at the inn for two days. Perhaps she's sick…"

"Wha— Wh-wh-wh-wh-wh-wha-WHAAAAT DID YOU SAAAAAAAAAY?!?!"

Everyone present froze in shock at the High Priest's surprising loss of composure. The priests tried to call out to High Priest Skargo with trembling voices but watched in dumbfounded amazement as he ran off at the speed of light. Even Agaido was stunned by his vanishing act.

Meanwhile, Cayna was holed up in her room at the inn, completely unaware she was the center of the madness. Rolled up in her blankets, she had become a silkworm in its cocoon.

Several days had passed since the distressing revelation. All her plans had been blown away, and now she had no idea what she was supposed to do.

Perhaps it was a late case of the winter blues or some sort of strike. No, to be honest, she was just sulking in bed.

The werecat proprietress and the other inn staff worried greatly about her. She felt bad, but in recent days, she wanted nothing more than for everyone to leave her alone until she got back on her feet.

But she could keep this up forever.

Cayna was living in this world.

She thought about cutting all ties and hiding away in her tower, but such an existence couldn't be considered "living." After all, she knew how miserable being unable to do anything except lie in a hospital bed was.

She needed to eat something, and now she had plenty of new friends. Plus, she'd promised to see Lytt again. She couldn't let Mai-Mai and Kartatz's cheerful smiles fade, either.

Even so, she couldn't ignore the fact that, no matter how long and hard she searched, she'd never find any other players. Even if she revived all the towers, no one would be there to greet her.

"There's gotta be something that'll get me out of this funk...," she murmured.

Just then, Cayna heard a commotion coming from downstairs. She stuck out only her head from the covers and looked around. All she could see were the walls and ceiling.

However, someone was racing up the stairs in a frenzied panic.

The very next moment, the door to Cayna's room came flying off its hinges as it opened.

Shortly before this, the werecat proprietress had looked up at the ceiling with concern. The cause of this was the female high elf Cayna, who was lodging there long-term. The girl had sunken into depression a few days earlier and locked herself away in her room without ever coming out. When the proprietress went to go check on her, Cayna didn't appear to be ill but rather seemed listless from lack of motivation.

The proprietress saw many people come through her inn, and she soon realized the girl's affliction. It was one that struck many who made their living as an adventurer. Something must have happened during a request that made Cayna realize her limitations. It was an ongoing pattern among those in the occupation, and many shut themselves in their rooms for several days. Whether someone got back on their feet and kept going or gave up and returned home all depended on the individual.

The proprietress had learned from experience that such a problem could only be solved with time, and she decided to gently watch over the girl. If Cayna wished to talk, the werecat would listen for as long as needed. She wasn't one to underestimate.

That said, she had no way of actually knowing the real reason Cayna was down in the dumps.

"I wonder if Miss Cayna is okay."

"Well, she's sayin' she ain't sick. That means it's all good, right?"

"Maybe she's sad about something?"

The inn's regulars were worried and now voiced their various speculations. When all was said and done, though, it seemed to raise solidarity among the races.

That alone made the proprietress think maybe starting up the inn had been worthwhile after all.

When the proprietress hushed the conversation in the dining hall and listened closely, she could hear a commotion slowly building in the street outside.

By the time the remaining guests in the inn noticed, it was already too late. The entrance had been magnificently blown away.

…Then they saw him.

"THIIIIIIS IS THE PLAAAAACE!!!"

With those few words, a refreshing breeze swept through the inn, followed by a head of beautiful, shining lemon hair. The priest's azure robes immediately drew everyone's eye.

He was the most famous of the famous, an unparalleled beauty coveted by every woman in the capital. And frankly, you could hardly expect to see someone of his stature at an inn like this on the outskirts of town.

The new arrival was indeed none other than the capital's third-in-command, High Priest Skargo.

""DWAAAAAAAAAGH?!""

Everyone in the inn, down to those in the farthest corners, was dumbfounded and let out a unanimous frantic shout.

Skargo took no notice of their panic, and his priest's robes, glittering like veritable stars in the sky, only further accentuated his presence.

The High Priest brushed his hair back with a "Hmph," his dashing smile charming men and women alike. His perfect pearly-white teeth gleamed audibly.

After managing to somehow recover, the proprietress smoothed things over with a bow.

"H-however may I help you…High Priest, sir? If you are dissatisfied with this inn in any way…"

"This has nothing to do with your establishment. I have no

intention of rebuking you in any manner. I have but one target: a single guest of yours."

The proprietress had seen more than her fair share of customers over the years, but this man's captivating gaze and its ensuing sparkle made even her heart skip. She pressed her hands against the counter to keep herself from falling.

"I believe my mother dearest is staying here," Skargo continued. "Where might she be?"

"……Huh?"

Everyone present—not just the proprietress—was visibly baffled.

"What the heck is this big celebrity talking about?"

"Did he just say his mom was here?"

"Yeah, right. Don't be ridiculous…"

"What high-class noble like that would be staying in a place like this?"

As the guests voiced their skepticism, High Priest Skargo—as dazzling as the light of the morning sun—smiled brightly.

"I shall get straight to the point. Where is my mother dearest, the woman known as Cayna?"

The room froze. No, time itself stopped.

Indeed, there was a female elf named Cayna at the inn.

She was an adventurer and…the High Priest's mother?!

Everyone understood these words as their minds raced and connected the dots to this person before them…or not.

""WHAAAAAAAAAAT—?!""

Another shriek just like the previous one shook the inn.

Not the least bit fazed, Skargo locked onto his target—the stairs to the second floor—with literal stars in his eyes. He brushed his fingers through his silky hair with a *swish!* and gave a single cough. He opened both arms wide as a Backdrop Brimming with Hope casually appeared behind him, and he dashed up the stairs in a single bound.

The proprietress and the inn guests stood in abject shock, still trying to make sense of what had just transpired.

Just as Cayna heard an unknown noise from downstairs that was either a strange scream or an enraged shout, all grew quiet. Then someone started running around in a mad dash.

When the person she could only assume was the cause of the commotion came bursting through the door, Cayna went on full-alert mode. Thinking the intruder had to be either a stalker or a thief, she jumped from her bed.

Her gaze met lemon-colored shining hair and gentle green eyes. A lean face and slim body.

A beauty in blue priest's robes hemmed in gold stood before her.

Why do I feel like I've seen this guy somewhere before...? Wait—no way?!

The moment she tried to speak to this person, the identity of whom she was almost certain...

...the gorgeous figure went "Oh!" and closed on her in an instant. He wrapped her hands in his own with a cry of "Mother Dear!" and kissed the back of Cayna's hand with a "It has been too long."

A chill ran down her spine and froze her solid.

The beauty before her gave a smile so blinding it could practically stun a person. He took a step back and bowed deeply as if he were addressing royalty.

A flourish from an elegant wind instrument played as he opened with "Forgive my tardiness..." and declared, "It is I, your eldest son, Skargo," his narrow almond eyes dripping with pearly tears as he continued, "here to repay my dear mother's love." A garden of roses

CHAPTER 5

instantly surrounded them as Skargo then declared with a dazzling smile, "I have arrived."

Wordless and expressionless, Cayna stood stock still next to her bed, her face as white as a ghost.

"Wha…wha…wha-wha-what…the…?"

"I heard you were feeling most unwell and rushed over as fast as these legs would carry me." *Shing!*

His intense gaze took hold of Cayna. As she sat there, strength gently returned to her trembling arms. A number of Active Skills automatically kicked in.

Seeing her like that, the handsome Skargo deciphered that his mother must not be feeling well and spread both arms wide. A Field of Blooming Sunflowers backdrop spread out behind him. His wide smile seemed to be welcoming all who looked upon it.

"You…y-y-you CREEEEEEEEEP—!"

Panicked and repulsed, Cayna threw a fist that directly connected with his smile. Although fighting wasn't her calling, all the battle skills she'd acquired made that single hit a considerable one.

However, even if he was a creep, her mental brake kicked in and prevented the blow from being fatal.

All the same, the taller elf easily went flying. Skargo, who wasn't used to being sucker punched, went into a tailspin and got stuck in the ceiling. Seeing as he didn't give the slightest twitch, he'd presumably fainted at the moment of impact.

Her eyes glazed over, Cayna glanced at the priestly art installation hanging from her ceiling, cast Isolation Barrier, which muted any outside noise, then huddled up in her blankets and sulked.

Immediately after that, a new intruder burst into Cayna's room.

"Hey, Skargo! Do you really think a High Priest can go runnin' around in the middle of…town? …Huh?"

Mai-Mai had heard about Skargo's eccentric behavior from a nun

201

at the church and raced over to collect her brother. She looked up at Cayna's ceiling and saw him hanging from it.

Isolation Barrier acted as a blanket of sorts that completely separated the room from the outside world.

Mai-Mai stared aghast at the sight before her eyes.

"Huh? U-um, Mother?"

Even though she called out, her voice naturally wouldn't be heard. Isolation Barrier was a Magic Skill that protected villagers who couldn't fight in quests. The skill itself was problematic. Not only was the caster the only one who could interfere with the barrier, but they couldn't receive alerts from the Admins or messages from other players. It was useless outside of defense, so it was the type of skill that gathered dust after you acquired it.

Mai-Mai could use it as well, so she understood its unique properties. She'd discuss this with her brothers later, but for the time being, she had to do something about the idiot stuck in the ceiling.

She tiredly called out "Okay, come in" to someone outside the door, and a mysterious group dressed head to toe in black came rushing in. They put up a ladder, dug out the High Priest's head, and dropped back down to the floor. They then filled in the hole, put Skargo in the coffin they'd brought, and quickly withdrew.

Mai-Mai glanced around the room to make sure they weren't forgetting anything before whispering, "I'll come back another time," and excusing herself. She then bribed each person in the inn with a silver coin to keep word of the matter from spreading.

The black-clothed group gracefully carrying the coffin through the busy streets of the capital was a strange sight indeed. However, the people simply looked on at the funeral-like procession with exasperation and said, "Ah, it happened again…"

High Priest Skargo—a celebrity among the capital's inhabitants in more ways than one.

*   *   *

"Uh, I don't think that's gonna happen at this point."

"I need you to take this seriously, Kartatz! What will we do if Mother locks herself away forever?!"

To keep away from prying eyes, Mai-Mai and her brothers had gathered in Skargo's more appropriate office. After escorting her stricken brother home with the funeral procession, Mai-Mai had called on Kartatz to meet and come up with a game plan.

The eldest now sat deep in thought at his desk with a conflicted expression on his face. Unsurprisingly, the results of his long-awaited chance reunion seemed to have taken a large toll on him.

Mai-Mai thought he was just reaping what he sowed, but that wasn't the issue right now. It was their mother.

"Anyway, if Mum shut you out with everything she's got, do you really think we'll be able to break past that barrier?"

"Ngh…"

Her younger brother's logic shut down any counterargument Mai-Mai might have had. There was no denying their mother was a high-level mage who reigned as one of only twenty-four transcendent chosen ones during the Seven Nations Era. Cayna was also recognized as the Master of the Sacred Ruins from the Age of the Gods (per her sons' rose-colored account of events).

It was all too easy to see that no average mage like Mai-Mai could possibly compare.

"If your skills are average, Sis, then people these days gotta be the lowest possible rank…"

Kartatz tried to cut in as Mai-Mai mumbled to herself, but it didn't seem to do much good. He scratched his head with a *What do I do now?* expression and figured he'd try turning to his older brother.

Just as he was about to, the troubled Skargo exclaimed, "That's it! I've got it!" and stood up with surefire resolve burning in his eyes.

"Wh-what's up, Bro? You figure out a way to get past the barrier?"

"No, but I know why Mother Dear hit me!"

A Raging Wave rose up behind him, and he took out his official ceremonial robes from his closet. Its bright golden glimmer made him stand out even more than the king, so all concerned parties had made him stow it away. He proceeded to put it on as the ocean spray scattered around him, and he struck a sharp pose followed by a *sha-shing!*

"I'm off to see Mother Dear! As I suspected, such shabby clothes were an offense to her most supreme presence!"

A bolt of lightning struck behind Skargo with a *crack!*

"In a way, you're braver than all the rest of us, Bro..."

Kartatz could feel his sister's magical energy growing and decided to leave the room before he got caught up in it. His skills mainly consisted of low-level healing magic, support magic, and architectural Craft Skills, so no matter how many lives he had, he'd never survive a fight between those two.

At any rate, he decided to pay a visit to the inn in question to see if they could talk things out.

He pretended not to hear the explosions coming from the other side of the closed door.

...However, on the way there, Kartatz ran into some good—or perhaps maybe not so good—fortune at the market.

He spotted Cayna buying a skewer of meat and tripped over himself. Enduring the curious stares from the market staff, he used every muscle in his body to shakily stand back up. He chased after his mother with his last bit of strength.

"M-Mum?! Weren'tcha holed away in yer room?!"

"Oh, Kartatz. What are you doing here? You want some meat, too?"

Kartatz watched his mother merrily tell the vendor, "One more please, mister!" Dejected, the rest of his energy left him as if to say, *What the heck were we so worried about?* Sitting down next to her on some of the wooden crates lying around, Kartatz watched Cayna with a deep sigh of relief as she ate her meat skewers and bit into some fruit.

The cause of all this distress smiled at him as if to allay his anxiety and bowed her head.

"Sorry about that. It looks like I worried you. There've been some things that threw me for a loop, but then I got hungry. After eating sweets and stuff, all that didn't seem to matter anymore, and I felt better. Heh-heh, pretty silly, right?"

"Geez. Sis is acting like the world's about to end, y'know. Go see her later."

Cayna smiled and gave a "Sorry, sorry," but then her face immediately fell.

"By the way, about that blond pervert I sent flying..."

"Ah, I heard from Mai-Mai that Bro came rushing in and you let him have it."

"I knew it. So that *was* Skargo..."

Kartatz figured out what had happened based on the glazed-over look in his mother's eyes. He sort of pitied her for what she must have witnessed.

Both he and Mai-Mai, too, had been in Cayna's shoes before, and he wanted his mother to know about Skargo's idiosyncrasies as well. Now was as good a time as any.

"Yeah, Bro lives by the doctrine that you are above all else. He's always like that, so prepare yerself."

"*Always* like that... Where did I go wrong?"

This, of course, had to do with how he'd learned his skills. She had never guessed he'd pick up Special Skill: Oscar—Roses Scatter with Beauty so perfectly. In a way, he had natural talent.

His personality, however, was another matter entirely.

Even so, perhaps one might say this was what had swept her shock away; when faced with such a sight, she couldn't care less about the other players and whatnot. She realized the current issue at hand was how best to deal with her son.

"I've got it! After I completely destroy his personality, I can reinstall a new, decent one!"

At this "like mother, like daughter" statement, Kartatz slipped off his wooden crate. Cayna was liable to turn both Skargo and the entire capital to ash. Kartatz crossed his arms as if hugging himself and opposed her head-on.

"Hold on there, Mum! What're ya thinking?! You gonna kill Bro?! He might be like that, but he's always thinkin' about the country and has worked real hard so far. He's put his whole heart into establishing order among the people so you could see what a fine man he's become. Don't discount everything he's done!"

"Kartatz..."

The backstory her son suddenly had blurted out warmed Cayna's heart a bit. After all, she could see he truly believed in Skargo, at least on that point, and felt a little embarrassed that she'd judged her eldest son as completely one-dimensional. She'd merely wanted to chastise him for throwing his skills around all over the place and sticking out like a flashy sore thumb. It was a bit shocking that Kartatz would think she'd try to kill him for such a reason.

"Yes. You're right. He's changed, at least partly... I registered him with the Foster System, so I guess I can't really judge..."

"*Siiiiigh.* A-as long as you understand. Agh, you really had me going. Gwagh!"

Kartatz's voice veered wildly as his mother, next to him, suddenly hugged him tight. He squirmed against her philanthropic love, and she murmured a quiet "Sorry."

"If you mean that, then pay attention to other people's feelings!"

"Hmm? ...Oh?"

Cayna noticed the market visitors and unoccupied vendors stealing glances at them and whispering to one another. A dwarf who was old enough to know better being hugged by a lovely young girl was enough to draw suspicion.

She grew a little red but could confidently say she didn't feel as if they were doing anything wrong. After all, she was merely a parent hugging her child.

"Hee-hee-hee, I'm glad."

"There ain't nothin' to be 'glad' about! Put yerself in my shoes!"

He forcibly tore away from her with all he had and looked at his smiling mother with bewilderment.

"You've changed, ain'tcha, Mum?"

"...Hmm, you might be right. After all, I have you three."

"What're ya talkin' about? Ain't it obvious we're here because of you?"

"Hee-hee-hee, that's true. Thank you, Kartatz."

Why am I moping all because there are no other players? I still have family, and that alone is enough. I'll be okay here.

"So shall we go see Skargo?" she asked.

"Eh?"

To that battle zone between his brother and sister?

He'd gotten caught in the middle enough times to understand, and Kartatz's face froze as he recalled the scenes of chaos.

"Hmm? What's wrong? Is Skargo feeling that down?"

"No, it's not that. Those two are in the middle of a huge fight right now..."

"A fight? Well, yeah, I guess that sort of thing does happen."

To his mother, a fight between master mages was apparently insignificant enough to just be summed up as "that sort of thing." Kartatz really had no idea what went through her mind.

207

Unaware that her son was thinking things like *I hope the church doesn't get blown away*, Cayna urged him on.

Kartatz returned to the church, and the sister who had turned Cayna away before came out to greet them.

"Oh, Master Kartatz. If you wish to see Master Skargo, he's still in the room with Lady Mai-Mai…"

"They're *still* at it, eh…?"

"A-and, ah, who is this woman?"

"Oh, right. You said the sister sent you packing before, right, Mum?"

"…Eh? *Whaaat?*"

Hearing the High Priest's younger brother call this obviously young girl "Mum" sent cold sweat running down the sister's spine.

The girl herself brushed back her hair, and the slightly pointed ears that marked her as a high elf peeked through. She gave a "Nice to meetcha" and bowed.

"I'm lettin' you know right now that this right here is our mum. If yer rude to her, you'll face my brother's wrath."

"Kartatz… I gotta say that as your mother, it kinda hurts for you to call me 'this right here'…"

In no mood to be listening to the familial comedy act, the sister immediately fell prostrate and apologized for her previous blunder.

"I-I'm terribly sorry! I may not have known, but that does not excuse my awful manners! Please forgive me!"

"Ah, no worries. You had no idea, and it didn't really bother me. Please raise your head."

"Yeah, it ain't like Mum holds any kinda position."

After the two pacified the church knights who had come running to check out the commotion the sister had caused, they stood before the door to Skargo's office.

There wasn't anything particularly odd about the door, but the corridor where it was located lightly swayed on occasion.

"They set up a barrier in this room beforehand. That's why there's no damage outside."

"How 'bout that."

Cayna took out a vial filled with yellow liquid from her Item Box, opened the door a bit, tossed it inside, then quickly closed the door again.

Immediately afterward, there was an odd, explosive *BA-BAAAAAM!* The item she'd thrown was like a flash grenade that stunned enemies with light and sound. Its creator was the worst person Cayna had known, so this special concoction had more to it than just flash and bang.

A huge sweat drop rolled down the back of Kartatz's head, and he looked back and forth between the door of the now-silent room and his mother.

After a full minute, Cayna opened the door. Inside, yellow smoke wafted across the floor. She used Wind Magic and opened up the windows in the room and corridor to clear it out.

The room didn't actually look too bad. The furnishings had been fixed in place with magic, and only the chairs and desk were strewn about. Mixed into this were Skargo and Mai-Mai, who had been knocked unconscious.

Once the two were put in a corner, Cayna and Kartatz cleaned up and set the chairs back in their original places. The youngest sibling then dragged his brother and sister over by their collars, and Cayna produced small icicles, which she then used to poke her two unconscious children.

""HWOOOOOOOOO?!""

The two let out a strange yell and jumped up, then looked on in bafflement when they noticed their brother and mother laughing at them raucously.

"Mother Dear!"

"Mother?!"

"Hey, guys. Sorry about that. Looks like I had you worried."

Cayna had Kartatz sit down on the sofa and Skargo and Mai-Mai kneel on the floor; then she got down on her own knees and bowed deeply.

"I'm so sorry I upset you two."

"W-wait, Mother! Why are you bowing?! We're the ones who should apologize!"

"That is correct, Mai-Mai. You are the questionable one. You mustn't cause Mother Dear such trouble…"

"Hey, Bro, wanna try shutting up?"

Kartatz gave a dark smile that lacked all humor and aimed his Guillotine Ax right at Skargo's throat. Sure enough, Skargo decided to keep his mouth shut.

Her head still bowed, Cayna continued her apologies.

"I fell captive to my egocentric thoughts and despair and treated you cruelly. I have failed as a mother, and for that, I am deeply sorry."

The siblings exchanged glances. Their mother was earnestly remorseful.

Kartatz put away his ax and joined his brother and sister in a kneeling position.

Mai-Mai rapped herself on the head and shook hands with Skargo, who pulled himself together with a shake of his own head.

Skargo then removed his coat, patted Cayna's shoulder, and lifted her chin.

The three siblings then bowed their heads low.

"Just as in the old days, I look forward to spending time with you, Mother Dear."

"Yes. Me too, Mother."

"You're the only mum we've got."

"Yeah. I'm glad to have you three!"

Cayna wiped tears from the corners of her eyes and smiled. This instantly passed on to her children, and the room was filled with bright smiles.

"*Phew.* When Skargo went charging in, I wasn't sure how things were going to turn out!" Mai-Mai exclaimed.

"I was simply worried because I heard from Lord Agaido that Mother Dear was ill."

"How would he know something like that?"

"Come to think of it, he did say something about his spies…"

"Spies?! Has he been watching Mother?"

"Maybe he's just keeping an eye on me from a distance? I don't really mind. I'll call him out if he starts getting in my way. Besides, I've got Kee as my watchdog."

"I am not a watchdog."

"Ah, it seems you have made a contract with a Divine Spirit, Mother Dear. You are as exceptional as ever."

"Sheesh, when you called on me, I had no idea what I was in for…," Kartatz chimed in.

It was here that Cayna murmured, "Oh, right," and pressed one fist against her palm.

"I have something I want to talk about with just the two of you. Oh, Kartatz, you left work, right? You can go back now."

"Okay. Well, I'm outta here. There's no way I can leave everything to those guys."

"For now, you two kneel over there."

Skargo and Mai-Mai had returned to standing positions, but the dark aura Cayna had surrounded herself with using Intimidate, Glare, Evil Eye, Pressure, and Fear made their faces twitch. They immediately froze like frogs being stared down by a snake, and a penetrating chill rattled through them as if they'd just come down with a cold.

"Wh-wh-wh-wh-what is it, M-M-M-M-Mother...?"

"M-Mother Dear?! Wh-wh-what may I ask has angered you so...?"

"I heard a lot from Kartatz. From now on, you're forbidden from fighting with magic. I have to at least teach you that much common sense. Of course, that also includes your excessive use of Special Skills, Skargo."

Her expression was like that of a man-eating fiend, her smirk a red crescent moon. The siblings trembled in fear at the sight of their mother, who had transformed into a Demon King without any Special Skills whatsoever.

Upon closing the door behind him to return to work, Kartatz shut out their terrifying screams. He gave a big stretch and cracked his neck.

"You guys got whatcha deserved."

Several days after the uproar at the church...

Elineh visited Cayna's room and set events in motion with a single question.

"Lady Cayna, won't you consider traveling north?"

"Hmm? North?" she replied halfheartedly. In one hand, she held a round red fruit known as a ruche. It was a present from Elineh, and she saw it as a kind of dessert you could casually munch on.

As she ate, she considered whether to leave the capital.

Thinking Cayna would cave if he just pushed her a little bit, Elineh unleashed his trump card.

"After we visit that remote village, of course."

"I'll go! ...Ah."

She replied without thinking and soon understood. The kobold's expression was difficult to read, but she glared at the trembling merchant's shoulders as he suppressed his laughter.

"Nghhh, that's not fair, Elineh! You knew I'd never refuse if you said that!"

"Goodness, no. Don't say such things. I simply said we would stop by for a visit on our way to the north, did I not?"

"Geez, you really are a sneaky one, Elineh… Um, it's four silver to get to the village, right?" she asked, recalling how much it cost to get to the capital and wondering how much a longer journey would be.

However, a crease formed on his brow, and he shook his head.

"I don't mind treating you as a guest as far as the village, but after that, I would like you to serve as a guard…"

"Huh? Is the north that dangerous?"

Cayna thought that if it merged with the Black Kingdom (also known as the Kingdom of Demons), it probably was. However, Elineh replied, "Actually, it rather is," and began talking about recent product distribution. He opened up a map and traced a generalized trade route with his finger.

"First, there are trade routes that go around the outer edges of the continent. Then, there are inner routes that run alongside the nations' borders. This country has two to the north and south of the river. Last, there is the continent's main traffic route that connects each nation's capital to the others."

Thinking, *It's like the trains passing through different capitals*, Cayna nodded wordlessly. Elineh tapped the country's western border and continued his explanation.

"Right now, the capital of Felskeilo and the capital of Helshper to the north are connected by this main route. Our outer route to the west is closed off, so the current plan is to pass through our inner route to reach the outer one to the east, cross the river, then take their inner route to reach Helshper's capital."

"Is the road blocked off because of a landslide or something?"

"No—bandits," Elineh responded not a moment later.

Cayna could sense the degree of nervousness in his answer, and she gulped. Elineh pointed slightly north of Felskeilo's western border.

"There's a weathered old fortress here, but apparently, the bandits made it their hideout recently and started expanding here and there."

"Ah…"

"Their leader isn't to be messed with under any circumstance. Even the knights are in over their heads, and they say it's turned into a deadlock."

"Wow, I didn't think there was still anyone that strong left in this world… Whoa, Arbiter?! When did you get here?"

"Hmm, I guess from *the*."

""That doesn't help at all!!"" the two retorted together.

Arbiter murmured, "I somehow always make the young miss mad," and left the room. His words put a sour look on her face, and she asked Elineh, "Am I really always that angry?"

He responded with trembling shoulders and barely contained laughter. Needless to say, this put Cayna in an even worse mood.

Since she'd be leaving the capital soon, Cayna thought it best to give a quick word to anyone who needed to know of her departure.

This was primarily because she saw how the daughter she'd recently reunited with fawned over her. The hot-and-cold attitude wasn't enough of a reason not to see her. However, paired with how her daughter clung to her like a big cat, snuggled up close, and behaved like a spoiled child each time they met, this three-hit combo was slowly becoming too much for even Cayna. Frankly, she was at a loss as to how to deal with it. She felt bad for Mai-Mai, but she wanted to put some distance between them and get a mental break.

Despite everything Cayna had said to her children during

Mai-Mai and Skargo's bickering, she had no experience with children far older than her. Consequently, she wanted to come to terms with this and sort the matter out herself.

"What?! You're leaving the country, Mother?!"

"Don't act like I'm running away, Mai-Mai. It's for work. I'm going to be guarding a merchant caravan."

Elineh had told Cayna they were planning to leave the next day, so she had visited Skargo first. However, he seemed to be in a meeting with the royal family and wasn't at the church. Cayna worried whether it was wise to share that sort of information with a third party. When she asked the elderly sister assisting her, the woman assured her that Skargo was a man of integrity and this was merely his policy.

Cayna put her head in her hands. She didn't know whether to go after the church for freely divulging secrets under this policy of "integrity" or her son who insisted on it in the first place...

"If I get involved with this, I have a feeling their policies will switch over to my way of doing things."

If Cayna told Skargo to stop blabbing confidential info, she had no doubt he would immediately shift the church's policies to whatever Cayna said to him. She couldn't have one mother's opinion turn the entire church on its head, so she decided to keep quiet on the matter.

Cayna often saw Skargo preaching out on the main road, but the brilliant, shining flowers that bloomed around him only brought her anxiety.

Truthfully, Skargo's reputation among the townspeople wasn't bad at all. Although he did give sermons, the spectacles that erupted behind him seemed to play a large role, and they were easy for children to understand. Even so, the populace's ability to accept these displays as "normal" gave Cayna a headache. This was apparently because Skargo had been serving as High Priest for around two generations.

Cayna next walked a bit farther to the Academy to break the news to Mai-Mai. Incidentally, since her children held positions of authority in both the church and the school, she could practically walk right in.

Mai-Mai could tell Kartatz the news for her, so she wasn't particularly worried about pinning him down. Cayna was grateful her youngest son was the easiest to distance herself from, though there were still bad habits he'd learned from his older brother.

"Hmm. Still, you're going to Helshper, right? Perfect timing. Mother, do you think you could deliver a letter for me?"

"I don't mind. Do you have a friend there?"

"Heh-heh-heh. Actually, Mother, I was hoping to introduce you. I'm thinking this might be a good opportunity."

Mai-Mai's devious smile didn't raise any red flags for her mother. It seemed relatively harmless, so Cayna didn't think much of it at the time.

However, she never could have guessed that Mai-Mai's failure to reveal her plan would later create chaos that wore away at her very sanity.

The next day, Elineh's caravan readied for their departure outside the capital's east gate. The wagons were well stocked with carefully selected merchandise, and all the Flame Spear mercenary guards were present. Only Cayna, the smallest among them, looked out of place. Even if she took out the sword at her side, one would think her nothing more than a traveler.

Normally, no one would be there to see off a single caravan, but two people were speaking with Cayna.

"Mother! Come back soon!"

"*Oomph?!* Hold on, Mai-Mai, it hurts when you hug that tight!"

Locked in a bear hug, Cayna protested as she peeled away from her daughter. Although a mere side note, Mai-Mai's chest was so small that she didn't really feel as if she was being suffocated or anything. This was because there had been an unnecessary interruption during her character creation.

Both Skargo and Mai-Mai were taller than Cayna, who could easily be mistaken for their little sister. Kartatz, on the other hand, was a bit shorter than her. However, hardly anyone looking at the two side by side would think they were parent and child.

"Not sure we really need to worry about you, Mum, but take care."

"Right. Careful not to get hurt at work, Kartatz."

Cayna gave her younger son a big smile. From behind her, Arbiter called out, "Heeey! We're leavin', miss!"

"Ah, coming! Well, then. I'm off, you two."

"Oh, Mother. Here is the letter I mentioned yesterday. Thanks in advance."

"Right, just leave it to me. Who is it addressed to?"

"Caerick of the border town. Take care, Mother!"

Cayna took the letter, confirmed the recipient's name, and asked Kee to make a note of it. Once she put it in the Item Box, there would be no losing it.

She waved good-bye to her son and daughter as she chased after the caravan that was already heading out. The two continued waving until the procession disappeared into the distance east down the main road.

Kartatz and Mai-Mai stood there for some time, a conflicted expression on his face, a calm one on hers.

"Hmm, Mum as a guard… No caravan in the world could be safer."

"Rather, wouldn't you say Mother could destroy the bandits' den in one strike?"

"Well, she's an adventurer now. No point puttin' in the work if there's no profit."

"Yes, that is true."

"Anyway, that letter you gave her. Is it, y'know, for *those* guys?"

"That's right, hee-hee-hee. Mother will surely be surprised."

"I'm pretty sure she's gonna faint…"

Kartatz crossed his arms, sweating bullets. He never could have guessed the impact it would have.

"Hey, miss. What did that woman give you just now?"

Even though he'd been standing far away, he'd apparently seen Mai-Mai give her something or other. Thinking to herself that he had some serious twenty-twenty vision, Cayna re-evaluated her rough image of him.

"Perhaps it is a love letter? Lady Cayna's charm captivates even the ladies."

"I don't know what either of you are talking about! It's just a regular, plain old letter! She said she had a friend in the other capital and asked me to deliver it. I've got absolutely nothing to hide."

"Is that right? Well. I'm takin' that story with a grain of salt."

"I'm telling you, there's nothing fishy going on. What's so weird about me talking to my own daughter?!"

"Wha—? That was your daughter, miss? Who was the dwarf, then?" a separate merchant asked.

"My youngest son."

She answered this question honestly, and a cold wind whooshed through the entire caravan. Cayna ended up having to go on an impromptu tangent about why she had a dwarf for a son and secretly wondered if she had any skills that would help eloquently smooth things over.

Last time, the journey took about ten days from the remote village to the capital. This time, she wanted to try out a number of Magic Skills she had picked up and came to Elineh with a proposal.

"Elineh, can I talk to you for a second?"

"Yes? Is something the matter?"

Cayna had agreed to be a guard during the journey, but the fact was that she had no experience. Thus, she talked it over with Arbiter, and he allowed her to join the Flame Spears. He placed Cayna in the center of the caravan and had her mostly serve as Elineh's personal guard. She was right next to his carriage, which made it easy to have a discussion.

"I was thinking I'd like to boost our movement a bit. You don't mind, do you?"

"Boost...our...movement?" Elineh repeated, tilting his head at the strange question.

Cayna called out to Arbiter, who was busy giving orders to the mercenaries throughout the caravan and repeated the same question.

"This 'boosting our movement' thing won't have a major impact on us, right? It won't tire us out or nothin'?"

"That's right. Any distance we cover will be with the help of magic, so we won't be exhausted at all. If you like, I could even call out lots more golems to serve as night guards!"

As Cayna pumped her fists in a display of strength, Arbiter patted her shoulders with a "Hold on there" and calmed her down. He was glad to have someone take over night duty. However, when he pictured the creepy golem from before wandering freely around the camp, he somehow felt uneasy.

"For now, show me what you can do. It might help us out, depending on the results, but if it looks like it'll cause trouble for us or the horses, I'm putting a stop to it."

"Understood. Okay, here I go!"

Magic Skill: Movement Up

A glittering green light spilled from Cayna's raised hand and spread across the ground to wrap the entire caravan ahead of her in its aura. It affected not only the mercenaries and horses but the carriages as well.

This spell would increase their speed by 20 percent. The range of effect was anywhere in their line of sight. During *Leadale*'s wars, which made up most key Events, it could maintain the marching pace of allied armies for about five minutes. Since about three or four hundred people were assembled and moving together, the effect had a short duration time. However, since those who could use the magic would recast it at the last second, not many actually worried about this.

This time, the spell covered the caravan carriages, the horses, the men, and Cayna. It would last for over two hours.

It was the first time she'd used it outside the world of the game, but it was pretty fun to suddenly walk as if she were gliding. Although Arbiter and the others couldn't hide their uneasiness at first, they seemed to quickly get the knack of it.

As night fell and they made it beyond their initial stopping point, Elineh's eyes lit up.

"That was splendid, Miss Cayna! By all means, please use this every day! In fact, stay with our caravan forever!"

"I can use it every day, but I'm afraid I'll have to turn down the permanent position."

"Well, it ain't like someone who's havin' fun adventuring would suddenly attach themselves to a single caravan."

Elineh's invitation didn't stand a chance against Arbiter's rebuttal. However, an unwavering light still burned in the kobold's eyes. Cayna wondered with a sigh if she'd have to turn him down every time they'd meet.

*   *   *

The estimated ten days became eight, and the caravan arrived at the remote village. It felt as if it had been forever, but really Cayna had only left about a month and a half ago.

Even so, the place was different.

At the entrance, there was a one-story building where the rest stop for carriages once was. The door seemed to be open 24/7, and the sounds of hammering that come with construction echoed from within. It seemed some sort of factory had moved in.

In addition, the abandoned houses farther inside had been cleaned up, and smoke from food preparation flowed from their chimneys. There appeared to be newcomers.

The villagers who came to greet them despite it already being nightfall came rushing forward when they saw Cayna among the caravan. She was soon surrounded, and the crowd swept her away to the inn. Elineh and Arbiter watched with wry smiles as the townspeople took her captive with nary a chance for the two of them to protest.

"Hey there! If it isn't Cayna! It feels like it's been forever! How've you been?"

"Hi, Miss Cayna!"

Marelle and Lytt welcomed her warmly, and Cayna gave a sigh of relief. It felt as if she'd returned home and could finally relax and let go. Hot bread and stew appeared before her unbidden.

The mother and daughter broke out into laughter when Cayna, comforted by the familiar dish, quickly tried to take out her wallet. This passed on to the other villagers, and soon enough, the tavern was in a riot. That night, the inn filled with tales of her days in the capital, the requests she took on, and her children.

The next day, before the sun had even risen, Cayna hurried to the silver tower, told the mural Guardian that the Ninth Skill Master's tower was reactivated, and once again tried asking what had happened two hundred years prior.

"I only know what the other Guardians told me, but it looks like the other masters said 'Bye,' then up and left just like that."

Doing so didn't really change anything.

The region she stood in was formerly part of the outermost edges of the White Kingdom, and if one headed east, there was unexplored territory not found on the map. Cayna had no memory of seeing anyone other than players looking to challenge the silver tower. She remembered talking with members of her guild about a new area that might be introduced in future updates, but in the end, she had no way of finding out whether it had.

After replenishing her items, Cayna left the tower and returned to the village. However, as she was eating breakfast, unfamiliar faces approached her.

There were three dwarves and a lanky woman wearing glasses. Getting straight to the point, they said they were technicians from Helshper and wanted to ask about the well's water-drawing mechanism.

"We heard you were its creator, but how did you do it?"

"Huh? I just used Craft Skills and followed the recipe."

"Ohhh, so you have these 'Craft Skills'?! In that case, we would like you to teach us your ways."

"Just a fair warning... There's a lot of prerequisites."

She took out a log about the size of an arm from her Item Box and cast Craft Skill: Processing: Buddha. A small green tornado leaped from Cayna's hand and completely enveloped the log. It disappeared for a few moments before revealing a wood-carved Kannon statue that was about twenty centimeters high.

This was one of the skills that came with pre-existing conditions if you wanted to learn it but became completely useless after you did. The quest had you offer up a doll to the master of the lake in place of a human sacrifice, and for some reason, it created random ancient Japanese Buddha statues. Cayna had occasionally seen players use stone and wood ones as golems, and that really was pretty much all they were good for.

"If you can't do at least this much, you won't be able to use the skills even if I teach you. Got it?"

Cayna winked and put on an impressive air, which sent the four shaking in their boots. Hearing them say things like "Th-this is the work of the gods" and "Is that out of legend?!" gave her a good grasp of the situation.

She remembered why Kartatz didn't use Craft Skills to build ships. Unless he used his apprentices and employees to build everything by hand, nothing would be passed on to the next generation.

Come to think of it, didn't Mai-Mai once say something about skills degenerating and dying out?

As Cayna ruminated over her daughter's words, she noticed Lytt tugging at her sleeve.

"Yes, Lytt?"

"What's dat?" She pointed to the wooden Kannon statue in Cayna's hand.

She had only made it as a demonstration and didn't care much about it one way or the other, so she said "Here you go" and handed it to the little girl.

This, of course, also caught the attention of Marelle on the other side of the counter.

"It looks pretty nicely carved. You sure it's okay for her to have it?"

"I don't mind at all. I don't have much use for it."

Lytt's eyes sparkled as she put it on the table and stared at it as if spellbound. It was still breakfast time, so it caught the attention of the caravan and the Flame Spears as well.

Incidentally, since she was persistently asked what it was modeled after, Cayna told them it was a goddess of kindness in her home-town. Naturally, they mistakenly thought this meant it was a goddess revered by the high elves. It was too much of a pain to correct them and explain further, so she just decided to let the matter drop.

However, to Elineh, it was a profitable handicraft.

He declared, "We could sell these," and soon Yakushi Nyorai, Ashura, Miroku Bosatsu, and even a *jizo* statue appeared one by one on the table. Needless to say, since the statues that popped out were completely random, there were quite a few doubles before they got the complete set.

After Elineh saw them, his enthusiasm dominated all conversation in the tavern, and the technicians were completely forgotten. As the tavern neared closing time, Cayna finally took notice of them. As an apology for leaving them in the dust, she drew the gear's mechanisms on a piece of paper. Saying they would take it back to the workshop and investigate further, they left.

The caravan planned on leaving the next day, but the village elder said he had something he wished for them to look into. The delay ruffled a few feathers.

"Hey now, Elder. The young miss is working for our caravan right now. She can't just drop out halfway," Arbiter exclaimed.

Backing out of their guard request before Cayna's duty was complete wasn't an option. Although Elineh had asked her directly, the request had more or less still gone through the Adventurers Guild and would require the proper procedures to nullify it. Besides, since Cayna was currently under the command of the Flame Spears, Arbiter was the one who negotiated with the elder.

Hit by his sound argument, even the elder fell silent. She could see that both he and the several villagers who had joined him were troubled. They understand how much Cayna had done for the village and how much they depended on her, but now that she was an adventurer, it wasn't as if she could give a simple *Yes, of course.*

Arbiter knew he, too, didn't have the final say. Elineh was her real employer. If he nodded his head in approval, Cayna would be temporarily put on loan. He was being harsh on the villagers, but it was only out of a familial concern for Cayna, whom he didn't want selling herself short as a new adventurer.

"I see. We've earned ourselves a few extra days thanks to Cayna's magic, so I suppose one more day here wouldn't do any harm."

Elineh counted the number of days on his fingers, and as Cayna stood nearby and stared at him with puppy-dog eyes, he couldn't help but give permission with a wry smile. By this point, it was difficult to tell which of them was the real canine. Elineh heaved a heavy internal sigh.

There was no rush, but merchants only allowed themselves a certain amount of leeway during a journey. Since having her come along with the caravan shortened their time to the goal, he decided they could spend one more day in the village.

Relieved, Cayna had just turned to the elder to ask for more details when Arbiter again cut in. His rough visage broke into a sneer, and he held off the elder, who had thought with relief that his wish would finally be granted. Cayna was about to complain, but the mercenaries' second-in-command told her "You'll have your turn" and left her with no choice but to reluctantly obey.

"Hold it there, Elder! If you're gonna hire the young miss, that means you can cough up the funds, right?"

Forming a circle with his index finger and thumb, Arbiter negotiated with a bright smile plastered on his face. The offended elder argued that although she was an adventurer, she was still a novice. However, Arbiter, Elineh, and the mercenaries didn't take well to this viewpoint.

"No novice could take down a horned bear with a single kick," insisted Elineh.

"And you can bet no newbie could defy all logic and walk on water," added Arbiter.

"No beginner could get golems to do odd jobs, neither!" said Kenison.

"How did you know about that?!" cried Cayna.

Numerous fishermen along the river had witnessed her display with the rock golem—not that Cayna was aware of that.

Elineh's caravan had aided the village for many years, so the elder had no choice but to offer legitimate payment.

"Well then, how much will it cost to hire her?"

"Eight silver coins," replied Arbiter.

"Eight?!"

Just as the elder gulped, a cry of "Whaaaat?!" came from the caravan party. Arbiter and the others gave a dumbfounded look.

"Why are you actin' all surprised, miss?"

"But I owe the village so much. One silver coin is more than enough…"

"No way. What'll happen if you sell yourself short, miss? Think a single working day and assume half a day is five coins. If you work for one silver, the real newbies will be forced to work for only one bronze coin. I'm not sayin' it's bad to be modest, but don't let it affect other adventurers. Got it?"

"…Yes."

As Cayna looked down dejectedly and gave a slow nod, Arbiter ruffled her hair. The other worried members also patted her shoulders and back in hopes of cheering her up.

Arbiter once again turned to the elder and asked, "So you'll pay?" to seal the deal.

The inn was essentially the one place in the self-sufficient remote village with a decent amount of outside currency, and their only other longtime guest besides Elineh's caravan was Cayna. Considering they primarily bartered with the caravan in goods, the village would most likely have to pull together to come up with the scratch.

The village elder furrowed his brow, and just as he began to mull all this over with a "Hmmmm," Cayna pressed her fist against her palm. She declared, "Okay, let's do this," and stepped forward.

Arbiter and Elineh had a bad feeling about that smile.

"What if the elder keeps the money and I get twenty free days at Marelle's inn?"

The old man had thought he'd have a major problem on his hands, so his eyes went wide to hear this. Arbiter and the others gave a wry smile of *I knew it*. Cayna was somehow obsessed with the place, and it seemed like just the sort of answer she'd give.

"If any number of days equals the amount the elder owes, the free period will end," she continued.

"Yes, in that case, we can work things out as we go along. I understand and accept your conditions."

"Just hold on there, miss. Adventurers should get real cash, y'know?" Arbiter warned.

However, Cayna had plenty of money saved up from her time playing the game. Even a year of eating and sleeping at the inn in the capital wouldn't make a dent in it. For someone like Cayna, who couldn't even move before, she was happy as long as she could be healthy and eat delicious food.

She couldn't be too open about it, but a part of her heart modestly thought, *I don't need anything else!*

"Well then, what would you like me to look into?"

"Right. About that…"

A few minutes later, Cayna and the others were lined up in front of the well at the center of the village.

"Why are Arbiter and everyone else here…?" she asked.

"Ah, well, I was kinda worried our temporary member might make a real mess."

"I would never do anything like that."

"But your whole existence is weird, y'know? Better safe than sorry."

"That's so mean!"

While Arbiter and Cayna were working on their comedy routine, the villagers helped remove the well device. They seemed to want her to investigate the inside of the well. Arbiter peeked his head inside, but he could just barely see the glimmer of the water's surface at the bottom.

Even if something strange was going on with the well, it would be hard to tell from their current location.

"You'd like me to look inside here?" Cayna asked the elder.

"That's right."

As he gave a deep nod, Cayna thought for a moment and spread her arms wide. She instantly switched into an outfit completely different from the robe and leather armor she had been wearing.

"Whoa, what in tarnation is that?!"

"Miss?!"

Cayna now wore a black wetsuit that covered her neck to her ankles and ran along every curve of her body. Large acute-angle fins were attached to her arms, legs, and back. Used in marine warfare, it had extraordinary abilities and was known as "the Black Dragon Suit."

However, it was one of the serpent-style outfits that most female players disliked. There was another similar equipment item called "White House on the Battlefield," but Cayna didn't have it.

Back in the game, players' character bodies couldn't deviate very far from their real-life proportions. Thus, there weren't many people whose outfits fit them perfectly. This was because of either excessive confidence on the Admins' part, their lack of shame, or because they were idiots who weren't thinking at all.

These sets were generally called "The Pervy Admins' Desire Series," and female players despised them.

Summoning Magic: Load: Water Spirit Aqua Level 2

Cayna used a Summoning spell to invoke a one-meter-long flying fish—or rather, it looked like a flying fish but was actually a Water Spirit whose body was almost entirely liquid. It was so transparent that you could look right through it at the person on the other side, and it swam gracefully though the air around Cayna like a natural satellite.

"Hey, just whaddaya plan on doing?"

"I'm going to check things out for a bit. Elder, can you tell me what exactly about this well is so strange?"

"We hear moaning coming from inside it in the middle of the night."

"Moaning? It looks like we'll never know what's happening unless we go down."

As far as Cayna knew, a well quest never required you to actually go in the well itself. There was a quest about moaning that came from a mine, but the cause of that was a dragon. If the sound was coming from the well's water source, there was a chance something similar had made its home there.

Before anyone had time to stop her, Cayna jumped in the well. She cast Float before hitting the water to cushion the impact. She'd slam into the bedrock if the well was shallow.

However, it was fairly deep, and Cayna's entire body sank into the water.

"GAH, COLD!"

Shocked by the frigid temperature, she cast Insulation. This was a spell that wrapped the area around yourself or the target in a thin layer of warm air.

Having dispelled the cold, Cayna followed the Water Spirit through the underground water vein. As long as this spirit was nearby, it could control any water around the user down to the muddiest stream. It could even move a waterfall with ease.

The underground water vein was still pitch-black regardless of using Night Vision. Even if one did produce some sort of light, one would only see rock surfaces slippery from long years of water exposure.

When slowly making one's way through tunnels that veer up, down, left, and right, one's sense of time and distance gradually grows murky. Since Cayna had Kee, she didn't lose track of how long they'd been wandering around.

There were unpassable areas as well. In those cases, the Water Spirit shaved off sections as Cayna used her magic to create a make-shift pathway while being mindful of the ground around them.

Even so, it took thirty minutes to progress through one hundred meters of the winding current.

"I have picked up weak vibrations."

"Kee?"

This was the situation they found themselves in when Kee gave his report. It seemed to be a sonar-like sound that ran through the water and could not be detected by human or elven ears. They hadn't progressed very far and so continued along the water vein.

"There is a cave above us."

"Got it."

Led by the Water Spirit and Kee, Cayna popped her head above the water and saw an enormous cave with stalactites hanging from the ceiling like icicles.

Kee's precise location capabilities indicated they were near a mountain range east of the village. As expected, the water in this tunnel was melted snow that flowed from the mountain. There seemed to be some sort of glowing moss in the cave and faint light sources found here and there. When she took a look around, not everything seemed to be submerged.

Before lifting herself up onto a nearby rock, Cayna radiated Intimidate in every direction. It was another way of checking for any hostile monsters or animals. Even so, Cayna boasted the highest level of excellence in this world, and the energy she emitted reflected that.

For the small animals whose vision had deteriorated from living in the cave, it was like being bathed in poison. Small lizards, crabs, and fish collapsed and quickly dropped like flies and ascended to the great beyond in an instant.

However, Cayna heard a small voice go "Eek!" from somewhere in the dim cave.

"Who's there?!"

"…?!"

Just as the voice suddenly rang out, there came a splashing sound. Mixed with the reverberations and the noise of flowing water, it was difficult to pinpoint its location.

"Who are you? We mean you no harm!"

Although she was using Night Vision, the random boulders and stalactites got in the way and prevented her from seeing in greater detail.

Deciding she'd have to brighten things up if she hoped to spot anything, Cayna cast another spell.

Summoning Magic: Load: Light Spirit Shye Level 7

A ten-meter-long dandelion tuft manifested from the magic circle in front of Cayna.

This was a level-770 Light Spirit. Not only did each piece of fluff shine brightly, giving it a slight shake produced smaller versions of itself. This multiplied its numbers, and they lit up the cave in an instant.

The light was especially effective on the cave's living creatures.

Their little bodies squirmed, and they quickly crowded together in the few remaining shadows. Those that failed to secure a spot sought shelter from the rays and threw themselves into the water one after the other.

Among them was a large, human-shaped creature writhing in the shallows.

Despite the harsh, undulating conditions of the cavern, the Light Spirit obeyed Cayna's will and gathered its pieces together to form a spotlight that revealed the figure.

"I-I'm sorry! Please forgive me! D-don't eat meeee!!"

The upper half of a mermaid broke through the water, and she artfully pleaded for her life.

"I'm not gonna eat you! Don't accuse me of cannibalism!"

Cayna couldn't tell whether the mermaid was trying to dive into the shallows or was just floundering. Cayna sat on a nearby rock in an effort to calm her, and her words made the mermaid stop.

"...You're not gonna eat me?"

"Do I look like some sort of mer-meat gourmand to you?"

"...No, you don't."

She smiled at the mermaid as she lifted her head and stared at Cayna with tear-filled eyes. Looking somewhat relieved, she peered past Cayna and froze when she saw the giant flying fish.

"Oh, this here is just a Water Spirit," Cayna reassured her. "Nothing to worry about."

"A-a Water Spirit?! M-my apologies!"

Watching the mermaid prostrate herself before the flying fish was really funny.

*　　*　　*

"Ah... So the Water Spirit is your guardian deity."

"Yes. The legend of my village says that it takes the form of a whale, but I was unaware it could take the form of a flying fish."

It was possible to summon a monster similar to a white whale, but as far as Cayna knew, the only Water Spirit available in *Leadale*'s game system was a flying fish.

The mermaid she'd somehow managed to calm was named Mimily. As to where she came from, even Mimily herself only seemed to know that it was from the depths of the ocean. After all, there was no way seafolk would recognize places by the names people on land gave them like "XX Ocean" or "OO Bay."

"Why are you in this underground cave, Mimily? Aren't you kind of far from the sea?"

"Well...I was actually swallowed up by a black hole that suddenly appeared near our village, and..."

"You ended up here?"

"Yes..."

Cayna might have been able to understand had this been the result of an accidental summoning, but she had no knowledge of any black holes. She asked Kee, but his only response was *"I do not know."* There was no foreseeable way of helping the mermaid return home.

Mimily read this in Cayna's expression, and her shoulders dropped dejectedly. Silence momentarily wafted through the brightened cave.

"Mimily, can you breathe normal air?"

"Yes, I'm doing so right now. After all, it's not as if I live underwater all night and day."

"Would you mind being somewhere that's kind of warm and cooped up?"

"I suppose that would be fine...but why do you ask, Cayna?"

Unsure where the high elf was going with this, Mimily tilted her head. Cayna pointed up at the ceiling as she replied.

"Conveniently enough, I've got some free nights at the inn. I thought maybe you could stay in the village."

"Huh?"

The mermaid's eyes and mouth went wide like a *haniwa*, one of the clay figures traditionally buried with the dead. Cayna took Mimily's hand and pulled her up onto the back of the flying fish. She dispelled the Light Spirit for the time being and summoned an Earth Spirit instead.

A spirit in the shape of a chess pawn about two meters high appeared.

"At any rate, let's get out of here."

Mimily had apparently tried to leave the cave countless times. However, the complex underground water tunnel was nothing like her ocean, and she was unable to figure out where she was going. On top of that, there were many spots even a mermaid couldn't pass through, and eventually this was the only place she could stay. Outside predators couldn't reach Mimily in the large cave, but catching tiny fish was her only source of food. She'd also occasionally sing of the home she so dearly missed. It seemed her voice would echo strangely through the tunnel and come out through the village well like a moan.

A mermaid's voice had some pretty incredible volume.

"Do your thing, Thog!"

As Mimily rode atop the Water Spirit and Cayna magically walked on air, the pawn piece hauled them up via gravitational pull.

It then charged right into the ceiling, stalactites and all.

As opposed to the mermaid's wide-eyed surprise of *Huh?* and *What?*, Cayna smiled sweetly.

"Wh-what is this?!"

"Pretty neat, huh? We're boring straight through the earth."

The Earth Spirit, which could literally manipulate the ground at will, moved without needing to open up a tunnel. By becoming the earth itself, it permeated straight through the soil and bedrock.

Those under its divine protection shared this ability, so they could observe themselves rising through the strata. However, the sensation of dirt passing through them was likely to nauseate the uninitiated.

A few minutes later, Cayna and the mermaid emerged somewhere in the forest. Across the main road, the village wasn't even fifty meters away.

Surrendering herself to the Earth Spirit's gravitational magic, Cayna continued floating lightly through the air as she returned to the village's main entrance.

She didn't forget for a second to switch from the wetsuit back to her usual outfit.

"The heck?!"

"Whaaaaat?!"

The voices of Arbiter and the others who had been anxiously waiting for Cayna's return by the well were shocked when she called out to them from behind. They were further surprised to find a giant pawn piece, Cayna floating in midair, and a mermaid.

Cayna then recounted how she came across Mimily, and they unanimously nodded in understanding. In fact, the level of absolute trust the villagers had in her tale worried her.

"Well then, as for the elder's payment that we discussed earlier, I'd like you to let this girl stay at the inn."

Unsurprisingly, the villagers were silent in the face of Cayna's request. After all, even if she was asking them to take care of a mermaid, none of these landlubbers had any clue how they were supposed to go about that.

However, Cayna figured all they'd have to do is feed her. As long as they could talk it out, all would be well. It was far easier than asking them to take care of a horned bear that couldn't speak at all.

When Cayna told them this, Arbiter and the villagers gave an "Oh, I see" and nodded in satisfaction.

It was a last resort, since there was no way they could take a mermaid on their journey, but the elder and the rest of the villagers seemed to warmly accept Cayna's proposal. The mother hens of the village couldn't stay silent upon hearing there was a lost child.

After discussing it with Marelle, they decided to turn the women's side of the village's public bath into a living space for Mimily.

They created a narrow waterway leading from the bath to the inside of the house that served as a changing room and dug a vertical pit she could sit up in. When asked, Mimily had said that mermaids sleep while floating in water, so she wasn't particular about her bed.

After that, Cayna created a golem that looked like a coffin with four legs sticking out. She cast magic on it and created a mechanism that would produce water and fill the coffin with it. These would serve as Mimily's legs, which would take her to the inn when she was hungry.

The mermaid herself had been completely left behind, and she watched in wonder as Cayna prepared everything Mimily would need for life in the village.

As she stood there dumbfounded by Cayna's efforts, Elineh and Arbiter put their hands on her shoulders.

"You've got it rough, Miss Mermaid," said Arbiter. "Well, live your best life."

"Your luck ran out the moment Cayna caught you. Hang in there," added Elineh.

Mimily's expression tensed with worry at these well-thought-out words of encouragement. She began feeling despondent from the anxiety of having to live with humans as well as from something else.

"Oh, but please don't misunderstand. I guarantee, without exaggeration, that being taken in by Cayna and this village is indeed a great blessing."

The kobold Elineh's gentle persuasion eased her fears a bit.

"Cayna might look like a young lady, but she's got three kids. Not that I think it'll bother ya too much, miss…"

"WHAAAAAAAAAAAAAT?!!"

Mimily's voice cracked in shock at Arbiter's statement. She had assumed Cayna was around her age, but perhaps Cayna had been treating the mermaid like a poor lost baby from the very beginning. Mimily sadly thought it was very possible that a high elf could see her that way.

It was a huge misunderstanding, but since no one knew the truth of the matter, from that point on she assumed Cayna saw her as a mere child.

They left the village the next day. This time, there was no excessive send-off.

The women of the village told Cayna to leave Mimily to them. She felt a sense of trust in them as they proudly sniffed and thumped their chests, but she was a tiny bit anxious. Cayna promised Mimily she would come check up on her from time to time and that she'd also look for the mermaid's village while she searched for the towers.

After traveling north from the village for two days, they ran into the Ejidd River's main stream. Although several tributary branches flowed downstream to converge here, it wasn't as wide as it was in the capital.

Even so, it was still about two hundred meters to the opposite shore.

"How are we going to cross this?" Cayna asked.

"There was a log bridge here 'bout half a year ago, but…," Arbiter started.

"A flood washed it away," Elineh finished.

"I see…"

"…Well, this is where your job truly begins, Lady Cayna."

"It's all on you, miss."

"Huh?!"

Cayna stood in momentary shock as they dumped everything on her. Slowly realizing where they were going with this, she put her hand to her forehead and tried to hold back a headache.

"It's all up to me, huh…?"

"Something like this is nothing for a mage of your caliber, right, Lady Cayna?"

"Well, yeah."

The river wasn't flowing all that fast, but the sheer amount of surging water concerned her.

Arbiter put his hand on her head in a reassuring gesture.

"Well, don't push yourself too hard. The client will understand if some things just can't be done."

"We've come this far, and everyone is counting on me. I can't just give up now."

Arbiter couldn't help but laugh as he watched Cayna mull things over with a "Hmm" and face the river with her arms crossed.

A few minutes later, she had two proposals.

First, there was plan A: build a bridge.

"You can do that?!" Arbiter exclaimed.

"What?!" Elineh chimed in.

Utterly baffled, everyone had *That's crazy* written all over their faces. Only Cayna, who had proposed the idea to her shocked audience, was frowning with utter perturbation.

Reading her expression, Elineh quickly rejected the idea, and needless to say, Cayna was relieved. After all, it would require chopping down dozens of trees.

"Can't you freeze it over or somethin'?"

"It's not a question of what I can and can't do, but the river would get dammed up, and we'd most likely get swept away as a result."

"It's kinda amazin' how you basically just said you can freeze the river…"

Cayna was merely stating the risks, but the listener could only smile wryly at her exceptionalism.

Since making the horses walk on an icy path placed a heavy burden on them, the plan was scrapped.

Next was plan B: use either the Pull or Water Walk spells.

"What's this Pull thing do?"

"It can pull individuals in its field of vision straight toward it. I use it to climb cliffs and things like that."

In fact, that was precisely the sort of quest she'd undertaken in order to get it. However, one point stuck out to Arbiter.

"'Individuals'?"

"Yes, up until now, it's never been used on anything other than people. If you cast it on a carriage, it's unknown whether only the carriage would come or if the contents inside would be safe."

Elineh immediately disapproved. Neglecting his products would sully his pride as a merchant.

"I suppose we'll have to use Water Walk, then."

Only Cayna knew how to cast Flight, and she had recklessly considered using Summoning Magic: Dragon to get them there. However, once she heard there was a Helshper checkpoint less than a day away, she decided that explaining it to eyewitnesses would be too annoying and gave up.

One advantage to Water Walk was that as long as you were on the water, the effect never wore off. The downside was that you were limited to completely flat surfaces, and if you stepped onto anything else halfway, the spell was broken.

Several people appeared confused by her explanation, so Cayna provided an example.

"In other words, if I cast this spell, we could ride this current all the way to the royal capital even lying down. However, if you stepped on a rock or some driftwood, you'd sink."

Hearing this, Arbiter divvied out guard assignments among his team. Each carriage would be led by one outrider, while another stayed vigilant to make sure nothing was flowing from upstream.

Arbiter and Cayna would cross to the opposite shore first to make sure it was safe and secure a clear area.

"Arbiter, you just want to be the first to go across, don't you?"

"Man, this is amazin'. Your magic really can do anything, miss."

When Arbiter timidly stepped onto the water's surface, an astonished cry of "Ohhh!" rose up from the other members.

The two checked to make sure nothing was in the water as they made their way forward. Even so, the water wasn't very clear, so the most they could do was make an educated guess.

Once Cayna and Arbiter reached their destination, they patrolled for any possible threats. Since none were found, the soldier remained behind. Just to be safe, she cast Summoning Magic: Water Spirit and ordered it to keep him safe.

"I dunno, being protected by this thing makes me feel kinda pathetic..."

The flying fish was much smaller than it had been the day before. It could now fit in a person's hand.

Arbiter grumbled and watched skeptically as it pranced around him.

"If danger comes calling and you throw yourself into it, this little one will protect you."

"Quit foolin' around. It's gonna ruin my reputation."

But no matter what he said, she couldn't have him secretly asserting his authority as captain while on the opposite shore. After getting him to somehow understand, Cayna returned to the other side.

First, they had Elineh's wagon act as the vanguard. She cast the spell on the three horses, the wagon, and two mercenary members, then followed behind them as a precaution.

Everyone kept an anxious eye out as they crossed and let out a cheer upon their safe arrival. However, after Arbiter's sharp glare and harsh shout of "Idiots! Wait until everyone has crossed before you celebrate!" they quickly fell silent.

Since he suggested noise would likely ward off wild animals and believed there was no way they could keep the guards apart for a long time, they had them cross quickly.

They continued, and just after a carriage and covered wagon crossed over, Cayna cast magic on the remaining two covered wagons and guards. One patrolled ahead of them and another checked upstream while Cayna followed up from behind.

Trouble brewed as they were about to finish crossing and the opposite shore was a few meters away. The horses connected to the foremost carriage suddenly let out a high-pitched whinny and reared up. Faster than the mercenaries or Cayna could react, an armlike creature rose up from the water, grabbed the horse downstream by the neck, and dragged it under the water.

Naturally, the reins and other equipment still attached to the horse caused the carriage to tilt diagonally, and the remaining horse started going crazy. Just as Arbiter yelled "Cut the reins!" from the opposite shore, the panicked members hurriedly found them sinking beneath the surface and did so.

Catching up to them, Cayna used Beast Master to calm the remaining panicked horse and quickly set it on the shore.

"D-didn't see that coming..."

Unused to expecting the unexpected, as soon as Cayna crossed over, she sat on the ground and let all her nerves melt away. She had put a number of cautionary Active Skills in place beforehand, but since the creature hadn't posed a direct threat to her, they'd apparently been overall pointless.

However, the caravan members showered her with praises of "Nice going!" and "You saved us!"

Arbiter rebuked his men for their delayed reactions, then looked at the blood-tainted water with a bitter expression.

"What was that just now?"

"Gotta be a laigayanma larva."

They glanced into the water and spied a shadow bigger than a horse. It quickly disappeared into the depths, and Cayna shivered.

"Scary..."

"I guess makin' a ruckus doesn't work on somethin' that big... Sorry, sir. It looks like I got careless."

"It seems that no people or merchandise was lost. Looking at that alone, we've fared very well. This is also thanks to Lady Cayna, of course."

Elineh has just finished checking on his wares in the carriages and sympathized with Arbiter as the man bowed his head.

The problem now was that they had lost one horse and the other had panicked while still attached to the wagon and injured its leg.

"Lady Cayna, could you heal it?"

"Yes!"

Magic Skill: Simple Substance Recovery Dewl Level 9: Ready Set

The healing magic she cast brought a faint blue light to her hands, and she healed the horse's injury in the blink of an eye. While everyone else remained fixated on her magic, Arbiter and Elineh talked about replacing the lost horse for the time being by taking one from the three-horse carriage.

"The caravan's speed will more or less drop, but thanks to Lady Cayna, we have shortened our travel time by a few days. I do not mind."

"No helping it, really. Can I pay you back for my failure later?"

"Sir Arbiter, you have no reason to blame yourself."

As they figured out a way to get out of their predicament, they heard a commotion rise up behind them. The two turned around to see a white magic circle appear before Cayna.

"Hey, miss. What're you plannin'?"

"I'm going to call replacements for the horse."

"Huh?"

A white flame swelled from the circle, and black shadows jumped out of it toward them.

Everyone gathered together from a safe distance to stare at the second replacement Cayna had summoned.

"Whiiine."

What caught their attention was the animal itself.

For one thing, its strange, otherworldly form frightened even the hardened mercenaries.

"What?! You don't like the idea?"

"It's gonna scare the other horses, so yeah!"

Arbiter just barely inched forward to tell Cayna this was no good. Her spirits fell, and the cerberus licked her cheek in an effort to cheer her up.

She had summoned it because it was roughly the size of a horse, but everyone had gone running the moment it appeared. Cayna

243

looked around at the caravan members and panic-stricken horses scattered in several distant directions.

"It cannot be helped, mine master. After all, they art of the human race. We are most incompatible with one another."

The one who consoled Cayna with artful prose was a heroic-looking man with curly red hair and a fine mustache and beard. He was sparsely dressed in leather armor, held a spear in one hand, and had the lower body of a horse. The centaur was the first replacement she'd summoned. In the game, he was a gentle soul, but when she explained her reason for summoning him, he shook his head.

"My deepest apologies, my lady. I wish to refrain from partaking in packhorse activities."

He totally shot her down.

Not to mention, his ability to hold a conversation had come as a surprise to her. Cayna wondered to herself if his warrior-like way of speaking was some sort of programmed setting, but given no one else could possibly know that, it wasn't as if she could ask.

Having no other choice, Cayna decided to summon a third.

As Arbiter pleaded with her to calm down, a fluffy boar piglet popped out from the magic circle and greeted Cayna with a *"Pii!"*

"What do you think? You can't complain about something this cute, right?"

Big round eyes. Little tusks peeking out of its mouth. A chubby body that looked like a sweet potato. An itty-bitty, funny tail that spiraled from its bottom. Anyone with a love of cute things would be unable to resist the urge to run up and give it a big hug.

Arbiter, on the other hand, gave that opportunity a hard pass.

"...Maybe if it wasn't so big."

It was about twice the size of its summoner, easily standing almost three meters high from the withers and about one size smaller than a covered wagon.

"Sorry Li'l P. Would you mind pulling this carriage for us?"

"*Pi-pi!*"

It tried to press its nose upward as one might thrust forward their chest with pride, but its roly-poly body seemed to make that a difficult feat. It gave a gleeful *"Pi!"* as Cayna patted its head.

Aside from its sheer size, the piglet really wasn't scary at all. The Flame Spears came out from the shadows of the carriages with sighs of relief. Cayna decided to keep the cerberus and centaur around and place them at the very back just in case anything happened. A lot of people kept looking behind them nervously, so she cast Invisibility to manage this.

They couldn't attach the baby boar to the carriage, so they had it hold the reins in its mouth. One of the caravan members nervously petted it before questioning Cayna.

"I've never seen a beast like this before. What is it?"

"I don't know how many are left, but it's a baby crimson pig."

The people who had gathered and even Arbiter suddenly froze. A few peered around them trepidatiously.

The crimson pig was well known as the biggest wild boar on the continent, and a few were occasionally spotted in the southern mountain range. Their name came from the flaming mane that flowed from their heads to their backsides. An adult was ten meters high at the withers, and they could reach up to twenty-five meters long. Despite such an impressive appearance, though, they were relatively tame beasts.

However, one had to be ready for retaliation if they laid hands on a mother and piglet. Their charge had a destructive power beyond all imagination, and they could break through a city wall as if it were paper.

Thus, when they heard the baby of such a creature was right in front of them, it was only natural that the party's eyes would grow

shifty in fear that the mother would come looking for it. It was a rare monster during the Game Era, and everyone had hated its tough, raw, and stubborn power. Even Cayna had avoided going up against them solo.

While it was a conundrum for everyone, the group's priority was staying on schedule, so they left immediately instead of dawdling around. Cayna was the one who had to command the baby boar, so she stood near the covered wagon it would be pulling. The invisible cerberus and centaur followed a safe distance behind, and the caravan set off.

Arbiter and Elineh explained that since there was a Helshper checkpoint not far off, that was where the group would be spending the night.

Cayna looked forward to setting up camp and enjoying a night of conversation with the Flame Spears. Everyone would always chat among themselves as they comically dramatized tales of where they'd been so far and what happened there. She loved their nightly gatherings around the open campfire, and the thought of future ones put a smile on her face.

Suddenly, however, the trees' voices whispered into her ear.

"Be careful."

"There's evil afoot."

It mingled with the rustle of leaves in the wind, and a quiet commotion stirred among the nearby trees. It grew louder and multiplied.

Lightly tapping the boar's back, she excused herself from the mercenaries walking nearby and headed toward the front.

She wasn't used to group fighting, so Arbiter had told her what temporarily working as a guard in the mercenary unit would entail. It seemed that "reporting for duty" didn't change no matter where you went.

"Arbiter!"

"Hey, so you noticed, too, miss. There's a weird aura floatin' around. It's probably comin' from *that*."

Arbiter had already perceived quite a bit, and he pointed to the checkpoint visible ahead of them. There was a gatepost that looked as if it could fit two carriages side by side and white walls to the left and right that continued into the depths of the forest. Two sentries holding spears stood there, but from the looks of them, they were extremely slovenly and didn't seem concerned with their jobs in the least.

Arbiter called over his second-in-command and ordered the caravan to stop. He then approached Elineh's wagon and told him there was a chance of attack.

"Would Helshper truly do such a thing…?"

"Not necessarily. But if somethin' happened between our countries, they won't let us through easy."

The road wasn't very wide, so Elineh quickly gave the order to stop and form a diagonal line. Arbiter instructed Cayna and two other mercenaries to stay by the wagons at all times, then called out loud enough for the soldiers standing at the border gate to hear.

"Hey! Hurry up and get out here! You've been found out!"

These words rode along the wind, and with a click of a tongue, a pale, black-robed man holding a wand appeared next to the Helshper guards.

Cayna could sense several other vulgar voices echoing from within the forest and conveyed this to the second-in-command. She then cast Invisibility on herself and moved to the back of the line to give orders to her summoned creatures.

"Can I leave the hidden ones to you two?"

""""Woof!"""""

"Please leave it to us, my lady. Those despicable ruffians shall become the rust on my spear."

She ordered the cerberus to take care of the ambush in the forest on the right and had the centaur take care of the enemy guards who were to the left of the carriages. She then got on top of a carriage, canceled the Invisibility spell, and focused on using Assistance Magic to provide support. Her position made her an easy target for archers, but she intended on making herself a decoy, since she had greater defensive strength than anyone else.

Arbiter already realized her plan. Although he normally called her "miss" and labeled her a lady, Cayna was deeply thankful that he disregarded gender when it came to who performed what duties.

In the Game Era, Attack Magic differentiated even between friends and foes who shared the same space, but she hesitated to use it now that she was in a melee. They were also surrounded by forest, so she held back.

"Gotta say, yer pretty sharp. Unfortunately, this is the end of the line. We promise to make good use of your women and goods."

The man let out an ugly laugh and waved his wand as he basically ordered them to surrender.

Arbiter gave a shrug and snorted.

"Dirt like you ain't ever gonna win over the ladies. Right, miss?"

"They also look pretty weak…"

"Y-you bastards! I'll make you regret them wor…"

"GYAAGH?!"

Before the ill-faced man could finish his sentence, a scream that was a mix of fear and despair rang from the forest. At the same time, a beastly howl echoed, sending a chill running all the way up from their feet.

It was the cerberus's ranged attack Hell Howl, which came with an added Fear effect. Since the mercenaries guarding the caravans only seemed slightly shocked, the attack seemed to distinguish between friend and foe.

The ambushers were stricken with fear. One after the other, soldiers strapped with bows, arrows, and short swords against their leather breastplate armor ran out from one side of the forest in total panic.

Magic Skill: Superior Physics Defense Up: Laga Proteck: Ready Set

At the same time, Cayna had a chant waiting in the wings and cast it on her allies. Twinkling blue sparkles covered everyone from the mercenary guards to the caravan members, the horses, and the carriages. Arbiter was a little shocked to find himself glowing a faint blue, but he didn't forget what had to be done and fired up his men. They attacked the terrified bandits with no intention of sparing their lives.

As Cayna looked out upon the scene, a sour feeling welled within her heart that she forced back down. This scenario had also been explained to her ahead of time to keep her from getting upset. She didn't know much at all about this world and didn't think it was her place to interfere. Cayna's turmoil was inconsequential, and the end of the fighting was nowhere in sight.

She didn't know whether they were too eager in the pursuit of glory or simply saw their chance, but several bandits came similarly running out of the opposite side of the forest.

But although they were invisible, the summoned beasts that served as the caravan's line of defense were still lying in wait.

As one of the bandits approached the carriages, he suddenly went flying straight upward. Another was hit was such force that his face squished as he was repelled sideways, and still another was suddenly impaled midair by a spear that came out of nowhere.

The form of the centaur who so swiftly took out the three appeared front and center. Raising his weapon that was still wedged in the thief, he announced himself loud and clear.

"Verily, verily! Those watching from afar, draw near and listen well! 'Tis I, Heigl of the famed centaur clan!"

This sent a shock through both sides of the battle. Arbiter's spear stopped midswing, and he said, "Hold on, this ain't all about you," with a wry smile.

The pale-faced thief, on the other hand, grew unnerved and exclaimed, "What's somethin' like that doin' here?!" while taking a few steps back.

As for Cayna, she murmured, "So he had a name...," which was probably crueler than anything else anyone said.

Deciding things would come to an end if they crushed the heads of the fake sentry bandits at the checkpoint, Arbiter pressed forward.

However, the Water Spirit protecting him flew out and used Water Cutter to slice them both in half with blinding speed. Arbiter, spear readied as he prepared for a fight, felt a bit let down.

Thanks to the strenuous efforts of the mercenaries and Heigl, the brigands were mowed down one after the other. They were all dispatched, leaving only their pallid leader to watch in horror. Mercenaries who had extra time captured several who were still breathing.

Cayna got down from the wagon, and the cerberus approached from the forest. She was a bit unsettled by the red stains around its mouth. As she gingerly patted its head in appreciation, a unison of three happy whines rumbled from its throats.

"So what're ya gonna do now? You're out of minions."

"Sh-shit! I've still got *this*, though!"

The Flame Spears were collectively provoking the ghastly brigand leader with composed smirks. The man's face twisted with hatred, and he lifted his wand as if about to put on a show.

Figuring he was just being a sore loser, Arbiter was about to speak when the bandit leader let out a Command Word:

"Boot Up Fireball"

An instant later, a flaming sphere that was multiple shades of red appeared over his head. Before anyone could say a word, it rotated and

251

grew larger and larger in diameter until it was big enough to swallow a person whole. At its caster's command, it gave a howl and shot forward.

Straight at Cayna.

Her back had been turned as she thanked the two creatures she'd summoned, and as soon as she noticed something was amiss and turned around, the fiery being caught hold of her and exploded. A shock wave erupted from the blazing flames.

Everyone's ears pounded as black smoke and ash scattered in all directions, and a cry came from the caravan. The place where Cayna had stood was enveloped in a raging fire and smoke.

"Miss?!"

"Ha-ha-ha-ha-ha! Now you know what happens when you defy me!"

The mercenaries gripped their weapons with a look of hatred, and the urge to rush in ran through their bodies.

On the other hand, the man remained unaware of their rising battle lust and continued his loud self-satisfied laughter.

…It was comical, really.

"How foolish. Do you honestly believe such piddling flames would harm the lady?"

"Woof!"

The man's face remained frozen in a smile. Arbiter and the others turned toward the direction of the voice as well, to the site of the fiery explosion where any normal person would have met their end.

A light-blue phosphorescence rose up from within and easily swept away the fire and smoke.

Heigl stood there lazily holding his spear while the cerberus bared its fangs menacingly.

Cayna appeared between them without a single burn on her.

`Come forth, beauty of ice and snow!`

With this Command Word, the arm guard on Cayna's left arm instantly morphed into a silver bow and began releasing Ice-type magic power. Anyone with even the slightest experience with magic could tell how ridiculously powerful it was.

A moment later, a white circle appeared beneath her feet. The pale light endlessly pouring from it intensified and converged between the bow and bowstring in her left hand.

As snow scattered across the ground, there was a crackling sound, and the area around her turned into an ice field. The pale-faced bandit leader, along with Arbiter and the others, watched a terrifying magic beyond anything in their world swell between the bow in her left hand and the taut bowstring in her right hand.

A pure-white arrow constructed from a powerful spell materialized in Cayna's hands.

"D...damn you! Wh...what's that magic?!"

"If you want to hurt me, you'll need to be able to pull off something like this!!"

Magic Skill: Convert: Blue Ice of White Night, Liza la Giga

Shoom!

...The sound of its release was far too swift.

To most people, the noise alone was foreboding enough. However, the impact would be far more impressive.

Who would ever believe such an unthinkably powerful treasure woven from the most supreme magic, something that was the embodiment of despair said to bring death to all, would be coming right at them?

The bandit leader heard someone cry out, "This is what gets the Demon King in fairy tales, right?!"

Too deranged to realize these words were coming from his own mouth, that was the last thought he ever had.

There was the sound of shattering glass, and pure-white flowers bloomed along the forested road that ran through the two nations. Constructed from hexagonal ice prisms both big and small, in the center of the transparent, flowerlike blooms now rooted in the earth was a snow sculpture whose face was twisted in horror.

This was indeed the bandit leader himself.

All was silent for a moment, but then the left and right arms that were spread open wide snapped off. They struck the ice flowers and broke off into tiny pieces, but this was only the beginning; cracks spread throughout the sculpture, and it wasn't long before it completely crumbled.

"...*Phew...*"

"That was marvelous, my lady."

"Woof!"

"*Pii!*"

Though her summoned entourage praised her, Cayna felt rather melancholy, and everyone around her stared in overwhelmed amazement. Even Arbiter sensed the heavy air but sighed seeing Cayna notice the reactions around her and the subsequent lonely unrest in her eyes. Shaking his head, he locked away this horrifying sight deep into his memories, then slapped the girl's back. The noise rang out, and everyone gasped as they returned to themselves.

"Gwagh!"

"That was amazin', miss! You got hit with all that, yet there's not even a scratch on ya!"

He meant it as a compliment, but he saw a dark shadow appear on Cayna's face and grew flustered.

"Wh-what's the matter?! Are ya hurt anywhere?"

"No, my hair just got a little singed..."

"…Geez, don't scare me like that. I thought there was somethin' seriously wrong with you."

"Hey, now… You shouldn't say such things to a girl! Your lover will quickly tire of you, Arbiter."

"Do I look like the type of guy who has someone like that?!"

"Whaaaat?! You mean you don't?! You're so caring that I was sure you'd have two or three girls following you around…"

"Miss. Let's talk about how you really see me. All the way until morning."

"You'll try your dirty tricks on me, too?!"

"Who said anything about dirty tricks?!"

As the two engaged in witty, sibling-like banter, the rest of the caravan began smiling.

It was evident to everyone the sort of powers Cayna possessed, but it was clear to all on this journey that she was not the type of person to throw her strength about recklessly. Even so, Cayna did occasionally use it in rather unexpected ways.

"Come to the back of the capital inn right now!"

"Where?! And how?!"

Interrupting their friendly bickering pained the second-in-command, but he steeled himself and stepped between the two.

"…Boss, Miss Cayna. I would ask that you set this aside and properly continue until the morning hours at a later day. For now, please relay your instructions regarding postbattle affairs."

"Even you think it's decided, co-leader?!"

"Ah, right. First, clean up the bodies. Once we've done that, there's a clearing on the other side of the border. We'll have Sir and the others set up camp there. Get two people to go with them as guards."

"If it's guards you need… Heigl, Li'l P, do you mind?"

"Understood, My Lady."

"Pipipi!"

By the time everyone mostly finished cleaning up and had dinner, the sun had well set. As they searched the area afterward, they found four badly charred bodies. Having passed through the border countless times before, Elineh confirmed they were the original guards who had protected the checkpoint. Once they arrived in the Helshper capital, he would report to the Merchants Guild and return the deceased's personal effects.

"The bandits' base of operations is out west. They're already this widespread...?"

"So it seems. If they've gained this much territory, they must be quite formidable."

As if attempting to dispel the heavy atmosphere, merry voices echoed profusely around the open fire. Guards and merchants alike recounted their experiences with a decent amount of exaggeration, and both Cayna and the others burst into childlike laughter.

In the shadow of the carriages, Arbiter and his second-in-command discussed the bandits' movements and carefully handled the wand of the fallen leader from that afternoon.

Elineh hadn't known what it was, but Cayna had appraised the wand and found the answer. It was an all-purpose item that wasn't particular about who wielded it and could cast Fireball with a simple Command Word. It was abnormal in the fact that back during the Game Era, even the newest players could use it immediately.

"This...is disposable but can be used up to ten times. It still has seven attacks left in it."

"Somethin' like this was all over the place two hundred years ago...?"

"You can get good money if you sell it, don't you think?"

"We cannot say whose hands something like this would pass into, so wouldn't it be better for Sir Arbiter to have it?"

"Wha—? Me...?"

"In that case, shall I make a new one that can work up to three hundred times? That would be more convenient, don't you think?"

"Don't you dare!!"

"Please don't!!"

She had smiled like a normal girl, but one might say it once again reminded them of her unbelievable capabilities. They probably also had to thank their lucky stars that their relationship with her remained unchanged.

"It's certainly a good thing she's on our side," said the second-in-command.

"That makes you feel better...?"

In a way, Arbiter honestly shared the same sentiments his comrade quietly murmured.

As dawn rose on the border between Felskeilo and Helshper, Elineh's caravan and Flame Spear guards inspected the boundary line's facilities and accommodations.

They were there the night before, but there were still plenty of things only seen in the light of day. After they had the surviving bandits spill how they'd reached the checkpoint, they disposed of them during the night. After all, it wasn't as if the caravan could take them along, and if they banished them, there was no guarantee they wouldn't commit the same atrocities somewhere else again. The group piled up the bodies and cremated them, and that was that.

The log cabin apparently being used as a barrack for the soldiers was in wretched condition. Even excluding what the bandits seemed to have brought, desks and shelves had been leaned against the walls and used for knife-throwing practice. A few were still stuck in both those and the walls. The food stores had been ransacked with only whole vegetables being left behind. The absence of any kind of meat was clearly thanks to them as well.

Elineh documented the disastrous scene and composed a letter from the Merchants Guild reporting his findings to Felskeilo.

The bodies of the soldiers would become undead if they weren't dealt with, so Cayna wrapped them in sheets purified with Holy Magic and buried them side by side in a place with plenty of sunlight. To help any possible investigation teams, Arbiter and the others carved grave markers from wood and placed them on top. After a moment of silence, the caravan left the border.

Even though you could normally hear voices here and there as the caravan kept moving, after they crossed into Helshper, no one said anything. Even the Flame Spear mercenaries would occasionally look behind them with sorrowful expressions before once again facing forward.

Cayna only ever stopped so she could summon the crimson pig Li'l P, since they needed it to pull one of the carriages. She didn't forget to cast Movement Up on everyone, either, and called upon the Wind Spirit to patrol the area and alert the group if any armed figures were approaching. After all, if she just told it to attack, disaster might befall some unwitting adventurer. Furthermore, since she'd heard that the road ahead was surrounded by forest as well, the trees would surely tell her if any malicious characters were nearby.

In this vigil-like atmosphere, Arbiter, the one usually leading the way, dropped back to the center. Cayna was tasked with protecting Elineh's wagon, while Li'l P pulled another one behind it.

"Oh, Arbiter. How's the front?"

"My co-captain is keeping an eye out. I'm gonna have to breathe some life back into these guys in the back later and get rid of this shaky mood."

It seemed he was committed to making sure each and every member was cared for. Cayna thought this deep consideration was why everyone followed him despite his brusque demeanor.

He spoke briefly with Elineh before coming up beside Cayna.

"Are you doing okay, miss?"

"Huh? Oh, yeah. It's so quiet that it makes you wonder if it's okay to talk at all, don't you think?"

When Cayna was in the hospital, she had been susceptible to sorrow. At times like those, the always-present nurses and the other child patients would come talk to her and take her mind off things.

However, now that she could move freely and try calling out to someone else, Cayna couldn't seem to get the timing right. The grannies also staying at the hospital had been so good at it, it made her want to sigh.

"It's gonna be a rough ride if you're this down already."

"Huh? Wagh?! Hey! Ow, that hurts, Arbiter!"

He tousled Cayna's hair, patted her lightly on the shoulder, and walked away.

Immediately afterward, an angry bellow roared from the back.

"C'mon, you worthless goons!! How long you gonna mope around for?! Don't go slackin' off! You think a half-assed job is gonna cut it?!"

She could hear the "Gah!" and "Gugh!" sounds that accompany kicking and punching. Despite the alternations between the mercenaries' cries and Arbiter's scolding, Cayna did her best to ignore it and instead focused partly on the shared consciousness she had with the Wind Spirit.

"Miss, you're actually insanely powerful, aren't you?"

"Huh?"

Arbiter asked Cayna this the second day after they crossed the border and had set up camp. Now that they had covered three days of distance in two with the help of Movement Up, Elineh and the others were exceedingly grateful to her and saw her as a great boon.

Over the past several days, she had received endless words of praise and gratitude from the caravan members. By this point, she wished they would stop with the *Thank you* mega blowout sale.

According to Elineh, there were two villages they could stop by along Helshper's outer trade routes. Since Helshper had a mountain range that ran along the ocean to the north, gentle slopes continued to the east and west. These inclines provided it with excellent irrigation and cultivated rich fruit trees.

The village near the border had already long seen better days. The group soon went about inquiring with the townspeople, and apparently, the bandits hadn't caused trouble for years. It seemed the ones from the other day couldn't have passed through the outer trade route. Since the village didn't have so much as an inn for even a few adults and the sun had been at its highest, they asked their questions and moved on through.

"So what's goin' on?"

"*Sigh...* Um, may I ask what makes you ask such a question?"

"Sure."

They had just finished eating dinner, and besides the guards on patrol duty, everyone was taking a momentary breather.

"When that robed guy attacked you, you said, 'If you want to hurt me,' and whatnot. Plus, you got hit directly by a fireball but don't have a single burn to show for it. Wouldn't anyone call that pretty intense?"

"Ah, well, I guess you have a point."

Yes, even Cayna didn't have enough time to come up with a convincing lie as to why she wasn't hurt by a fireball. The wand was a generic item whose power rose and fell depending on the magic of its user.

For someone like Cayna who'd reached max levels of Attack and Defense Magic in the game, any spell from an enemy like that did nothing. To give a clear example, it was like setting off a pinwheel firework in front of a massively tall, thick steel door.

"The caster was simply low-level."

"Really? He seemed pretty competent from what I could tell, but I guess that's not the impression you got."

Cayna thought she could see the light in Arbiter's eyes change from mere curiosity to "battle junkie."

"It looks like that backfired on you."

Kee! What's that supposed to mean?

"You'll find out soon enough. In any case, do be careful."

Of what?

Unnerved by Kee's warning, she tried to press him but was unable to. This was thanks to the spear tip suddenly thrust at her.

"Arbiter?! What're you doing?!"

"Heh, so you could dodge it. Wanna do a bit of sparring with me, miss?"

"...Huh?"

Arbiter smiled at Cayna, who had instantaneously used Passive Skill: Perception to give herself a momentary pause. The mercenaries who had been nonchalantly watching their exchange jolted at Arbiter's words and rose up halfway. The second-in-command walked over with his shoulders squared and grabbed his arm.

"What are you doing, boss?! Picking a fight with Miss Cayna is utterly childish!"

"If there's someone strong, you challenge 'em. Ain't that only natural?"

"She isn't like the knights, so please refrain from your old problematic behaviors!"

It seemed Arbiter had once been part of the knights and had been known for causing trouble even back then. As to why he'd been hiding this bad habit of his until now, well, that was because he hadn't come across anyone as strong as him. Now that Cayna had revealed her incredible power right before his eyes, this sleeping predilection had finally awakened from deep inside him.

"Agh, that wasn't good…"

Cayna watched grimly as, at the co-leader's command, the other mercenaries pinned Arbiter's arms behind his back.

"You're already a grown man, so please act like it, boss!"

"Hey, what're you guys gangin' up on me for?! It's just a mock battle."

"We know that won't be enough for you!"

"That mess during the admission exam was the worst. I'm beggin' ya, don't make anyone deal with that again!"

"Didn't we tell you it was time you grew up?!"

Their leader had apparently inflicted various traumas on his subordinates. Each brought up their own past experiences as they admonished Arbiter.

Elineh and the others were equally troubled by the situation, and they frantically looked back and forth between Cayna and Arbiter, who was now stuck in a mercenary sandwich.

"I see no harm in accepting."

Huh?! Kee!

Cayna was floored by Kee's sudden, risky statement. More than anything else, mock battle or not, she didn't have the nerve to fight someone who had done so much for her.

Half the reason was also because even she didn't know her full specs. Even if she considered herself mostly a rearguard position, she was still a Skill Master who could more than likely handle serving in the advance guard as well. However, just because she could do it didn't mean she'd be a master at it. It made her reluctant.

"*This is fortunate. It is a good opportunity for a trial run, is it not?*"

Are you serious?! I have no idea what will happen if I use my weapons!

"*You have the Go Easy skill, do you not? If you use that, I am certain he will not die even if something does happen.*"

Uwagh?!

It was hard to argue with Kee, who knew more about Cayna than Cayna did herself. Back when she was in the hospital, the most he could give was advice. Inside, she was glad they could now have conversations like this.

She did sort of think it wouldn't hurt to listen to Kee. However, she lacked the composure to realize her less-than-stellar friend used this form of persuasion as well.

"All right, I accept."

"""WHAT?"""

The mercenaries around Arbiter instantly froze at the sound of the consenting voice behind them.

"Hold on, miss! The boss's strength ain't anything to mess around with!"

They were worried for her, and Cayna was sincerely grateful for their desperate attempts to dissuade her. She bowed her head.

"I think I'll be all right. Arbiter would never recklessly hurt an opponent in a mock battle, right?"

"Y-yeah! Of course not!"

The way they became tongue-tied was a little suspect, but Cayna burst into laughter as the mercenaries thumped their chests confidently.

"Let's begin, then," she said. "We have an early day tomorrow, after all."

The second-in-command gave an exasperated look but quickly

ushered the two contestants away from the campsite. Cayna summoned a Light Spirit and fixed it in the sky overhead. A dark battlefield didn't affect her in the least, since she had Night Vision, but that skill didn't extend to Arbiter or those watching. As long as the Light Spirit illuminated them overhead, they wouldn't have to deal with poor visibility.

"What about a weapon, miss? Wanna borrow one of my spare spears? It's not like you can use that sword you got there."

The Rune Blade was at Cayna's side. At first glance, it looked more like a one-handed club, but it was actually a full-fledged sword. The weapon transformed into its blade shape when infused with magic and inflicted the same amount of damage no matter who wielded it. In the world of the game, it was a magic weapon with fixed damage that new players up to level 100 found highly useful.

"No need to worry. If you're looking for something longer, I have just the thing."

Cayna gave a light smile and took off the roughly three-centimeter-long rod-shaped earring from her right ear. The small object had gold rings on the left and right side of it, and with Cayna's single command of E x t e n d, it became a staff longer than she was tall.

The merchants and mercenaries observing began stirring up a commotion. Not many saw such a weapon in their world, but among all those in Cayna's possession, this one was not particularly rare. It was a magic staff with unique qualities that looked exactly like the weapon carried by Son Goku in the Chinese tale *Journey to the West*. In the story, it was a tool used for surveying and managing rivers, but here it got longer or shorter, and that was about it.

Normally, she kept it on her right ear as an accessory. Cayna had never measured it herself, but she guessed that in the game it extended to about five meters. She'd never actually tried it out, though.

The second-in-command stood at the center to act as the referee.

"Listen well. You are both absolutely prohibited from hurting each other."

"Got it!"

"Of course."

"Well then, begin!"

As soon as both parties accepted the terms, he quickly waved his hand downward.

Cayna had planned on waiting for Arbiter to make the first move, but he wasted no time closing the distance between them and unleashed a sharp thrust. She brushed his spear tip toward the edge of the arena while getting out of his direct path.

Shing!

As the sound of clashing metal rang out, the wild crowd of men let out a unanimous cheer of "Yeaaah!" With cries of "She blocked his first attack!" and "Not bad, miss!" their excitement rose to a fever pitch.

Cayna, however, couldn't afford to listen to the bystanders. Arbiter's sharp thrusts drew meandering, misleading arcs that aimed straight down the middle. It was all she could do to avoid each oncoming attack and deflect it outward.

Initially, the game world of *Leadale* had hardly any form of official martial arts. The development team had mostly set weapon motions to several different patterns, and these race-based moves had been the reason players gave high elves a wide berth, but that was a story for another day.

Later versions allowed individual players to use fake forms of martials arts, and an era of chaos ensured. Everyone would pick and choose whatever they liked from the database and download it. Cayna had been unable to find Staff Techniques, so she had downloaded some *naginata* ones and treated those as Staff Technique skills. Since it was all part of the game, one could pick these techniques like they were nothing and defeat enemies in their chosen style.

There was also the blessing of skills, which made it all the better. The Perception skill that allowed you to read your foe's trajectory. The Move skill that optimized the target's movements. It was only natural that players combined these to avoid a foe's attacks. This also meant there were times when so many skills overlapped that the game system couldn't handle it.

However, this was not a game, and skills were no longer bound by such limitations. Passive Skills could be used at any time. If you knew Active Skills, you could set them in motion.

Although clumsy at first, Cayna meshed these all together, and her movements grew more and more polished. She read every movement of Arbiter's spear, threw off his timing by stepping forward instead of dodging, swept aside the incoming strike, and counterattacked by twirling as if in a dance.

Opposite her, Arbiter was unnerved by this change.

Initially, he figured she'd either get hit or avoid his attacks at most, but within several bouts, it was clear her movements were getting sharper. By these few clashes alone, it was as if a beginner martial artist had just gone through a year of intense training.

In fact, he carefully absorbed his opponent's talent as they exchanged blows and couldn't hide his astonishment at how she was turning into a first-rate soldier. It had evolved from receiving one of her hits for every nine he gave out to about half and half. Now Arbiter was at a disadvantage. Only about 10 percent of his strikes landed, while hers succeeded about 90 percent of the time.

Fortunately for him, Cayna had no intention of winning. Even if he threw off her rhythm, if Cayna went all out, Arbiter would undoubtedly lose.

Unfortunately, he had no intention of losing to her, either. Realizing she was going easy on him and continuing a prolonged game of back-and-forth frustrated Arbiter but also roused him.

Letting out a wild howl, he heatedly went to force her back, but she completely sidestepped it. He was soon left fighting a completely defensive battle.

For those watching on the sidelines, it was clear what was going on. The true power of "that little lady" left them at a loss for words. At this rate, the fight would never end until someone's stamina ran out.

Even the second-in-command, who watched the battle in utter bafflement, noticed the shadow in Arbiter's expression and hurriedly moved to stop them.

"That's enough, you two! We're finished! Any more than that, and things will get dangerous!"

Cayna, who had fallen into a trance and kicked off with one leg, heard an internal warning from Kee and quickly put away her magic staff. She hadn't noticed before, but she was sweating profusely.

Not only that, she was feeling pretty refreshed.

If exercise feels this great, I should have gotten more serious.

"Had you been any more serious, he would have died."

Just as Cayna was starting to have a positive outlook, Kee chided her and dampened the mood.

As for her sparring partner, Arbiter sat on the ground and leaned against his spear.

"Are you okay, Arbiter?"

"*Huff, heave, haah...* Don't make an old man wear himself out. You got me good, miss."

"No, you were great as well. Let's do this again if we get the chance!"

"Sorry, I think I'll pass."

As if those words had taken the last shred of energy out of him, Arbiter fell backward.

Not expecting this at all, Cayna reached out to him, but the mercenaries scrambled to grab him first.

"Are you okay, boss?!"

"Hang in there!"

"What'll we do without you?!"

"I ain't dead yet!"

Simply glad for a chance to finally rest, Arbiter angrily shouted at his men for overreacting. He then grinned, and one by one, the circle of mercenaries erupted in laughter.

"They're all such good friends. I'm envious."

Cayna thought back to the similarly chaotic guild of her past.

Epilogue

After that, the enraged second-in-command ordered them all to bed. Having determined that the wood golem Cayna created on their way to Felskeilo posed no issues as a night guard, this time he had her use several.

Having the wood golems patrol at night also allowed everyone to get a good night's sleep, which made the golems a big hit. However, that was if you could put up with the extreme discomfort of passing one when you got up to go to the bathroom in the middle of the night...

Before Cayna went to sleep, Arbiter came to her to apologize.

"I'm real sorry, miss. I shouldn't have told ya to suddenly spar with me like that. I got a little crazy."

"'Crazy'?"

"Yeah. When I charged at you, for some reason, I felt like I had to. After it was all over, I realized that wasn't like me at all. So I'm real sorry!"

Arbiter put both hands together in front of him in an apologetic gesture, and Cayna replied, "You really are serious," with a smirk.

"Honestly, I didn't even get hurt or anything," she reassured him. "I went overboard, too. I'm sorry."

"No kiddin'. I never would've figured you were that good. Sorry for underestimating you."

"You've done more than enough apologizing. Let's call this one a draw. Otherwise, I'll owe you even more."

"Huh? You mean like when I told you about all that stuff? That was just advice I wanted to pass down from one adventurer to another. Just forget about owin' me for any of that."

"*Sigh*. Okay, if you say so."

Cayna noted (that is, told Kee) that she'd make it up to him once they reached Helshper.

As the two conversed quietly, a warning came flying at them from the second-in-command.

"You two!"

""Y-yes?!""

They hurriedly flew away from each other and slipped under their own covers. They were relieved to avoid any further reprimand.

Cayna's sleeping area was a hammock tied between two carriages. Another carriage nearby had been turned into sleeping quarters for the merchant women.

She was still a bit tired from running around. She'd surely sleep soundly once she calmed down. Cayna released the tension from her body but opened her eyes when a report came in from Kee.

"Around the start of your mock battle, there was evidence that Buff had been cast over a wide area of people in the campsite."

"Huh?"

As if in answer to her question, Kee brought up a screen in front of Cayna, displaying the log from her and Arbiter's sparring session. Sure enough, it said *"Enhancement Effect Denied."* While the merchants had been getting ready for bed, Cayna and the mercenaries who had gathered at the center of the campsite had been cast with some sort of enhancement magic.

Furthermore, the mere fact that the second-in-command had been elsewhere and was the only one who'd remained calm helped Cayna come to a realization:

The effect itself was weak enough that it got interrupted by the slightest disturbance.

"That may explain the unnatural aspects of Sir Arbiter's apology."

"Oh, right. You mean the part about 'feeling like he had to' or something?"

"I believe it was most likely a form of sound-wave hypnosis that carried on the wind and ordered him to attack."

"...Seriously?"

"It is only a conjecture, but I can confirm there is about a seventy percent probability."

Since Cayna hadn't been the one to cast it, she didn't think it was too big a deal, but this was one seriously roundabout and elaborate prank.

Furthermore, while the list of people she knew who might do such a thing was short, she had a pretty good guess.

"You've gotta be kidding me..."

However, even if the person was trying to send a message, there was no sign they were going to suddenly appear out of the shadows and laugh upon being found out. On top of that, Cayna had no idea what was to be gained from doing something so roundabout.

"I'm kinda nervous to find out what else is in store."

Her mind a complicated mix of anxiety and joy, Cayna obeyed the call of sleep and closed her eyes. She prayed she wouldn't wake to find that person's traps greeting her the next morning.

She also had a feeling this was somehow the only good night's sleep she was going to get.

BONUS SHORT STORY
A Workplace Inspection

Cayna had adjusted to life in Felskeilo by that time.

"Come to think of it, I wonder what they normally do?"

And it was then that her questions about her children began.

She'd originally created them with the sole intention of selling them off to the Admins. Who could have ever imagined she'd be able to meet them face-to-face and carry on conversations like this? When Cayna thought back on it, she could clearly remember the moment she'd made her foster characters.

She also happened to remember her terrible, horrible, no-good friend.

For better or worse, this friend was like a slightly annoying in-law. No one irritated her more. Even so, Cayna couldn't help but wonder what had transpired now that they hadn't seen each other in a while. If that person ever found out about this curiosity of hers, she would be sure to send a flying kick their way. Definitely.

It happened while she was creating Mai-Mai.

"You're projecting onto your daughter way too much. If she's related to you, there's no way she'd be that busty. Make her as flat as you."

"I get it. You're just trying to pick a fight. Go away!"

At the time, a team of four girls and one idiot had stayed behind at Cayna's base and were looking worse for wear after a multiplayer battle.

In all honesty, Cayna's character did indeed leave a lot to be desired. However, that issue had to do with a function common throughout the genre as a whole. Most VR games created a basic character skin by scanning the user's real body. Players had to be prepared in the event that their in-game body's movements were drastically different from their physical body's; after all, there were multiple incidents of people logging in and out so many times that their brains malfunctioned and could no longer return to reality.

Since Cayna had started the game when she was admitted to the hospital after her accident, it created data based on a skinny, paralyzed body. For this reason, one might say it was also inevitable that she was smaller and less developed than others her age.

"Cayna, you're getting distracted. Don't let your mind wander from the task at hand."

"Y-yeah, you're right. I can't go thinking about that idiot now. Begone, evil spirits! Away!"

"That isn't quite what I meant..."

A moment later, the moronic shadow was wiped from her mind, and Cayna nodded.

"Okay then, let's check out Mai-Mai's classes. We can go observe Kartatz's factory, too."

"You appear to be excluding Skargo."

"He'll probably neglect his church duties and come charging at me if he sees me, so I figure I really have no choice but to make myself scarce."

"...I suppose I can't refute that."

Alas, Skargo's behavior was something even Divine Spirits were aware of. And for all the wrong reasons.

*   *   *

Since dawdling and chatting with Kee wouldn't get her anywhere, Cayna headed out to tour Kartatz's and Mai-Mai's workplaces. Kee resided within her, so she was free to talk with him mentally.

To any outsider, however, it only looked as if she was laughing, nodding, talking, and surprising herself. There was no question she made people cringe. When a child passed by one day with their mother and said, "Mommy, what's that girl doing?" and the mother replied, "Shh, don't look!" it was pretty much a foregone conclusion.

Cayna once again turned over a new leaf and headed toward the factory on Felskeilo's sandbar.

She had originally planned to confirm his schedule ahead of time, but that was pretty difficult when you lived in a world with no telephones.

Actually, there were equivalent skills for that, but while her children had them, she had lost them.

So Cayna decided to just drop in. If he was there, great; if not, she figured she could ask the workers all kinds of questions.

From what she could see in the entranceway, Kartatz wasn't there.

Although it indeed appeared to be a shipbuilding factory, they actually seemed to be making other things as well. There was a waterway within the factory that held finished vessels until they were ready to be launched, and though the framework of a ship they were working on was mounted on a central pedestal, for some reason, workers also seemed to be making carriages at the outer edges of the factory.

One of the employees spotted Cayna poking her head in curiously.

"Huh?! You're the boss's girlfriend from before!"

"Wha—?! His girlfriend?!"

Since Cayna looked around sixteen or seventeen, it would have been reasonable to think she and Kartatz were grandfather and grand-child when you saw them next to each other.

The workers' eyes all fell on her, and she slightly recoiled.

However, there was no way she could keep letting them think she was his girlfriend, so she confidently asserted, "I'm his mother, not his girlfriend!"

""""""His mother?!"""""""

Their eyes almost flew out of their heads in shock. You couldn't blame them, considering this was coming from a girl who looked younger than them.

Cayna, however, was used to the surprised reaction, and she looked around the factory curiously.

"Is Kartatz here today?"

"Y-yeah. The boss had a meeting thing— I mean, he's in a busi-ness meeting. He'll be back in no time— I mean, I believe he'll return shortly."

Perhaps it was because he realized she was his senior, but the one worker clumsily tried to sound more polite.

"Oh, don't worry about sounding all formal. I just came to tour the factory on my own, so this has nothing to do with anyone here."

Hearing this, the workers gave relieved looks and relaxed. They apparently weren't used to speaking with superiors. Cayna took this to mean that the duty normally fell to Kartatz.

"Why are you making carriages?"

"Ah, this is kind of like a woodshop. We mostly make boats, but when orders for those aren't coming in, we also make carriages and wagons."

The workers were of all different races. The mild-mannered man who had explained this to her was an elf, while the one who had first spotted her was a werecat. There were also humans and dwarves just like Kartatz.

As for the ship-in-progress that currently only consisted of framework for the bilge, it looked as if they couldn't work on it without Kartatz. Rather than what the workers called "ancient arts," these were made with good old-fashioned elbow grease.

Cayna wanted to ask more about this, but since she couldn't very well march into the meeting they were off having somewhere, she decided to save it for next time. Later on, she heard that even if they did build ships and architecture with these ancient arts, no one could inherit and preserve those techniques. That was why Kartatz had first become the pupil of a shipbuilder in a large workshop and spent fifty years learning his craft. He then set out on his own and spent one hundred years in diligent study.

After that, Cayna had his pupils tell her more about the ship they were building as well as the process before bidding them farewell.

She also left them with a small request and overall thought it was a fun, productive day.

Kartatz returned shortly after Cayna left the shop, but...

"WHAT THE?! WHAT THE HECK IS THIS?!"

"Hey, boss. Welcome back."

The pupils and workers noticed Kartatz standing dumbfounded in the entryway. He stared aghast at the two almost-three-meter-tall rock golems standing in a side chest pose that highlighted their pectorals.

"What's going on?! What are those?!"

As their boss raged while still clearly confused, the pupils looked at one another and nodded with a "Yeah?" and "Uh-huh."

The rock golems Kartatz pointed at switched to another position, this time an abdominal and thigh pose that showed off their lower halves.

"Miss Cayna left those for us to use instead of the crane."

"Huh?! Mum did?!"

"Yeah, she was just here to—what'd she call it?— 'tour' the

factory. We all showed her around the place. The crane broke yesterday, right? When she heard about it, she built these guys for us."

As this explanation went on, the bodybuilding rock golems continued their unified posing with several grunts for emphasis. Kartatz started to feel a headache coming on.

The next day, Cayna visited the Academy.

The guard at the gate had been notified of her visit beforehand, so getting through was no trouble at all. Unfortunately, however, she was informed that the headmaster had left for a meeting that day.

"I really should have contacted her ahead of time."

"Lady Mai-Mai would have most likely skipped her meeting to see you."

There were no words to describe the picture that came to mind. It would have surely put a strain on the other attendees of this meeting.

Left with no other choice, Cayna wandered around the Academy. Perhaps it was just bad timing, but she didn't even run into Lonti.

Just as she was thinking that she should probably come by another day, she passed a familiar face in the hallway.

"Oh, Lady Cayna. It's been some time since we last saw each other."

"Ah, Sir Lopus, was it? Hello."

There stood a lethargic, messy-haired professor in a pair of grimy, shabby-looking overalls. It was Mai-Mai's husband, Lopus Harvey.

Despite being a member of the baronage, he was a lauded alchemy professor—at least, that was what Cayna had heard from Lonti, herself the daughter of a marquis. She apparently considered Lopus a rather tough nut to crack.

"You-know-who is out. What brings you here?"

"I thought I'd come see what her daily routine was like. Looks like I missed her, though."

You-know-who and *her* both referred to Mai-Mai. Even though

Lopus and Mai-Mai were married, when Mai-Mai wasn't around, Lopus referred to her in more casual terms.

He chuckled, and with an inquiry of "Got some free time?" he invited Cayna to his research lab in the Alchemy Department.

Lopus's lab was surprisingly tidy. Since he himself was worn-out and disheveled, she had just assumed it would be full of garbage.

"It's quite clean."

"Yeah, well, I'm sure I could find anything on the shelves even if I dumped them all over, but you-know-who would get mad."

"Ah, I see what you mean. You seem to have it tough."

"Sure do. She doesn't lecture when she gets mad. She takes control of my body and makes me clean it up myself."

"Your muscles must be very sore the next day."

Lopus grimaced at Cayna's grin.

That alone told her what skill Mai-Mai had used. Its description stated, "If used on a disagreeable subject, the subject's muscles will be overexerted." It was a nasty technique that left the body feeling sore immediately after it was cast, let alone a day later.

Cayna didn't remember ever giving Mai-Mai such a dark side and tilted her head questioningly. However, she decided to just accept that a lot can change in two hundred years.

She looked around the room and saw glass vials with orange liquid lined up along one of the desks. They weren't all necessarily the same shade. Some were slightly lighter, while others were a little darker.

"Are these poison antidotes?"

"So you can tell. This is a drek antidote, and this one is a doh antidote. And this one…"

Cayna started fostering some doubts about Lopus as he rattled off the names of antidotes she rarely heard about. Drek was a weed that was often mistaken for an edible grass that grew in the area. If ingested, it caused ongoing fatigue and fever.

"Do you mix a compound for each individual poison?"

"That's right. It's pretty standard these days. If you go to a place that specializes in medicines, the shelves are buried in nothing but antidotes."

"The world certainly has become inconvenient," Cayna murmured.

She stared at one of the vials and then looked up. She took a bright-orange vial out of her own Item Box and showed it to Lopus.

"Wh-what's this…?" he asked.

"It is an antidote made with what you folks call 'ancient arts.'"

"Ah… I see…"

Lopus took it in his trembling hand carefully and stared at it so hard he might have bored a hole into it. He hurriedly took out several vials from a shelf and lined them along the desk. They appeared to be filled with either blackish-brown or greenish-brown liquid.

"What are those?" Cayna asked.

"Poison."

Moments after answering, Lopus placed a bit of poison on several small dishes. He then poured some of the Cayna's antidote onto a spoon and dripped it on one of the poisonous dishes.

In less than an instant, the single orange drop he'd poured on the blackish-brown poison began undergoing a drastic transformation. An instant later, the two substances didn't mix but instead became completely transparent.

"WH-WHAAAT?!"

As Lopus stood there dumbfounded, Cayna, next to him, wondered what the big deal was. He then dripped the antidote on each poison one after the other and let out a cry of awe each and every time. Once it was all finished, Lopus's face was flushed, and he was brimming with the desire to research.

"Wow, this is amazing. I didn't think such medicine even existed in this world."

"I'll give it to you if you want. You can use it as a sample."

Cayna placed two more vials on the desk.

"Y-you sure? Don't get me wrong; I appreciate it. But I can't give you anything that's gonna come even close to this."

"Research fanatics are the same no matter where you go. Keep using that casual tone with me, and we'll call it even. Best of luck!"

"Thanks, I owe you one."

Realizing it'd only get boring if she hung around any longer, Cayna waved good-bye to Lopus and left the Academy.

When Mai-Mai returned later on, her husband was so engrossed in his research that he completely forgot about work. Eventually, he pushed himself too far and collapsed from malnutrition. Mai-Mai soon gave him the lecture of his life.

When she found out the reason a few days later, she angrily shouted, "MOTHER, YOU BIG DUMMYYYYY!!"

◆

"Wh-what the…?"

It would be problematic if Skargo caused an uproar in the church, so Cayna went to go check on him in secret a few days after visiting the Academy.

However, when she peeked into his office, she froze in place with a weary expression.

It wasn't simply because Skargo was there. The problem was his eccentric behavior.

To put a fine point on it: High Priest Skargo was dancing with a nun's habit.

One, two, turn.

Each time he did so, the sleeves and back of the habit fluttered.

His footwork and dancing were impeccably elegant, but the mere fact he was doing it was undeniably strange.

"Ah, Mother Dear. Won't you please hasten here to visit with me as well?"

Bright and shining verdant leaves cascaded behind him as a backdrop.

"I simply must guide you around my workplace while you wear this habit I made especially for you."

A gentle peach-colored wind fluttered his priestly robes.

"*Ah*. Won't you please join me soon, Mother Dear? I must offer up this love to you."

Before she knew it, the office had turned into a section of plateau with a vast white-ridged mountain range in the far distance.

The way an absolute space case like him could so masterfully control Special Skill: Oscar—Roses Scatter with Beauty was worthy of praise.

However, Cayna regarded him with neither admiration nor apathy—only the pitying gaze of someone looking upon a most unfortunate individual.

"...I'm gonna pretend I didn't see that."

Cayna silently closed the High Priest's office door and hurried out of the church.

"I need to find somewhere I can soothe this trauma..."

"*In that case, how about visiting the new street stall that recently opened?*"

"Oh, the one that folks at the inn were talking about, right? Sounds good to me."

A few days later, rumors rose that a dancing nightmare was sighted at the church, but nobody paid them any mind.

Character Data

Cayna

A level-1,100 player and rare high elf. The Third Skill Master.

A powerhouse on both the front lines and as a rear guard, but her specialty is using her endless supply of MP to wipe out enemies with magic. Her Guardian Tower sits in a vast forest and stretches high into the heavens; it can only be cleared if a player climbs to the top for twenty-four hours without stopping, which is (supposedly) considered the easiest of the thirteen trials. In the game, she was known and feared by her two sobriquets: the Silver Ring Witch and Ferocious Firepower.

Skargo

Cayna's eldest son, who was placed into public service through the Foster System. A level-300 elf.

Raised to specialize in holy magic recovery, status ailment recovery, and physical buffs. Incredibly adept at using Oscar—Roses Scatter with Beauty, a skill that had, for some reason, been given to him just for kicks. Freely throws around various effects on a whim. Surprisingly popular with the public. He serves as High Priest and is the third most influential person in the Kingdom of Felskeilo. A pain in the neck who adores his mother to the point of fanaticism.

Mai-Mai

Cayna's second child and eldest daughter, who was placed into public service through the Foster System. A level-300 elf.

Raised to specialize in general Attack Magic. Somehow, over the past two hundred years, had twins with her first husband and is now settled into life as a baron's wife with her second husband. Currently the headmaster of Felskeilo's Royal Academy and previously served as a mage at the royal palace. Acts like an adoring kitten desperate for attention when around her mother.

Kartatz

Cayna's third child, who was placed into public service through the Foster System. A level-300 dwarf.

Raised to specialize in construction. Can more or less hold his own in close combat with his ax or hammer. Works at a shipbuilding factory along the riverbank in Felskeilo. Loves and respects his mother and has the most common sense among his siblings.

Afterword

Hello, dear readers. It's a pleasure to meet you. Thank you very much for reading this book.

This work was actually completed six years ago. It was my first original work created from scratch and my first submission to such a large platform. My writing was all over the place at the beginning, and the number of misspellings and typos pointed out by readers must have caused them no end of trouble. Now that I think about it, I wonder if I was a problem child who made people ask, "Who do they think they are?"

With this current novelization, some parts have been revised, while others are brand-new. To be honest, it was enough to make my stomach hurt. Whenever I go to a big bookstore and see the lineup of novels that started out on the Shousetsuka ni Narou website, I ask myself if I'm worthy…then my stomach starts killing me even more.

When I first came up with this story, the idea of "being reincarnated as a game character" was still pretty unheard of. Since the official novelization got a late start, my days were filled with trepidation as I worked with my editor. Even now, I can't stop asking myself if things are really going to be all right.

To "K" of a certain site: If you hadn't told me "Just write!" when I was flustered by all the comments, this book would have never seen the light of day. I'm glad you gave me the push I needed.

Lastly, I am deeply grateful to everyone who helped publish my work:

My editor, whom I caused a lot of grief during our meetings; Tenmaso for providing such wonderful illustrations; and the publisher.

Thank you all so much.

Ceez

I'm Tenmaso, the illustrator of this novel.
I read the entire Web version immediately after receiving the
manuscript. In that moment, a definite image of Cayna popped
into my head. I thought, *This is it!* and put my heart and soul into
bringing her to life. I don't know if she turned out how longtime
readers visualized, but nothing would make me happier than to
see them pleased with my depiction.

Tenmaso